DIRTY SCORE

KENNA KING

CONTENTS

CHAPTER ONE

Penelope

I hear Phil Carlton's voice against my father's door as he opens it to exit but then stalls.

"I guess there's nothing we can do about it—Ryker's gone and can't return for two years. And he's right about who he thinks should replace him."

The walls in the corporate offices are relatively soundproof, but between their booming voices and the door being slightly ajar, I can hear every word.

I practically hold my breath as I listen to their conversation regarding the plan for filling Ryker's spot as our Center, though the captain position was already given to one of our alternates, Lake Powers. Ryker getting deported right before the playoffs has the entire franchise rattled. He kept the team in sync and was the glue that held everyone together.

And who did Ryker suggest should fill his center position?

"Pulling a player from our Canadian farm team makes the most sense, and the kid is a killer center. With playoffs starting April 17th", three weeks from now, he needs to be ready," Phil continues.

Wait... did he say that the Hawkeyes are replacing Ryker with a player from the Canadian farm team?

There's only one player on that team good enough to complete out on the ice with zero notice and be thrown in during a championship season. But my father would never do that to me.

He'd never bring back to Seattle the man who single-handedly ruined my chances at getting to compete for a spot on the USA Olympics figure skating team four years ago.

"And we have to make a move quickly. Coach Bex has been moving guys around to different positions they don't usually play in and using our roster to its fullest capacity to cover Ryker's absence the last month. Our team has risen to the occasion, but we've only narrowly won our last few games. Luck is about to wear out as we head for the playoffs. We can't sustain the gaping hole Ryker left for much longer."

"How does Coach Bex feel about the new recruit?" Phil asks.

"Coach Bex is concerned he's not a team player. He has a tendency to hog the puck, but I assured Bex that he can be coached out of it. And besides, we need a permanent replacement for Ryker, and we need it now. He's the best suited and is already a part of the franchise family. In addition, I think it will stir up the huge media attention that we're looking for," my father agrees.

"Definitely. Sports media is going to go bananas over this. I'm surprised a kid with that much talent has spent so much time on our farm team. He should have signed with an NHL team years ago when they all wanted to recruit him right out of high school."

Phil's words instantly hit a nerve, and I practically feel my blood run cold. I don't have to hear the player's name to know who they're discussing now. I know only one player who had multiple offers to play in the NHL and turned them down to attend college first.

Slade Matthews.

My father knows what Slade did to me in college, which is precisely why he delayed Slade's career and sent him to Canada to play for the farm team.

Still, to this day, I don't know why Slade agreed to go to Canada. Maybe it's because he was always the Coach's pet in college and has always worshiped my father. It's the exact reason he ruined my life all those years ago—practically my father's watchdog. Somehow, he got off the leash and took it too far. He scared away any prospects I had for a new partner to skate with for the qualifier at the Olympic tryouts.

My old couple's skating partner had broken his foot in three places during a skiing accident a month before we were supposed to compete for the Olympic team. I had been looking for a new partner, but Slade ensured no one showed up for tryouts with his stunt.

"I've already called up the farm team coach and he's agreed. He'll send him down tomorrow and our new center will start training the day after. That will give him a day to unpack and settle in at The Commons," my father says.

The Commons?

Most of the team's players live at The Commons, which is only a few blocks from the stadium and offers seasonal rates for the Hawkeyes. Will my father seriously let this man stay in the same apartment building as me?

"Very good," Phil confirms, opening the door wider.

Phil's stocky body, dressed in a navy-blue fleece zip-up and tan dockers peeks through the doorway as he turns again to say one last thing to my father. "This is the best option we have with such short notice. Let's hope he's ready to play at the championship level."

"Slade Matthews is ready. And he won't miss his opportunity, I can guarantee it," my father says.

My mouth runs dry at the final mention of Slade's name. For the last few moments, I held out hope that there was another player who mirrored my college tormentors' earlier professional prospects, but now that my father has uttered his name, the reality hits.

Slade Matthews will be skating back into my life within twenty-four to forty-eight hours, and there is nothing I can do to stop it... besides quit.

But I won't do that.

I won't run away again, though my stomach gurgles uncomfortably at the thought of working in the same franchise together.

I try to swallow, but there's barely any saliva left in my mouth, and the churning of my stomach has me wishing I hadn't devoured that entire sticky bun the size of my head at Serendipity's Coffee Shop with Tessa, Autumn, and Isla an hour ago at lunch.

Those delicious carbs won't taste nearly as good coming back up if I end up puking from the less-than-appetizing news.

How could my father do this to me?

He's the one who banished Slade all those years ago for ruining my chances to skate for my country, and now he's bringing him back? Why not just release him back into the NHL and let another team pick him up if he thought that Slade had served his time? But bringing him here?

To my city?

To my team?

To my apartment building?

It doesn't make sense.

Phil exhales, "I'm glad to hear it, and that's what I expect. This is our year, Sam; I want to see the Stanley Cup hoisted over our team's head this year and sitting in the glass display case in the stadium lobby."

"Then Slade is our best chance," my father says.

I see Phil's head nod.

I stand up out of my chair and stare back at Phil as he walks out of my father's office. I'm sure I look entirely dumbfounded, but Phil smiles back at me.

"Have a good day, Penelope," he says with a smile, walking towards the reception area's door.

"You too, sir," I say, though I trip over the words.

This new information has me completely rattled, and now I can barely speak.

All I can think about right now is rushing to my father's door and demanding an answer. I know as the administrative assistant to the GM; I don't deserve a reason for his decision. But as the daughter of the coach, whose protégé ruined my Olympic dreams, I think he owes me an explanation.

I watch until the door closes behind Phil, and then I shoot a look to see my father standing in the doorway, also watching Phil leave.

He doesn't look happy or upset about the decision they settled on. He has on his usual stoic expression.

The look of a man who leads an entire franchise and puts out fires every single day with calm, methodical decisions.

Not much rattles my father... until it comes to me or someone threatening the Hawkeyes. But to me, Slade Matthews does both.

That's why this doesn't make sense.

The second I take my first heated step away from my desk, my father's attention snaps to me.

He turns to head back into his office but if he thinks he and I aren't going to have a conversation about this decision to bring Matthews into the franchise, he's dead wrong.

"Dad..."

"Penelope," I hear him say, the sound of his chair already groaning to his weight. The man moves fast; I'll give him that. "... now isn't the time."

I walk past the wide-open mahogany door of his office to find him right where I thought he would be—sitting in his black leather chair and pretending to be engrossed in something on his computer screen that sits to the right of his desk.

As a GM, my dad's day is mainly filled with player and vendor contract renewals, being cc'd on legal's emails, ticket sales figures, and general revenues of how much the stadium brings in. So, I know that there can't be anything more interesting on his computer screen than what he and I need to discuss.

He's trying to avoid this conversation, but it will happen whether he likes it or not. Lucky for me, I control his schedule, and I happen to know he doesn't have another appointment for half an hour.

"Slade Matthews? Dad, is this some kind of sick joke?"

He lets out a sigh, realizing I'm not going to go away.

He glances over at me as I hover over his desk.

"Penelope, this isn't personal, and you know that. This is business," he says with a lifted eyebrow like he's scolding me for even thinking that this decision has anything to do with me. His voice stays calm as usual. "I'm making the right decision for the team and this franchise. It's my job... remember? And a big part of my job is bringing on talent who I believe can win us a Stanley Cup. My boss expects me to do whatever I have to do to make that happen. And if I recall, the Hawkeyes' name is printed on your paycheck, too."

He clicks the end of his pen against his lacquered desk, his version of a mic drop, thinking that he won that argument. But even if he has a point, this isn't over.

He gives me a low-brow look like I'm the one being ridiculous.

I hate it when he makes me sound like a spoiled brat. But if I am, it's because he made me that way.

"You know what he did to me. You expect me to be able to work with him now after all of that?"

"I expect you to do your job with as much pleasantry towards Matthews as is required by your position in this franchise. No more, and no less. Don't forget that you and I are just as replaceable as any player on the team, and Phil Carlton won't blink an eye if he thinks his franchise isn't working at peak performance. Making this place run takes a lot of money, and Phil doesn't mind cutting dead weight. Do you understand what I'm saying?" my father asks.

"Yes, sir, I do," I say with a nod.

I cross my hands in front of me while my shoulders slump as my father puts me back in my place.

I don't have to like my father/boss's decisions, but he's right. Back in college, my father was the head coach for WU. The following year, after Slade graduated college and joined the farm team, Phil Carlton offered my father the GM position, and my father took it.

He has a job to do and a boss who expects results—the same boss who graciously offered the administrative position to a college dropout... me.

I didn't keep the dropout title for long. I gave myself time to mourn the loss of my figure skating career and then reapplied to school, taking WU's online courses that fit around my working hours for the Hawkeyes.

Now, I'm pursuing my master's degree in sports management and dreaming of working my way up the Hawkeyes franchise. I needed a new aspiring goal, and now I have it.

The first female GM in Hawkeyes history.

We both owe Phil Carlton our best, and though I don't like it, with Ryker getting deported on such short notice, we have to take the best option we have... and Slade Matthews is our only hope.

"This isn't college anymore, Penelope, and Slade took his punishment like the champion he is. It hurt me to hold him back, and he sure as hell didn't have to do what I asked of him. He could have taken one of the many NHL deals offered to him and left. But he knew that when he hurt you, he hurt me, and he did what I asked of him. That kind of loyalty doesn't come along every day in this industry... I should know."

My father spent a lifetime in this sport. He was signed by an NHL team at the end of his senior year of high school, spent twenty-plus years of his life playing the game, and then spent ten years coaching college hockey. Now, he's four years into his career as the GM of the Hawkeyes.

He has the kind of career that many professional athletes would envy, and with three Stanley Cup wins under his belt, he's admired in the profession.

I need to trust his judgment. Not just because he's my father and my boss but because he has the years of knowledge to know what this team needs to become champions. I won't stand in the way of that.

"At least I won't have to see him that much up here on the third floor," I tell him.

He gives me a sideways look as he turns back to his computer now that he knows this conversation is coming to an end, and he won... again.

"That's the spirit, peanut," he says sarcastically.

I'll do my job as expected, but I won't waste a perfectly good smile on Slade Matthews. He doesn't deserve it from me.

I'll have to do my best to avoid him at all costs.

And anyway, there's nothing more he can take from me now.

CHAPTER TWO

Three days later

Slade

It's just after six am when I walk into the Hawkeyes stadium. It's not the first time I've been here, but it is the first time I'm walking through the service side entrance, and it's the first time I'm here as a player for the team and not a spectator.

I flew in yesterday morning and took the time to unpack into the roomy one-bedroom apartment at The Commons that the Hawkeyes rented for me.

It's a nice place—far nicer than the tiny, slightly run-down studio apartments the farm team put us in

The building maintenance guy was never around, so I had to become my own plumber and electrician when things went bad... and they did. I can't complain, though; it was free housing. All the other players on the team lived in the same building, experiencing the same conditions.

Because we traveled so much for games, I wasn't home often, so it didn't matter that much.

When I spoke with Sam over the phone last night about coming in early to familiarize myself with the rink before practice, he said that the janitorial staff usually come in before six in the morning. The Zamboni driver comes in around seven to smooth out the ice before the morning skate, which gives me an hour to get in some drills and warm up.

As I walk through the hallways leading to the home team locker room, I glance at the photos on the wall of players and wins that came before me. This team has a long history and now I get to be a part of that.

I see the double doors of the locker room and push through them. The slight musty gym-sock odor, overpowered mainly by the smell of commercial-grade bleach, fills the air.

The janitors must come in before practice to keep things smelling as fresh as possible. With twenty-three dudes making up an entire NHL team using the same facilities, I can see why the janitors have full-time jobs. And they do an excellent job because the place looks immaculate.

When I walk in, the first thing that catches my eye are the floor-to-ceiling lockers against the back wall, lined up next to each other in a large U-shape. As I approach, I search the lockers to see if I have a spot yet, and sure enough, I do.

S. Matthews #67 is engraved on a small brass plaque above the bench for my duffel bag and coat hangers for my gear to hang when not in use.

My locker stands between names of giants in this sport that I've only seen on TV—never met in person. Seven Wrenley, Kaenan Altman, Briggs Conley, Lake Powers, and Reeve Aisa. Players who will all expect me to prove what I'm made of on day one.

I turn down a hallway and see the large showers. The tiling and rain shower heads look new, just like most of this building, due to the expansive remodel I heard they did a few years ago. Then I head past them towards the player's tunnel just beyond the exit on the other side of the locker room.

The moment I pass through the locker room doors, I inhale the crisp, clean smell of ice and invite the sharp bite of the cold that touches my skin before I even see the rink.

Being in a hockey stadium—any hockey stadium—is where I feel the most at home. It's where I feel the most at ease and it's where all my father's disappointments with my choice of career fall by the wayside.

As I inch closer to the rink's opening through the player's tunnel, my ears perk up to the scratching of the ice by a pair of blades.

Someone else is here and already on the ice.

Disappointment strikes first.

I'd been looking forward to having time on my own to get acquainted with the stadium this morning before tomorrow's first practice with the team, but life is full of disappointments, and God knows I've had my fair share.

The moment I walk up to the edge of the rink opening, my attention grabs onto the black swirl of fabric from a figure skating leotard and a long blonde ponytail as a skater performs a layback spin with expert precision.

It only takes me a second to remember where I am and who the figure skater is out on the ice.

Penelope Roberts.

Coach Sam Roberts's daughter.

The GM's administrative assistant.

And the only woman permanently inked on my skin, who just so happens to hate my guts.

But I'm here with a new game plan and four years of paying retribution for what I did to her all those years ago.

I can tell myself I did it all to protect her, and I've spent many nights lying in bed in Canada, making excuses for why I did it. But in the end, my actions were as self-serving as they were to safeguard her.

I wanted her for myself, and I didn't want to share.

Not to mention that I had to teach a group of rich frat boys what happens when you mess with a pissed-off hockey player.

Now I'm back for two things:

I want to play at the top of my game in the NHL and prove that four years in the minors didn't take any edge off.

And finally, win the one thing that I haven't stopped thinking about day or night since the minute I saw Penelope Roberts standing in the kitchen of a frat party over four years ago, the first week of the fall semester of my senior year. I knew I had to make her mine the second my eyes latched onto her long blonde hair and stunning smile. She wasn't a conquest like the girls before her... I knew this would be different.

I knew Penelope would change everything.

Before I could take one step forward in her direction, my teammate and my left wing saw what I had my sight fixed on, and he dropped the bomb.

"You know who that is, right?" he asked.

"Mine," I said with a cocky smirk.

He laughed and took a sip of his beer.

"What? Don't fucking tell me you've already touched her," I said, knowing that you don't get involved with a teammate's ex-girl.

It's a line you don't cross. Though for this girl, I might have been willing to break the rules this once.

"Fuck no. I like my starting position on your left," he said.

"What the hell does that mean?"

"That's Penelope Roberts. Our coach's daughter transferred here from Michigan to study. She's really smart, too. I hear she tutors students in science and math. She's also one hundred percent off limits... unless you'd like to watch your senior year from the bench."

"Fuck," I mutter to myself, but he hears it.

"Yep, that chick's a goddamn land mine to your NHL career. I bet you $100 dollars that one of the idiots on our team trips the wire," he chuckles.

Yeah, fucker, and that idiot is probably going to be me.

Ultimately, I didn't introduce myself to Penelope that night because I knew my teammate was right. Getting with Penelope would cost me my starting position on Coach Robert's team—a price that no girl before her was ever worth paying. But when I quickly realized several days later that I couldn't think much of anything else besides her, I got her tutoring email from a professor in the science department. I reached out to Penelope under the guise of a senior college student needing tutoring before he lost his financial aid due to poor grades.

It's not that I needed a tutor. As a pre-med student, I was on track to graduate with honors. My dad had me memorizing biology, anatomy, and chemistry flash cards every morning since I could walk. His dreams of me following in his footsteps as a cardiac surgeon were dashed when I got a full ride on a hockey scholarship to the University of Washington instead of his alma mater.

And I wasn't in jeopardy of losing my financial aid since I was on a full-ride scholarship for hockey. However, my family's trust would have footed the bill if I hadn't. I would have been forced to go to an Ivy League if the family money was paying for it.

I just wanted to get to know her and doing it as Slade Matthews was out of the question. I was hoping I would find out that under that layer of beautiful ivory skin, platinum blonde hair and crystal blue eyes, she was just as much of a waste of time as any other girl I've met in my life.

But the more I got to know her, the more entangled I became.

From: WinForToday067
To:SkatrGirlPen
Hi SkatrGirlPen,

I got your email from my biology professor. I could use some tutoring in my science courses. I can't flunk out or I'll lose my financial aid and won't graduate. Are you available?

That's when one harmless email to Penelope turned into six months of opening up to someone like I never had before in my twenty-two years of life.

To Penelope, I was just WinForToday067, a C-point-average student who might lose his college funding if he doesn't bring up his grades.

But to me... she became my lifeline. Those regular emails turned from weekly homework and test scores to in-depth emails about our day. I told her things I had never told anyone else.

I had never fallen for someone so fast. Actually, I had never fallen for anyone at all. She was compassionate, good-humored, and selfless—qualities I rarely witnessed in my upbringing.

And then the day came.

It was the day I should have seen coming—the day I'd have to walk away from the best thing I've ever had besides hockey.

I made a choice to step in and protect her, but I didn't anticipate that the repercussions would cost me the one thing worth saving.

Her.

Penelope

I finished the performance that Toby, my old skating partner, and I had created for the Olympic qualifiers all those years ago but never got to perform because of his accident.

I don't always skate that routine. In fact, it's been years since the last time I skated it solo without Toby. I guess Slade's impending arrival made me nostalgic this morning and reminded me of someone else I had left in the past.

A college student I had tutored over emails a few weeks after I started school at Washington University. He was a tutoring student who eventually turned into a pen pal, and embarrassingly turned into a crush.

Evidently, he didn't feel the same because he wrote me a "dear John" email out of the blue and disappeared from my life.

I shouldn't think of Win anymore—it's been years. But he was the one person who understood what I was going through with Slade.

Now Slade's back, but WinForToday067 isn't, and I could really use his assuring emails with Slade's impending arrival.

Distant clapping echoes out around the stadium and startles me.

Who's here?

Who's been watching me?

My eyes dart wildly around the stadium, looking for the person or persons who have been watching me without my knowledge. The janitors and the Zamboni driver have all seen my routine a hundred times before. I'm sure they're bored of it by now, so one of them clapping for it seems odd. And none of the players, coaches, or my father will be in for another half hour at the earliest.

Finally, my eyes lock onto a tall figure standing in the metal frame of the tunnel's opening.

Slade Matthews.

I can already feel my blood pressure rising at the sight of him leaning against the side wall. His tattoos creep up his neck slightly past his shirt, and the colorful ink peeks out around his muscular biceps and then travels down his arms, stopping at his wrists.

He thinks he's so damn special. It doesn't help that everyone within earshot likes to tell him so. Especially all the college girls that came to hockey games far too scantily dressed and freezing their bare asses on the bleachers to get his attention.

I mean, he's attractive if you're into that tatted-up, self-absorbed, spoiled rich kid hockey player type... which I'm not.

And if it wasn't the puck bunnies trying to get his attention, the NHL recruits weren't far behind, all clambering to sign him.

They offered ridiculous contract add-ons and more pay than most rookie players get on their first-year deals.

I skate towards the rink opening; the closer I get to him, the more my heart races. I forgot how obnoxiously tall and broad he is. But now, four years later, he seems almost more significant. That college body is gone— he's filled out as he's aged.

I glance away quickly to regain my thought process and stop thinking about the body of a man I loathe deeply.

I take a look around to ensure we're the only ones in the stadium, and Phil isn't going to see me yelling at his star player on his first day of practice.

"This is my time, Matthews. No one is supposed to be here this early. What are you even doing here?" I ask.

"Sam said I could come in early and check things out."

My dad told him he could come in early even though he knows I skate before the Zamboni does its run?

That's a ballsy move from my dad, seeing as Matthews is his prodigal son that he thinks is going to save the Hawkeyes season. My father failed to consider that his potentially vengeful daughter is wearing ice skates that I recently had sharpened.

These blades could cut through a muscular thigh in one swift slice and end a hockey player's career.

Slade stands in the doorway, blocking most of the exit with his body, his shoulder still leaning against one side of the door frame.

His honey-hazel eyes stare down at me, his lips pulling up to a lopsided smile as if he can't help but turn on his cocky charm.

God, I hate that gorgeous pearly white smile and ruggedly handsome face.

Even after everything he's done to me, my girly parts seem to suffer from long-term memory loss. I swear I feel my uterus flip with excitement.

Stupid reproductive organs.

It's an innate primal response to want to mate with the strongest and most attractive man in your vicinity. To give the future population the best genetics you can pass on to strengthen your species for longevity.

I remind myself.

However, if Slade was the last man on earth and it was between procreating with him or letting the human race die out... I'd come to terms with the fact that humanity had a good run and let that be the end of it.

"Well, six to six thirty is my time, and I don't like sharing the ice. And you'd better not be in the locker room from six-thirty to seven because I use the showers," I say, pushing past him.

He moves a little to let me through, and I do my best to slide past him sideways so that we don't touch. The last thing I need with this man is physical contact.

Just as I make it successfully past him, the warm sensation of his fingers reaches around my right wrist.

Tingles shoot up my arm at his touch, and I want to shake them off immediately and take a hot shower to wash away any reminiscence of him that makes my body react to his touch like that.

"Hey, hold on," he says quickly.

I dart a look back at him, and he releases me instantly when he sees my eyes narrow at him for touching me.

"What?" I bark.

"I just wanted to say that you look good out there." His cocky smile disappears, and that sparkle in his eye fades.

There's something genuine in those eyes now... or at least I think there is, but then again, how can I trust anything when it comes to him?

I can't.

"Thanks," I say cautiously.

I'm uncertain about the credibility of his compliment.

I turn back and head down the tunnel.

"Penelope," he calls out again.

I turn my head to look over my shoulder, already making it halfway down the tunnel.

"It's good to see you again."

He slides his hands into his pockets.

I hate how genuinely he says it. Like he really is happy to see me. The cocky Slade Matthews from college seems to have faded, and now... who is this person, and why am I having this reaction towards him?

I nod quickly and then turn, walking a little faster than before. I need to get out of here as soon as physically possible.

I wish my hormones had an on-and-off switch right about now because Slade Matthews is on the short list of people I wouldn't mind wiping off the face of the earth.

But really, it's just a list of one.

Four Years Ago:

From: SkatrGirlPen

To: WinForToday067

I think we should meet up. We've been emailing back and forth for four months and I still don't know who you are. Don't you want to meet me?

From: WinForToday067

To:SkatrGirlPen

I want to, but there's a lot going on right now with finals. I need to get an A on the Anatomy exam. Can't you just keep tutoring me? I think I'll ace this test with your help, but I need to stay focused.

From: SkatrGirlPen

To: WinForToday067

Yeah... of course I'll keep tutoring you.

Two weeks before Win graduates...

From: WinForToday067

To: SkatrGirlPen

Pen,

I've been staring at this blank email for the last few hours, struggling with what to say, so I'm just going to say it.

I'm moving... internationally.

I don't know where I'm going or how long I'll be gone, but correspondence will be too difficult to keep up any longer, and this is goodbye.

Thank you for tutoring me through anatomy. I aced my last exam.

CHAPTER THREE

Slade

I had stayed up late to make sure I had all the plays memorized this morning before practice. Every few minutes, I caught myself watching the clock wind down to six am, knowing that Penelope would be out on the ice by then.

My finger itched to close the playbook and head down to the stadium, even if only to watch her skate, but I've been given the opportunity to redeem myself and play with one of the best teams in the NHL.

I need to prove to Sam Roberts and Coach Bex that they didn't make a mistake bringing me up from the farm team.

A few hours later, I walk into the locker room. This is my first time seeing a locker room full of players. I recognize faces from watching televised games and interviews.

In the back corner, I see Seven Wrenley and Reeve Aisa, our two goalies, discussing something.

Sitting in front of their lockers, changing for practice, I see Brent Tomlin, our left defense, Lake Powers, our left wing, and Kaenan Altman, our right defense.

I recognize more as I survey the players and then head toward my locker, which I spotted yesterday when I was here while the team had the day off.

The door behind me opens, and Briggs Conley strolls in, passing me with his team duffel bag slung over his back.

He flashes a look over his shoulder as he walks by and then realizes that I'm the new guy.

"Hey, Matthews, welcome to the team," he says, stopping for a second and turning slightly back towards me. That gets the attention of several other players, who now notice my arrival, too, and all give nods or slight waves in my direction as well. "Do you know where your locker is? It's next to mine," he asks.

"Yeah. I came in yesterday to take a look around. Thanks," I tell him.

A side door opens from inside the locker room, taking Conley's attention, which is fine with me. I don't need a welcoming committee. I just need to get out on the ice and show everyone that I deserve to be here.

Coach Bex walks out with two of his assistant coaches trailing behind him.

I met them all yesterday briefly after their morning coaches' staff meeting.

Conley turns back around and makes a beeline for his locker. I follow his general direction and head for my own locker.

Practice starts soon, and the last thing I need to do is be late for it.

"Alright, listen up," Coach Bex says.

The whole locker room goes quiet as the assistant coaches settle on either side of him, clipboards in hand and ready for practice to begin. No doubt everyone's going to be laser-focused on me, wondering if I'm worth all those damn zeros they signed me for when I've been sitting on a farm team for years.

I'm used to being underestimated when I walk into a new locker room.

It's nothing new for me.

"As you all know, we have a new player on the roster now. Slade Matthews will be replacing Ryker Haynes on the starting lineup."

Coach Bex looks over at me and gives me a slight nod, and I send one back.

"We don't have time for morning chitchat. We're all here to do a job, and we get paid well for it. I want to see a shiny new piece of hardware in our stadium trophy cabinet so you can all handle your introductions after practice. We're not in the playoffs yet and we have six more games to win. Nothing's a sure thing. We still have to go out and win one game at a time. So don't get cocky, and don't get sloppy, got it?" he asks, looking around until he sees a unanimous nod from all the players.

I can tell that Coach Bex's coaching style is the polar opposite of Sam's, but I can work with it. I appreciate Coach Bex calling it as he sees it. There's no sugarcoating in his delivery, which I prefer. Being direct works best for me, anyway.

"Did you study every play in that playbook?" Coach Bex asks, turning to me.

"As if I designed them myself," I tell him.

"Good," he says and then looks around at the players in the locker room. "Let's go play some hockey."

And with that, everyone jumps into action, grabbing gear and heading out to the rink.

Being in a group of guys trying to break out from the pack and prove themselves to get recruited into the NHL meant that although we were a team, there was still an underlying vibe of "every man for himself".

And as a kid that had spent enough years entering new schools where I had to fight for my spot and prove myself... I guess old habits die hard. Playing for Coach Roberts and being a part of the same team for four years was the first time in my life that I've ever felt the camaraderie of a team. It's why we were unbeatable during those years I played under his leadership. And it's why he gained my respect and loyalty... something I don't give out freely to anyone, so I went without question when he sent me to the farm team in Canada.

I had lost his respect. He was the first person I ever cared about who respected me, and I was willing to do whatever it took to get it back. If I was ever going to get Coach Roberts to see me as someone worthy of his daughter, I knew I had to prove that I could bury my pride and take my punishment like a man.

I hope that Sam bringing me to the Hawkeyes as their center means that I have finally earned back what I lost when I threatened Sean Klein, the soccer team captain, after he asked Penelope out on a date. If Sam knew the reason behind Klein's motive for taking out Penelope, he would have done much more than threaten to end Sean's soccer career.

Which is exactly why I never told Coach Roberts or Penelope why I did it.

CHAPTER FOUR

Penelope

After yesterday's run-in with Slade, I really need a meet-up with my friends at Serendipity's Coffee Shop during our lunch break.

I'm relieved not to have had another run-in with Slade this morning like we had yesterday, but it doesn't change the fact that I could barely sleep last night because I couldn't stop over-thinking about our interaction.

I can only hope that, like this morning, I don't see him around the stadium except on the ice during home games. And maybe I'll get lucky, and some team will make a trade for him, whisking him as far away from Seattle and this franchise as possible.

"Has anyone met the new guy yet?" Tessa asks.

She sets her latte and plastic table number for our lunch order down on the square table that Autumn and I are already sitting at in the shop's back corner.

Autumn, the Hawkeyes PR manager and fiancé to Briggs Conley, our right wing, proposed lunch at Serendipity's Coffee Shop to plan my birthday party in two weeks. Right now, turning twenty-five is the last thing on my mind with Slade back in town.

Ever since our run-in yesterday, I can't think of anything else. I walked out the door this morning with my blouse inside out, which is the physical evidence of how much Slade Matthews rattles me.

"I haven't, but Briggs tells me the guy is a beast. He's just worried about his anger issues on the ice and his unwillingness to share the puck. Briggs said that Slade carried the farm team his entire four years there. He was by far the best player on the team so he's used to making most of the shots but he's going to have to learn to play as a team if he wants to play for the Hawkeyes," Autumn says, and then takes a sip of her iced water.

I've been curious how this morning went, but I didn't want to ask my father, and he's spent most of his day in meetings or in Phil's office.

"His anger issues on the ice?" Tessa asks.

I haven't kept up on Slade's career since he left for Canada, but in college, he was known for spending more time in the penalty box for getting into fights than any other player on the team and I overheard my father tell Phil that Coach Bex is worried about Slade not being a team player which explains the puck hogging. That's an old habit that must have resurfaced after he left WU because he didn't pull that kind of thing while playing for my father.

"Briggs says he's heard that Slade can be a loose cannon against the opposition, but he's hoping that with the championship on the line, he'll watch his temper and share the puck," Autumn says.

I'm tempted to tell them that Slade has a temper on and off the ice. Especially when it comes to jocks who ask me out on dates, but then Tessa turns to me. "Your dad coached him in college, right? And didn't you two go to the same college for a while?"

The barista brings us our food, giving me a little time to think about how to explain Slade and my past.

I've mentioned before that I had someone in college that I didn't like, but I've never gone into the details of what happened. I can't avoid the conversation now, and if he weren't a player on the Hawkeyes team, I wouldn't care about airing out all the dirty laundry. I just don't want the gossip mill churning over this one. It's bad enough what Slade did in college. I don't need everyone at work watching our interaction under a microscope.

"Yeah, my dad coached for Washington University until Slade's last year. Then Phil Carlton offered him the GM position here," I say, pulling the plate with the turkey club sandwich, with no tomatoes, closer to me.

The smell of fresh-baked bread and bacon has my mouth watering already. On top of putting my blouse on inside out this morning, I also forgot to eat breakfast before flying out the door. My father and Phil had an early morning meeting with legal today, and since I take notes for all meetings, I decided to opt out of my morning skate to attend the prep session with my father and Phil at six a.m.

I was absolutely not, in any way, avoiding the locker room to ensure I didn't have a run-in with Slade this morning. That would be silly, and I won't let Slade ruin the Hawkeyes' stadium for me. This became my home first, and I won't be chased out of it by Slade like I was in college.

Now I'm starving, and the only thing I had was the dirty chai that Tessa bought me from Serendipity's on her way to work this morning.

"So, you know Slade well, then. Did you have classes together?" Autumn asks, spooning saltine crackers into her tomato bisque soup.

"Well enough that he felt compelled to scare away anyone who wanted to take me on a date and ruin my chances at competing for the Olympics pair figure skating qualifier," I say in one long, frustrated breath.

"Damn, that sounds like a long history if you ask me," Tessa says, pulling her own turkey sandwich up to her mouth and then abruptly sets it back down on the plate when something comes to mind. "Wait! Is this the guy that you wanted to be killed in our 'kill-pact'?"

"Tessa!" Autumn says, dipping her head low and looking around to see if anyone heard Tessa discussing our hit list that none of us were actually serious about. "Not so loud. People don't know you're kidding. And besides, you're marrying the man you wanted off'd... remember?"

Tessa waves her off. "I'm still taking it day by day. That man drank the last of my coffee creamer yesterday and didn't tell me so that I could stop by the store and get more. Lucky for him, Penelope needed an emergency drink order. Otherwise, he'd already be sleeping with the fishes."

An emergency drink order accurately depicts the dire straits I was in after seeing Slade yesterday. I'll need another one before I leave here.

"Speaking of, don't let me forget. I want to order another chai before we head back to the stadium. I can't seem to keep anything straight today." I tell Tessa.

"Is there any chance that being flustered enough to wear your blouse inside out this morning has anything to do with the hot tatted hockey player that you want dead?" Autumn asks, smiling slyly at Tessa.

Ever since Autumn immediately pegged Ryker and Juliet's relationship as a ploy to keep Ryker in the States, she thinks she's some kind of relationship whisperer.

"Oh my God! Do you have a crush on him? I thought you hated him?" Tessa asks, her eyes wide as saucers.

"No... I—"

"Isn't that always how it starts?" Autumn sends Tessa a wink.

Tessa flashes her eyes back at me. "Yep, you're totally going fuck him."

I hate how she relaxes back in her chair and finally takes a bite of her sandwich as if sleeping with Slade is inevitable.

"There's no damn way I'm going to touch that man," I say, taking a bite of my own sandwich to show I'm not bothered with their nonsense, though I would have thought that of anyone, Tessa would be on my side.

My preference would be not to live in the same country as the man, let alone have sex with him.

"You've guessed all of our romance story tropes pretty spot on. What story is this one going to end up like?" Autumn asks.

"The Titanic," I say simply.

"Wait, is that movie considered a romance or a tragedy? The hero dies in the end. Don't romances technically have to supply a happily ever after?" Tessa asks.

"Sure, but a happily ever after for whom? Because I'll get my HEA the minute that Slade goes down with the ship."

There's a short silence as they both look at me wide-eyed. I'm usually the optimist in this group, and I would be if we were discussing any other subject. But what Slade did to me is unforgivable.

"Oh shit, she's going to marry him isn't she?" Tessa asks.

Autumn giggles as they share a look.

"Well, thanks for the pep talk, ladies. I'm glad someone enjoys my misfortune," I say.

"Sorry, girl... we're just teasing you. I'm sorry he was such a dick to you in college. Maybe he's matured now and won't do anything else stupid?" Autumn says, hope sparkling in her eyes.

"Yeah, we're just playing around. Trust me, Slade Matthews is on our shit list for what he did to you," Tessa nods. "We hate him. Right, Autumn?"

There's the Tessa I know.

Tessa shoots a look at Autumn with a frown and her eyebrows drawn together.

Autumn takes Tessa's lead and nods.

"Right... yeah... we hate that guy."

I shake my head and can't help but smile. Slade might be my very own version of kryptonite, but I know they're just trying to lighten the mood. And maybe that's what I need.

Who knows... Autumn could be right about Slade. Maybe he has matured since college. I can only hope that's true.

"But out of curiosity... so that we know why we really hate his guts properly, how exactly did he single-handedly ruin your chances at trying out for the Olympics?" Autumn asks.

Autumn pulls her glass of ice water to her lips.

"Good question," Tessa says, chewing a bite of sandwich and leans in towards me to hear my answer.

"He threatened Sean Klein, the captain of the soccer team and a guy I was supposed to go on a date with. Sean canceled our date with a text, and when my college roommate cornered him at a party she was at that same night, he said that Slade Matthews threatened to break his kneecaps if any athlete at WU touched me."

Autumn's eyebrows stitch together in confusion, and Tessa looks downright pissed off.

"Did you confront Slade about it?" Tessa asks.

Her irritation finally resembles how I would expect a friend to react to what Slade did. Slade and I are nothing like Lake and Tessa. There is no underlying sexual tension there like they had for years prior, and Lake had fallen for Tessa even years before that.

My history with Slade is not even close.

"I couldn't. They were at an away game by the time I found out. The partner I had been skating with for six years got in a skiing accident the week before and was going to be in a full-leg cast and would be out for a year. My coach put together tryouts with a couple of new potential skating partners for me to skate with, but Slade's threat spread around campus and no skaters showed up. None of them wanted to take the chance that Slade would make good on his threat to end any athlete's career who came near me."

"Are you serious? He did that?" Autumn asks, her jaw practically hitting the floor at my explanation.

Tessa sits there with her arms crossed and a scowl on her face.

"Please tell me that the minute he came home, you kneed him in the nuts so hard, he'll never be able to conceive children," Tessa says. "Or, at the very least, tell me that you spread a rumor around campus that he has crabs."

Autumn lets out a snicker, and I grin to myself, thinking about how Tessa would have handled Slade if he had done it to her instead of me.

"No, I didn't. But my dad got the last word. He's the reason Slade spent four years on a farm team instead of playing in the NHL," I tell them.

It's not like I didn't think about taking out my own revenge, but I know why Slade did it. I didn't need to ask him.

It's not news to me that my father is overly protective. I had heard about my father's hour-long lecture in the hockey locker room the day before I transferred to WU from Michigan, where I used to live with my mother.

"No one dates my daughter, or you'll be benched for the rest of the season."

I had a reputation before I even stepped foot on campus soil.

But it didn't bother me at the time. I knew that dating one of my father's players would put my dad in a weird position. I know enough about dirty locker room talk to know that the last thing my father wanted to hear was stories about me with one of his players behind closed doors.

Still, Slade took it upon himself to scare away any prospective athlete boyfriend, which then bled into the world of figure skating. It isn't surprising that my prospective new partners learned about Slade's threat since the ice skaters and the hockey players all shared the same ice.

Whether Slade's threat to a potential skating partner was explicit or implicit, he was responsible for the damage.

"Nice work, Sam Roberts. I always knew I liked him," Tessa says with a grin.

"He can do that? Force Slade to sign on with a farm team instead of an NHL team?" Autumn asks with one eyebrow downturned like something doesn't add up.

I have to agree with her that it did seem odd that Slade would agree to be exiled when he had a heaping handful of the top NHL teams wanting his signature on their contracts.

It just serves my theory even further that Slade's nose is so far up my father's ass that he would do whatever my father told him to do.

"He didn't have to force him. Slade went willingly. And now he's back," I sigh.

It's been four years, and he's still taking marching orders from my father. He could have told my father to cram it at any point, but he didn't. He waited patiently in Canada like a good little soldier until my father's judgment was over.

Now it is, and of all the places my father thought to send him, he sent him right back into my line of sight.

"I can't believe Sam brought him back here. Though Lake says that besides an obvious chip on his shoulder, the kid can play hockey," Tessa says.

"Chip on his shoulder?" I ask.

"Lake just said that it seems like he's got something to prove based on the way he acts like a team of one who doesn't want to pass the puck. But I guess he sort of does need to prove he can play after coming into a team that's only one more win away from making it into the playoffs."

I just shrug. He has nothing to prove to me. I already know the kind of person he is, and I have no interest in learning anything else.

"The way I see it, the best-case scenario is that he and I find a way to avoid each other."

After another twenty minutes of finishing up lunch, we all head out to leave.

"Did you still want to get your chai?" Tessa asks.

"Oh yeah, thanks for reminding me. Go on ahead, the line looks long. I'll catch up with you girls later."

Autumn and Tessa nod and then head towards the exit. They have a meeting in ten minutes, and I don't want them to be late.

I walk to the end of the line with five people before me, but then I see him.

Slade Matthews is at the front of the line.

With his stature, he's impossible to miss, standing at least a foot taller than anyone else in line.

He's dressed in a pair of jeans and a t-shirt that shows off his muscular arms. My eyes follow the full-sleeve tattooed arms from the tight-fitting cuff of his cotton shirt down to where the ink stops before his hands.

He didn't have all those tattoos in college... or at least I don't remember them. And although he was in good shape then... Slade seems so much bigger now.

He runs his hands through his messy, long hair.

It's not long enough for a man bun, but just at the perfect length that when he runs his fingers through it, it leaves those feathered layers of dark chocolate strands running parallel along the side of his head.

He looks back over his shoulder and finds me staring. A smile quickly forms across his lips, and I dart my eyes away towards the coffee cart that holds things like Splenda packets and stir straws in an attempt to pretend I didn't see him.

"Penelope," I hear him call out.

I want to pretend I didn't hear him and ignore his existence, but my father's words echo in my head that I'm supposed to do my job to Phil Carlton's standards. And Phil would want me to be nice to the newest member of the team and our best shot at winning the Stanley Cup. And if I ever want Phil to consider me for the GM position in the distant future, I need to show I can be diplomatic.

I can feel the eyes of other people in line, also looking back to see the person who has Slade's attention.

"Oh... uh, hi," I say back with a small and insignificant wave.

"What are you drinking?" he asks, handing his card to the new barista.

I've never seen her here before today. The owner was giving her instructions earlier when we came in and ordered our food.

She's got her eyes set on Slade as he stares back at me. She seems just as smitten with his presence as every girl on campus was with him four years ago.

Nothing's changed.

I want to warn her to stay away from him. He's not the "bring home to mom and dad" type, but then again, she might not be looking for long-term.

Either way, I hate when women give Slade any undeserving adoration. He doesn't need any additional ego boost.

"And whatever she's having," he tells her.

Her smile falls a little when she realizes that he's talking about me.

Though her smile has no reason to waver, I'm sure as hell not going to arm wrestle her for him. She can have him for all I care.

Everyone else in line, including the barista, stare back at me, waiting for me to answer him.

"You don't have to do that. I can wait," I say.

"What are you drinking, Penelope?" he says, not taking no for an answer.

He's holding up the line and is playing on the fact that I'll eventually succumb to peer pressure and cave into his request. I don't like being inconsiderate by holding anyone up. Having people waiting on me for an answer is a small kind of torture.

"A chai," I say softly, feeling yucky about letting him buy anything for me.

It's like, somehow, if I let him buy me this small thing, he'll have made amends, and I must forgive him.

Fat chance that's ever going to happen. Even if he bought me the whole damn coffee shop.

No chai, no matter how delicious, will make up for what I lost.

"Dirty..." I say at the last second, fighting back the urge to close my eyes and wrinkle my nose by saying the word out loud.

My eyes dart to the older man directly in front of me wearing a fedora hat and attempting to look like a character from a detective novel. It's more likely he's a retired middle school teacher that none of his students liked. He gives me an odd look... the one I figured I would get for ordering my chai... dirty.

Then my eyes reluctantly glance back at Slade. A smirk stretches across his lips as he stares back at me.

He turns back to the barista. "Make it extra dirty," he tells her, and she blushes.

Of course, she does.

Not that I have anything against her. She's just human... she can't help it.

I blame him. It's the damn Slade effect. That's what my roommate in college used to call it as she rolled her eyes.

The barista inputs the drink order, swiping his card to pay for it and then hands it back to him.

He takes his card and slips it back into his wallet, then steps out of line and walks towards the pick-up window.

There's no more reason for me to stand in line as other customers walk into Serendipity's Coffee Shop and start lining up behind me.

I follow him to the left side of the counter towards the exit where the coffee cart and the pick-up window are located.

He leans an arm up on the bar-height counter and watches me take my sweet time, joining him at the corner of the shop.

"Thanks," I say simply.

I watch Mary, the other barista standing in front of the large metallic espresso machine, start concocting a hot beverage that I can only hope is mine so that I can get out of this situation as quickly as possible.

"No problem. I interrupted your skate time yesterday. I owe you," he says.

"You don't owe me anything," I tell him.

That's not true. He owes me an Olympic tryout. But since I'll never get that chance back and I've already come to terms with retiring from my professional skating career, Slade's ability to make it up to me is impossible. I'll settle for him pretending that I no longer exist, and we can both get on with our day.

My eyes shift away from him as I watch Mary, my favorite barista, at work.

She can barely see me over the tall machine, but she smiles the second she recognizes me.

She mouths a hello, though the loud screech of the milk steamer drowns out any possibility of her and I having a real conversation, which would have saved me from having to converse with the man taking up everyone's attention in the small coffee shop.

While everyone else is staring and whispering about Slade, he seems to only have his eyes on me, not breaking away for even a moment. I'm sure he's used to all the attention by now.

Even in college, Slade's presence in any room he was in always demanded everyone noticed him. We didn't have any classes together. He was in his senior year, and I was in my junior year, so our paths didn't cross all that often except at house parties or when I'd watch my dad coach during home games. But if there was ever a crowd of people forming somewhere on campus, Slade would surely be surrounded by the mob.

I never understood all the hype. Or... I suppose there was a brief moment when maybe I did.

On my first night on campus at a frat party, I saw Slade standing in the living room with a group of guys. Our eyes met for just a moment, and he smiled at me. I thought he would come over and introduce himself, but then my roommate asked me if I wanted a beer and when I looked back to find him again, he was gone. I didn't see him again that night, but it's just as well since my roommate turned to me when she saw who I was smiling at.

I still remember our conversation.

"You know who that is?" she asks.

"Who are you referring to?" I say, playing dumb.

"The guy you just undressed with your eyes," she teases and then pokes her elbow into my side.

"I just smiled at him," I say defensively, taking the beer she hands me.

"Well, stay clear of that one unless you want it hot, fast, and temporary. Word is he's good in the sack, but he doesn't do girl-friends," she warns.

"Who is he?"

"Some big-shot hockey player who has a temper and likes to hog the puck... so I'm told."

"Hockey player? What's his name?" I ask, making a quick sweep of the kitchen and living room again to see if he returned.

"Slade Matthews. I heard he has had five separate NHL teams trying to sign him into a multi-million dollar deal since the kid was a junior in high school."

Slade Matthews... I've heard that name before.

My father's protégé and a hockey player, which means I don't get to touch, or my dad will have an aneurysm and lock me up in some tall tower.

My dad mentioned that Slade had a temper when he first showed up freshman year. He didn't like making friends or shar-ing the puck, either. He also said that Slade's good enough to get away with it to win most games... but you can't win championships without a team.

Slade has been my father's pet project for the last three years. Between this being Slade's senior year, and the Hawkeyes trying to wine-and-dine my dad into moving to the NHL, Slade might be the last college player my father gets to coach.

They have some kind of bond I haven't been able to understand from Michigan. But now that I'm here, I have to admit that I'm curious about the player that my father raves about.

"Oh... I've heard of him. He plays for my dad. Why doesn't Slade just take the contract deals, then? Why play college hockey and risk an injury?" I ask.

With everything my father has told me about his star player, he never mentioned that Slade has had NHL offers since before he showed up at the University of Washington.

With hockey careers being as short as they are, why would he risk his best years playing in college if he could already be playing in the NHL?

"His family is wealthy. Like mega-rich, great-great-grandpa owned a baby shampoo company, wealthy. He has like a fifty-million-dollar trust fund that he doesn't get unless he finishes college first," she says and then takes a sip of her beer. "The kid is pre-med too. Why try so damn hard? I'd be taking basket weaving classes, and wine appreciation courses to fill my requirements. Just enough to graduate, and then I'd be living out my best days on a private yacht off the Greek islands."

She has a point. Why is he trying so hard?

But there's no point in wondering. I'll never be allowed close enough to ask.

Thinking back on that conversation with my roommate, it turned out that keeping my distance from the hot hockey player with whom I shared a quick smile at a packed house party didn't matter. Because a few weeks later, that same boy blew up my life anyway.

And now, standing next to him in the pickup line, waiting for my chai latte, brings back all those painful memories that I've tried to leave in the past where they belong.

I lost my partner because of his injury, missed my chance at the Olympics because of Slade, got rejected by Win, the only man I've truly had feelings for in years, and then dropped out of professional skating and college in the same week. Everything happened in the span of a few months, leaving me feeling empty, isolated, and honestly... a little depressed, which is not my usual default setting.

I gave myself three months to grieve my lost life, and the pen pal I had fallen for, and then I set myself on a new destination, making hockey my career path. Besides skating in the morning to keep a little bit of my old self intact, I'd never consider single skating, and I'll never find a replacement for the dynamic partner I had in Toby.

I've made peace with it, so the sooner I leave Serendipity's and put some distance between Slade and me, the better.

Slade

She's doing everything she can to avoid looking at me. I'm not used to women attempting to ignore me. I'm not used to anyone showing this much disinterest in me... unless it's my father's disappointing stare and condescending tone when he's telling me that I'm throwing my life away chasing a mindless career like hockey.

But he's not worried about me throwing my life away. He just thinks my career path will embarrass him at his board meetings or charity events when people ask why his only son didn't follow in his footsteps and become a doctor.

He always thought that if he pressured me long enough and required me to get a pre-med degree as part of the stipulations of my trust fund, I'd eventually see the light.

He even convinced my grandfather to draw up a document that I had to sign with the family trust lawyers, agreeing to the prerequisite to get my inheritance. But now, with my part of the deal complete, I'll get my trust fund in two months when I turn twenty-six, just like all my other cousins on my mom's side of the family. Since my grandfather passed away during my freshman year of college, my mom's oldest brother controls the family trust, and he doesn't like my dad, so there's nothing my father can do to stop it now.

It's not that I need the money. The hefty starting contract that Phil Carlton offered me is more than enough for my lifestyle. After my dad cut me off the day after college graduation when I told him I wouldn't be attending medical school in the fall, I learned how to live on less.

I don't need to show off like I used to in college. The expensive condo my dad put me up in and the brand-new Mercedes G-class he'd lease me every year. None of that was for me. It was so he could show off our family's wealth.

Image is everything to my father. As one of the top cardiac surgeons in the country and married to my mother, who is one of only three heirs to a baby shampoo dynasty, my father never warmed up to the idea that his only son wanted to play hockey as a profession.

When I joined the farm team, he thought it would be my final straw—that I would give up and go to medical school to be the doctor he wants me to be. What he didn't know was that I had offers from all the top NHL teams. I wasn't skating on the farm team to keep my hockey dream alive; I was skating on the farm team to make it up to her.

"Penelope," the barista making the drinks calls out, sliding the cup over in her direction on the bar.

"What makes a chai dirty?" I ask as she steps forward to take it.

I try to hide the smile stretching across my face but I fucking can't stop smiling when she's anywhere near.

She stares back at me, those crystal blue eyes with facets resembling cut glass. I've never seen a pair as beautiful as hers. I've waited four years to be this close again to see them in person and they don't disappoint.

"Can I ask you a question?" she says, sliding a coffee sleeve over the piping hot drink.

"Sure... fire away."

She can ask questions all damn day if she wants—anything to keep her talking to me.

"Is there an off switch for that?" she asks, rotating her coffee sleeve in place and not looking at me.

I shoot a look down at my crotch.

How the hell does she know that my cock twitches whenever she comes anywhere near me?

"Dudes don't come equipped with a control panel. There's no circuit breaker switch for that."

Penelope follows my line of sight and then quickly looks away, transferring her weight to the hip furthest from me.

"For the love of God, Matthews. I didn't mean that."

I glance up to find her rolling her eyes and grabbing a coffee stopper off the coffee cart behind me to put on top of her drink.

"Thanks for the drink, Mary," she tells the barista working behind the espresso machine and then gives her a wave, turning away from me to leave.

"What did you mean then?" I ask before Penelope can make her escape.

She stops and looks over her shoulder to answer me.

"That fuckboy smirk you wear around."

Do I have a 'fuckboy' smirk?

I'm guessing, by her tone, that it's not an endearing quality by her standards.

Then she turns and continues for the red door to the coffee shop.

"Thanks for the drink, Matthews," she says, continuing her leave.

I can't help but watch her toned figure skater ass walk out the door.

The view from here is nice, but I'm fucking tired of watching her walk away.

This is my last chance to get her to forgive me and I know it.

CHAPTER FIVE

Penelope

Running into Slade yesterday at the Serendipity's Coffee Shop was like a straight ice bath plunge into the reality that he's really here. He's no longer just a person I might occasionally see when I fail to avoid him in the stadium but an actual physical addition to my city. He can literally show up anywhere I am, at any time.

Before I woke this morning, I received a text from our HR manager stating that her seven-year-old had woken up with pink eye. With her assistant still off on maternity leave until next week, she asked if I could handle the new player intake forms for her today.

AKA, can I meet with Slade Matthews and scan in all of his new recruit paperwork.

I've done this a small handful of times in the past for new janitorial staff or concession stand employees, but never for a player.

It's not difficult work, and if it were anyone else, I'd be excited about the chance to meet our newest team member.

Unfortunately, she couldn't have asked me for a worse favor. I'd rather share an eye patch with her very contagious bacterial conjunctivitis-infected daughter than have to spend any amount of time with Slade.

But since she isn't offering that as an alternate option, I'll have to meet with the living, breathing bacterial conjunctivitis himself. God only knows what contagious virus he could be carrying around with him now.

He wasn't exactly a pristine little altar boy in college. His reputation was public knowledge, which is ironic since his mission in life from the moment I set foot on campus was to make sure I didn't get any. Or at least not from any athletes based on the threat he made.

Thankfully, this morning, my father decided to get breakfast with an old player from his NHL skating days who's in town.

With no early morning meetings, I get to decompress on the ice before my dreaded meeting at eight am with Satan... I mean Slade.

As I push through the locker room doors, the usual smells of dirty gym socks, sweaty male testosterone, and intense cleaning ammonia fill my nostrils.

No matter how much they clean or how often they've painted the walls, the smell is permanent and seems to seep back out of them. Though, I will say, as a figure skater, I've been in enough locker rooms to attest to the fact that our janitors do a much better job than most. However, I'd never shower in the locker room without shower shoes, no matter how often they bleach it.

Gross.

Walking through the locker room and towards the player's tunnel, I feel the unmistakable humidity that's usually created after my skating session when I take a hot shower.

I stop in my tracks, but I don't hear a single sound in the locker room, and I didn't see a single soul when I walked in.

I'd never use the men's locker room if I knew a player or a coach were in here. But no one's come in here before seven since I started working here four years ago.

I'm alone... as I should be for this hour in the morning. Maybe one of the janitors got here early and cleaned the showers first?

That isn't consistent with their usual cleaning schedule, but it could have happened.

I have too much on my mind to worry about, so I continue towards my end goal of the rink on the other side of the locker room.

I glide onto the vacant ice, and any thoughts of the locker room showers drift away.

Thirty minutes later, I'm dripping wet with sweat. Slade showing up again is bringing all the pain of losing my shot all those years ago back up to the surface. And skating the same program that my old partner and I choreographed for our Olympic tryouts fueled one of the best skating sessions I've had in years.

I put it out on the ice today, and as I skate towards the player's tunnel, I have to say... I feel better.

Something small and coffee cup-shaped catches my eye as I skate closer to the rink opening.

It's a to-go cup from Serendipity's Coffee Shop. I'd recognize that swirl-designed logo anywhere.

The steam from the cup still rises from the tiny opening of the black lid.

I look around quickly to see if the person who left the drink is somewhere in the stands but there's no one in sight. My first thought is Tessa, but I remember that she refuses to wake up until the sun does. She's probably just rolling out of bed now and won't be in for another hour and a half.

And Autumn left last night for Walla Walla to tour wedding venues with both her mom and Briggs's. She won't be back for a couple of days.

I pull the drink off the ledge of the rink sidewall and pull down the protective coffee sleeve to read the cup.

Penelope. It reads in black markers.

And then, just below the drink order, it reads...

Extra Dirty.

Cute... real cute.

I slide the coffee sleeve back on and more writing catches my attention

Chloe. Written in pen next to her ten-digit phone number.

Just below that is a marker-drawn heart with **"call me"** written inside.

Now I know the name of the new barista who couldn't stop staring at Slade yesterday.

Really Chloe?

You can do better. Or maybe you can't if you're still flirting with the guy who came in to buy the same girl's drink two days in a row.

Though Slade and I are far from dating, she doesn't know that... unless he told her.

I don't have to guess who left this drink for me.

There's obviously a particular hockey player somewhere loose in the stadium, and since I was so engrossed in my routine, I have no idea how long he watched me skate.

I look around one last time to see if Slade is sitting in the stands somewhere, but the stadium seats are still as empty as the last time I checked.

I step off the rink and head down the tunnel.

How long has he been here?

Was that steam from the shower from him?

Did he go to the coffee shop to flirt with the barista, or did he go to get me this drink?

And if he did go solely to get me this drink, does he actually think that buying my favorite beverage two days in a row is going to make me forget our history?

He might have forgotten what he did.

But I haven't.

Though I don't consider Slade a long-term relationship type, I hope he and Chloe will be very happy together.

Actually... I don't.

I hope she rips his heart into a million pieces and then glides over them with razor-sharp ice skates for poetic justice.

Slade

I'm not a big enough piece of shit to wish a child gets pink eye, but getting the HR manager's email this morning apologizing for her absence today and referring me to Penelope's desk seems like pretty good luck.

I took Penelope's warning and made sure not to come in during her skate time this morning. Instead, I came in an hour earlier than her to get my conditioning in and shower.

When I finished my morning warm-up, the Zamboni driver was already there. He polished the ice after me so that Penelope would have smooth ice for her morning skate. He must like Penelope enough to do the extra work. It seems like everyone around here likes her, and I can't fault them for it.

After my workout, I took a shower and then went down to Serendipity Coffee Shop to get Penelope her chai and a couple of their bagel breakfast sandwiches for me, along with a sticky bun and a lemon bar.

If I didn't play professional hockey for the love of the sport, I'd do it just for the number of calories I get to eat. Some days it's a curse to have to consume so much food, but most days, it's fucking awesome to eat anything I want and say it's for 'work'.

I follow the dark, wide-plank, espresso-stained wood floors down to Sam's office.

The first door that leads into the large reception area is already open. I walk through to find a small well kept small love seat and coffee table to my left, closest to the door.

Penelope is seated further in the large room at a desk that runs vertically to what I assume is Sam's office.

Sam has been down to practice the last couple of days, but he hasn't called me to his office yet. With tomorrow's game, win or lose, the Hawkeyes will know whether we're in the playoffs, and with that comes significant money opportunities for the franchise with sponsorship funds and deals with vendors that are keeping Sam and Phil busy.

"I'm early. I hope that's ok," I tell her, pulling out the chair on the opposite side of her desk.

My phone reads 7:53, but since it took me all of ten minutes to scarf down breakfast, I've been walking around the stadium aimlessly, looking for things I haven't discovered yet. Today is the only day off for the players this week, but the coaching staff will be in today for me to meet in person.

"Just as well. Let's get this over with," she says, not making eye contact with me as she shuffles through paperwork. "There should have been an email with paperwork to complete. Did you bring that in?"

"Yep, I filled it all out last night."

I hand her the stack of items I filled out after receiving an email from HR before I left Canada and slid it over the table.

She reaches over and grabs the documents, quickly going through the pages to ensure I brought her everything.

"Oh... before I forget," she says, reaching for the coffee cup that I presume is the one I left her this morning. She pulls off the coffee cup sleeve and hands it to me. "Thanks for the chai, but don't forget the barista's number next time. You wouldn't want to lose that since you went through all the effort to go down there and all."

She thinks I went down there to flirt with the barista? Nothing could be further from the truth.

"I didn't go down there to get her number," I say to correct her assumption.

"It makes no difference to me what your next flavor of the week is, Slade. But I would prefer that the remnants of your efforts don't taint my morning chai. No matter how dirty you order it."

I smile to myself, thinking she must have read the 'extra dirty' written on the cup.

"Are you sure?" I ask, curious to find out if she really cares about someone leaving me their number on her cup or if there's more to it than that.

Her eyes dart up to mine, and she stares back at me through her thick, painted lashes. There's no glimmer of interest in them, just straight irritation that I'm here in her space, breathing the same air as her.

I'd think she was jealous if she were any other girl, but I know better. She's still pissed at me for what happened in college, though she doesn't know the whole story... and I'll never tell her.

She might never forgive me for it, but that's what I'm here to find out.

"Am I sure if I don't want my coffee cup littered with the phone number and heart-shaped doodles of your next conquest?" she asks, her fingers pausing their rummaging through the documents I brought to her. I have no doubt she is looking for something I missed so she can call me incompetent and tell me to come back when I'm more prepared. Good thing I triple-checked the requirements before I walked in today. "Yes, in fact, I'm quite sure."

She turns her eyes and attention back down to the documents in front of her, checking a list she must have pulled up on her computer screen to ensure I brought in everything the HR manager requested.

"Is this really how you want things to be between us?" I ask.

I know it's a fucking ballsy question to ask an already unhappy Penelope. I can see the light skin of her chest starting to blotch with redness beneath the zipper of her fleece jacket.

Her eyes dart back up to mine. The coolness of her icy blue eyes makes me almost shiver at the coldness of her stare.

"If I had a choice, Matthews, there would never be anything between us at all, and you wouldn't be here," she says, straightening her spine now that she's checked a half dozen times and can't find fault with my paperwork.

"I'm sorry for everything I did that hurt you, Penelope. I swear it wasn't my intention."

She shakes her head like she has no interest in hearing what I have to say and then walks out from around her desk. I half expect her to keep walking out of the office and down the hall of the corporate offices, but she doesn't.

"Save your apologies for Chloe and whatever puck bunny comes after her... because your sorry is wasted on me. All I want from you is your driver's license so that I can make a copy," she says and then hangs a quick left inside a small walk-in closet-sized room.

Chloe?

Puck bunnies?

I don't want any of that.

The only thing I want is the woman who barely holds eye contact with me and flees the area whenever I show up. But I know better than to think that will ever happen.

Forgiveness and Penelope not hating my guts for the rest of my life—that's the best-case scenario here.

I follow her, reaching for my wallet in my back pocket.

I walk through the door of the tiny space.

It's a small printer room and it's barely big enough to be a coat closet.

If I sat down against one side of the wall and stretched out my legs, they'd touch the other side.

"Don't let the door shut," she warns me.

I'm right behind Penelope's back as she stands in front of the tall printer that reaches just to the middle of her rib cage.

She pushes a button to bring the printer out of hibernation.

"License, please," she says with a slight grumble in her voice.

She's not happy about being stuck in this small space together, that I'm sure of.

But even though she can't stand me, she's too polite not to ask nicely, even if her tone suggests that she'd like to plunge my license into the side of my throat and watch me bleed out.

I reach my left arm over her shoulder with ease. In her ballet flats, she's at least eight inches shorter than my six foot two.

The moment I outstretch my arm, I realize the image I just offered up for her to view. In only a t-shirt, my tattoos are easy to see, and the inside of my left forearm is right at her eye level. Pulling back is not an option at this point. It will only cause her to wonder what I have to hide.

And besides, it's too late.

She grabs for the license and her eyes zero in on the tattoo on the inside of my arm.

I had a pair of figure skates tattooed with peonies surrounding them. It lays etched permanently into my skin, serving as a reminder that making things right with her is my end game. Not that a single day has gone by where I haven't thought about what my actions cost her... or myself.

Hoping for more is a losing battle.

The odds aren't in my favor.

But I like a good underdog story, and I'm sure as hell willing to fight for it if she gives me any indication of that being a possibility.

Her eyebrows furrow as she stares at the tattoo, her fingers gripping the license, but she's too distracted with the ink on my skin to pull the card from my fingers, and I won't let go until she does.

"Figure skates? Was this a mistake by the tattoo artist? Shouldn't these be hockey skates?" she asks.

Those crystal blue eyes meet mine when she glances over her shoulder at me, an eyebrow half-cocked in question.

"No," I say simply, not pulling my arm away to cover it up.

Maybe this is exactly how this should go down.

Maybe spilling it all out now is for the best.

It's been years in the making, and maybe it's time for her to know why I went to Canada for four years and waited for Sam to bring me back here when I could have taken several other NHL offers since day one.

Though I'll never tell her the real reason that I threatened Sean Klein and any jock that dared to go near her.

If she finds out that a frat house full of bored rich assholes put a wager up for the first athlete who could score with the hockey coach's gorgeous daughter on the first date... I don't know how she would handle it.

It's that kind of shit that made me reject their offer when they wanted me to pledge years ago. I don't associate myself with rich pricks spending Mom and Dad's money and not giving a fuck about anyone else.

I rejected that life a long time ago along with their invitation.

Yet another thing I did that disappointed my dad.

"Why would you get figure skates tattooed on your arm? You're a hockey player. And what's with the blank banner across it?" she asks as if there is a missing puzzle piece to the tattoo.

I suppose she's right.

There is a missing piece.

"I haven't decided what to put in the banner. And the tattoo is for someone."

"For a girl?"

I nod.

She stares back at the tattoo, and I finally let go of the license, pulling my arm back. All of the sudden, this conversation is getting too real. She has to have already seen the small initials P.R. hidden in the dark shading of the back of the blade of the second skate.

She couldn't have missed it. She's too observant.

And the banner with nothing in it? I thought about putting the date I left or, maybe, adding the date she finally forgives me. I left it blank until I figure it out.

"Yeah," I say, dropping my arm to my side.

She turns to face me. Her shoulder grazes past my chest from our close proximity.

The door to the tiny closet is still open, but I don't dare take a step back away from her, even though I don't know how she'll react to seeing her initials on my skin.

I'll stand my ground and take whatever backlash I get for tattooing her on my arm after costing her the Olympic Tryouts. And the embarrassment that my threat caused, leading her to drop out of school a week before I left for Canada.

"Is she a girlfriend in Canada?" she asks, staring down at my left arm, now hanging down by my side.

Girlfriend in Canada?

Her question confuses me. I've never had a girlfriend before.

"No. It's for the one that got away."

Her eyes flash back up to mine, and I think...

This is it... this is the moment when she realizes it.

But I see only a void in her pupils. A distrust that I wish I could wipe clean.

I'd give anything just to see her smile at me as she did from across the room in that frat house where she was standing with a group of friends around the kitchen island all those years ago.

"She dodged a bullet," she says. "Lucky girl."

Fuck... ouch.

Does she really hate me that much?

And should it surprise me?

Then she swiftly spins her head back to the printer and lifts the top flap up, laying my license on the flat glass. She sets the printer flap back down and hits copy on the control panel.

The loud sounds of the machine gearing up to make a copy of my ID fill the space around us.

She has no idea I meant her.

She thinks I met someone in Canada and that I got this tattoo for that relationship.

I'm not so sure that setting the record straight at this point will help things. But I don't want to let her believe that there is anyone else... or has been anyone else.

I want back what I had with Pen—or, I guess, what Win had with Pen. She was falling for him; I could feel it because I was falling for her. But if I tell her that I deceived her to bypass Coach Roberts' rules in order to get closer... I might end up getting slapped with a restraining order and kicked off the Hawkeyes team.

All I can hope for now is a ceasefire and at least coming clean with her about why I got the tattoo in the first place.

"Penelope," I say, taking half a step closer, though there's little room left. "I need to tell you something."

My chest presses slightly up against her back.

We're close—closer than we've ever been. I can smell the sweet essence of vanilla in her hair and a hint of the spicy chai that I brought her to drink earlier.

The loud sound of the AC unit kicks on behind us from somewhere, causing us both to look back over our shoulders towards the door.

The door to the closet abruptly slams shut at the forced air vent that must have come through the ceiling and pushed the door closed behind us.

"No!" she yells, dodging around me and jumping for the door, but it's already shut.

"What?" I ask quickly, not understanding her panic.

I watch as she shakes the door handle vigorously without it budging.

"The door is locked from the outside. You can only open it from the outside," she says, her voice mumbling against the solid wood door.

Oh... shit.

"You can't open the door from the inside? What stupid design is that?" I ask.

I reach around her and try the door myself. What contractor would put a doorknob like that in any office, let alone this one?

She seems to give up for a second as I try the door a second time. Her shoulder slumps into the door as if she already knows our fate.

Her head rests against the door now, too, as she watches me jiggle the door handle in vain.

"It's one of the last original doorknobs from before the big renovation they did to this office a few years back. I've called the janitorial staff, and they've been too busy to get to a non-emergency item with the long list of items they need to get to in the stadium before the playoffs."

"I'm guessing this isn't the first time you've been locked in here?" I ask.

"Yeah... that's why I asked you to make sure the door didn't close," she says, rolling her eyes as if I locked us in here intentionally.

This wasn't my intention, but now that we're stuck in here for God knows how long, she'll have to hear out my apology. There's nowhere else for her to run.

"I guess that means we have some time to discuss what happened four years ago—" I start, but she cuts me off.

"I don't want to discuss this with you, Slade. It's in the past. Nothing you can say will fix it, so... just forget it, ok? If you want to make it up to me, you can do it by pretending that we don't know each other."

That stings harder than I want to admit.

"Penelope—" I say, turning away from the door and facing her straight on.

She moves around me to try to avoid this conversation, going back to the printer and pulling out a copy of my driver's license. There isn't much room to move around in here, so I don't know how she thinks she'll run away from hearing me out.

The sound of the outside office door opens, and Penelope's ears perk up instantly.

She pushes past me towards the closet door and starts pounding an open palm against it.

"Help! Help! We're locked in here!" she yells and starts to jiggle the handle again

I stand behind her as she rails on the door handle, and within a second, the door rips open while Penelope is still holding on.

I quickly grip her waist and pull her back before she face-plants from being pulled forward abruptly by the person on the other side of the door.

It's a knee-jerk reaction, and I pull too hard that she whacks hard against my chest, and we fall backward.

I pull her protectively to me so that she doesn't hit her head as my back smashes against the front of the printer.

I hear the loud crack as my back connects with the printer plastic, and a small groan escapes my lips, but it's not even close to the hardest hit I've had in my life as a hockey player.

"Penelope?" I hear a familiar voice say.

I look up to find Sam Roberts standing in front of us with the door pulled back and the handle still in his hand. His eyebrows stitch together in confusion at the scene in front of him.

His daughter, who hates me, is sitting in my lap on the floor with my arms wrapped around her.

Then his eyes connect with mine.

"Matthews?"

Penelope pushes out of my lap and quickly stands out of my grip. "They still haven't fixed the door," she huffs.

She immediately exits the printer closet as fast as she can, whizzing past her father and taking a left towards the exit instead of a right to her desk. "They're going to hear from me in person... right now," she says in a grumble and stomps off with the copy of my driver's license still in her hand.

Sam watches her for a second until I hear the door to reception slam closed.

She left.

His eyes revert back to me.

"Matthews... in my office," he says with one eyebrow downturned like I did something wrong.

A look I know well enough after playing for him for all those years in college that means he's disappointed in me.

"I didn't do anything. It locked us in, I swear," I say, scrambling to my feet.

"Anything to do with you and my daughter never seems to be nothing," he says, opening the door wider and then turns to head for his office. "My office, Matthews. Let's go."

Glancing over at the printer before I follow him, it doesn't look any worse for wear even though I hit it hard. Though I'm not so sure I'll fare as well in Sam's office.

I reach over quickly and lift the top of the printer to retrieve my driver's license first and quickly stuff my license in my wallet as I head for Sam's open office door.

Sam stands on the other side of his desk; his hands pitched at his hips as he watches me walk in.

"I brought you here because I thought you were up for the challenge of coming in here and helping this team bring home a Stanley Cup."

"I am, sir, and I'm up for the task."

"Then why the hell am I walking in on my daughter locked in a printer closet with you?" he asks, a frown across his lips.

"It was an accident, I swear. You can even ask her. The AC vent above the door blew it closed. I didn't know the door locks from the outside or I would have been more careful," I explain, but he doesn't seem any less irritated with the scenario.

"In the last four years, my daughter has never been locked in any room with a player on this team. And then all the sudden, you walk into this building, with the ink on your contract barely dry, and this is what I find you up to in my office," he says, his eyebrows raising in surprise at the situation he walked in on. "With the history between you and my daughter, I find it too coincidental to be an accident."

"Coach Roberts—" I start but he holds up a hand to stop me.

"I'm not your coach anymore, Matthews. I'm your GM. You can call me Sam from here on out," he says, his eyes a little softer, remembering that we have history, too.

A four-year-long history of state championships and a winning college hockey team that I captained for most of our time together during those years.

With my father's constant disappointment in me, Coach Roberts is the first male role model I've had that's believed in me. Every other coach, teacher, or potential mentor has only seen me as a spoiled trust fund kid with anger issues.

Though I was a hothead and got myself in more trouble than Sam would have liked, he's always believed in me. Then, when I went and put a black stain on our last year together by coming near his daughter and causing problems for her skating career, I unknowingly started a chain reaction of gossip around the school that didn't do well for her or Coach Roberts.

I nod.

"I can assure you that the only thing we did in that room was take a copy of my driver's license. She couldn't wait another second to get me out of this office. All I tried to do was protect her from falling face-first into the wood flooring."

"You know I've heard this before, right? When I confronted you about the rumors circulating about you threatening every jock in the university not to touch Penelope, you told me that you were trying to protect her. But you never told me what you were protecting her from. And then she lost her chance to compete in the tryouts."

Trust me, it's better that you don't know.

I want to say it out loud, but then he'll attempt to force it out of me. His knowledge of the humiliation and rumors that *could* have gotten around campus about Penelope if I hadn't stepped in would have been worse than my threats.

No good can come from telling Sam or Penelope the truth.

And a part of me can't shake the feeling that going after Penelope might have been retaliation from the fraternity towards me for turning them down, though I can't prove it.

"I know."

I nod, sliding my hands deep into my pockets and shrugging my shoulders.

I'm not the person I was then, and our roles on this team are far different than when he was my coach.

I'm no longer the dumb-ass, reckless kid he's trying to mold into a decent player. Now, I'm a highly paid recruit on the team who he has to put his faith in. And I have to trust that he makes sure that the Hawkeyes is a healthy team and stays a healthy team so that I have a place to play.

I'm here to do a job, and so is he.

"Penelope begged me not to bring you here, but I assured her that years have passed and you deserved your chance. Am I going to regret that decision?"

"No sir, you won't regret this," I tell him.

Penelope mentioned she didn't want me here, but hearing that she told her father that too, lets me know that I'm even further from making amends with her than I thought.

Maybe I underestimated how deep her hatred for me runs. I thought time might have lessened it but I couldn't have been more wrong.

"I'm no longer your coach, and you and Penelope are grown adults. This isn't college—there's far more on the line than just a college championship. We're playing with people's money now," he says. "You and I have the same boss, and Phil Carlton wants a Stanley Cup. I can't bench you for going anywhere near my daughter like I could in college. That's Coach Bex's job now. But I can trade your ass if you don't perform, so whatever you're up to, it better not distract you from what we hired you to do. Otherwise, I'll find someone else to fill your spot."

"I understand," I say. "I'm ready to win. I'm going to make you proud of me again," I tell him.

He stares back at me for a second.

"I've always been proud of you, Slade. That's never changed."

I wasn't expecting him to say that, and it takes me off guard. My father would never have words like that for me, not even when I graduated with honors in the courses he required of me.

"Thanks, coach," I say as a last respect for the relationship we've grown out of.

I know I lost some of Sam's respect the day that he found out about the rumors, but to hear that he's still proud of me means that one of the things I set out to accomplish by coming back to Seattle is done and I'm going to continue to earn Sam's approval.

Now, I just need to win over his daughter.

I have one more trick up my sleeve—a last resort. I planned on leaving this one in the past where it belongs. I chanced it for too long and it almost got me caught. If Penelope finds out that I'm WinForToday067, and that I basically catfished her to get close to her, I don't think she'll ever forgive me.

Then again, without persuasion from someone she trusts, she may never let down her guard.

I'm going to have to run the risk and hope it pays off.

"Ok then," he nods with a sigh. I'm not sure if it's one of relief or one of knowing he has no control and has to relent anyway. I hope it's the first. "Don't do anything stupid, Matthews."

Thanks for the famous last words, Sam.

Because when it comes to Penelope, it seems the only things I know how to do... are stupid.

CHAPTER SIX

Slade

Excitement seems to fill the large aircraft as we board our flight for our away game, the second to last week of the regular season.

Everyone seems to have their usual spot next to another teammate—two players per row of three seats on either side of the aisle, with coaches and other staff mixed in among the rows.

I notice that most of the back of the aircraft is still empty. It puts me closer to the lavatories, which isn't favorable, considering I'm on an aircraft full of athletes who eat more calories than the average human, and what goes in has to come out eventually. But it also gives me a better opportunity to sit alone.

I'm still the newest member on the roster, and throughout my entire career, except for college, I'm used to not forming tight relationships with my teammates since my father moved us around so much.

I'm used to coming into teams as the new kid, having to prove myself, and then leaving just as I hit my rhythm with my teammates.

I'm used to the players on the team staring at me, assuming that my talents are all overstated and inflated, and having to prove myself on the ice over and over again.

The farm team felt like an extension of that, except that all the players seemed to feel the same way. Either they were buying their time until they'd have to leave hockey altogether and retire into a desk job, or they didn't expect to be on the farm team for long because they thought they'd be getting picked up by an NHL team sooner or later.

Everyone was playing to stand out, not to blend into a team.

It's why I stay to myself. It's easier that way.

Every season since I started on the farm, scouts for NHL teams still offering me deals would ask me what I was doing, wasting my talent.

My father's calls after every loss to ask me why I hadn't thrown in the towel yet and applied for medical school didn't help either.

I was waiting on Sam's call, and I had to believe eventually, he would let me up for air. Now he finally has, and I'm in a position to do what I've come here to do.

I'm here to do a job, and that's what I'll do. I don't have to make friends. It's not a requirement for me to win.

I take my seat at the end of the last row, stowing my large backpack overhead to give myself leg room.

My larger bag is stowed under the aircraft with everyone else's.

I move into the last row and plop down in the window seat. It's early morning, and the sun is barely coming up.

I recline my head against the headrest and shut my eyes. A few minutes later, I hear the rustling around of luggage in the overhead compartment above me.

I peek open an eye to find Seven Wrenley stowing his backpack and then sitting down in the aisle seat in my same row.

I quickly glance in front of us to find that at least three rows ahead are still completely vacant. He didn't need to sit this close.

"Is this seat taken?" he asks.

When he asks, he doesn't look in my direction. He just starts to pull out his cell phone, a tablet, and a set of headphones. I get the impression that Wrenley doesn't ask for permission.

"Nope," I say simply.

Wrenley is one of the oldest players in the league, somewhere in his late thirties, and has had an unheard-of long career for a goaltender, which is why the fans coined the nickname "Lucky."

One is because of his legal name, Seven, and two is because he has one of the best and longest-running stats in the league's history as a goalie.

He's well respected in the league, though the media doesn't like him because he refuses to do interviews. If a reporter calls him by his nickname, Lucky, he'll ignore their question altogether.

I should be honored that Wrenley decided to take a seat in my row, but honestly, I'm not here to make friends. I'm just here to win a Stanley Cup or two, gain back Sam's respect, and get Penelope to look at me for longer than the few seconds it takes her to pass judgment or insult my way.

If we can at least tolerate each other, that's enough for me.

"There are other open rows if you'd rather," I say as if he missed them on his stroll through the aisle.

"I figured I should get to know my roommate," he says again, not looking in my direction as he puts his right Bluetooth earbud in his ear.

"Roommates?"

He finally looks over as he places the left earbud into his ear next.

"Ryker and I paired up as hotel roommates. You took his spot, so I guess that makes you my new roommate, rookie," he says.

He hits the play button on his tablet, and I can just barely hear loud music streaming through his earbuds. It's the most I've heard Wrenley say in all our practices since I showed up, but now he's done talking.

A man of few words.

Something I can appreciate about him.

It doesn't take long before the aircraft is filled up, two players to a row and only one vacant row in front of Wrenley and me.

An hour into our three-hour flight, I hook up to the jet's internet and pull up a video streaming service. I input Penelope Roberts pair skating, hoping to find the old routine she used to skate in college to confirm if it's the same one I watched her skate a few days ago.

I pull up the first one, but I can tell instantly that this program with her old skating partner doesn't start out the same way. It doesn't matter, I'm too mesmerized to stop the video and find a new one.

She's so goddamn beautiful when she skates. She pours so much emotion into her routine, even when she's just practicing, and to think that I'm the one who cut her career short kills me.

Her fluid motion makes it look like she's floating instead of skating.

I have no idea how to fix her missing partner problem, but there's one thing I can do... I can at least give her someone to skate with in the mornings.

I'm not a figure skater, and God knows I have zero training in lifts, spins, and death spirals. It's not as if I'll ever be good enough to skate competitively with her. I'm not built for it, and I'm a lifetime behind to be a real partner for her. But fuck it, if she'll agree to train me, I'll show up every day to spin her around that rink. Even if it's just for the hell of it.

I'm strong enough to hold her, and I can learn everything I need with her instruction.

There's one thing she can be sure of: I'll take a blade slicing through my skin if that's what it takes to ensure I never physically drop her.

I'm not an adequate fill-in, but it's the best I can do for now. That is... if she'll let me anywhere near her.

"Is that Penelope Roberts on the screen?" I hear Wrenley's voice cut through my focus from her routine.

I glance over to find his head still leaning back against the headrest and only his left eye open, peeking through and staring back at my screen.

I want to lock my phone as quickly as possible and deny his question, but it's not really a question at all. He knows it's her.

I don't appreciate him spying over my shoulder to see what I watch on my own time. I haven't asked him what music he's listening to, but I've been caught red-handed, and telling the most senior of the Hawkeyes team to pack sand won't serve me well here.

"Yeah. It's one of her routines from college," I tell him and then turn back to watch it.

If I'm already caught, there's no point in stopping now. It will only look like I'm hiding something or guilty for watching the video. Frankly, I don't care what he thinks about me watching the GM's daughter, but I do care that he keeps it to himself.

"I heard she almost tried out for the Olympics, but her partner got hurt," he says, now both of his eyes are open as he lazily watches the phone in my hands.

"Who almost made it to the Olympics?" I hear a player ask.

Brent Tomlin peers over a window seat two rows in our same aisle after he asks the question.

"Penelope Roberts," Seven says, giving Brent a quick glance and then his eyes come back to Penelope on my screen.

Another player, Reeve Aisa, turns in his aisle seat, two rows down and on the adjacent side of the aisle. His eyes lock with Wrenley's as he speaks. "I heard she was good enough. She and her partner were supposed to be the standouts during the preliminaries. A lot of people figured they would medal in the Olympics."

I see Brent nod in agreement on his side of the row.

"It sucks that her partner got in that accident. Why didn't she go out and find a new partner or skate singles?" Brent asks Reeve.

Aisa just shrugs his shoulders. "No clue. But it's too bad all that talent went to waste."

I could answer that question for him, but I don't think it will be well received in this group, considering how all the players and coaches avoid the rink during her skating hours so that she can have it to herself or how she seems to be best friends with half the team's fiancées. Even the Zamboni driver comes in half an hour earlier to polish the ice after she's done skating.

Reeve and Brent start discussing something about the history of Olympic sports, and I tune it out, turning back to my phone and watching the rest of the routine.

"So, what's with having a video of the GM's daughter on your phone? You played for Sam back at the University of Washington, right?"

Shit... I had a feeling he wasn't just making small talk earlier.

"I did. For four years."

"Then you already know how he feels about her," he says.

His voice is calm, and his facial expression is vague and unreadable. I have no idea where he's going with this.

"Better than anyone," I say back.

That's an understatement, considering my stint in Canada.

This time, he still didn't exactly give me his blessing not to date Penelope but admitted that he couldn't bench me since he's no longer my coach and she and I are both adults. His only recourse is to trade me if I fuck up on the ice. So, I'd better play better than I ever have in my life.

"Good, because Penelope Roberts is the unofficial little sister of this league, and if you screw with her or hurt her in any way, you'll struggle to find a single guy on this team willing to pull you out of the bottom of a player pile-up. Do you understand?" he asks.

His expression is still unemotional like he's talking about the weather. Still, the seriousness in his eyes tells me that I'd prefer being in a dark alley with a ninja holding a samurai sword than Seven with a dull butter knife.

"Got it," I say, not breaking eye contact with him and finally locking my phone by feeling for the side button.

I make a mental note to finish studying Penelope's routine in a more private setting from here on out since Seven mentioned that the entire team feels his sentiments about her.

"The Hawkeyes are more than just a team. We look out for each other. From my experience over the years that I've played for this team, outsiders coming in either embrace it... or they end up not lasting very long. It's your choice how this goes," he says.

"I'm here to stay," I tell him.

"Then the next time you're thinking about not passing the puck during a play, erase that thought and fast. This is a team sport. We travel as a team, we play as a team, we win or lose as a team. If you want to play an individual sport, go play tennis," he says and then hits play on his tablet and relaxes back against the headrest again, closing his eyes.

That must be the end of his motivational speech.

My guess?

Sam or Coach Bex put him up to it, and he wanted to botch it so badly that he made sure they never asked him to do it again.

Mission accomplished.

For the love of God, no one asks this guy to give a best man speech.

CHAPTER SEVEN

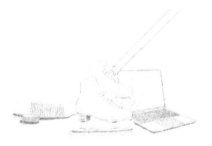

Penelope

The team is coming home today after being gone for the last three days.

Autumn, Tessa, Isla, and Berkeley have been over to my apartment for every game, and we've cheered on our team to victory for all three games. We're that much closer now to making it to the playoffs I can feel the nervous energy in the room. All of us girls sitting around the TV as we try not to bite our nails during every play at the net.

I hate to admit that Slade seems to be playing well, and sharing the puck better than I heard he had been last week in practice. However, he still spent more time in the penalty box than Lake and Kaenan combined over the last three games. An impressive record considering Lake and Kaenan spend a lot of time in the sin bin.

A record that I'm sure is making Coach Bex and my father want to rip out their own hair.

He's supposed to be playing on the ice, not watching from the time-out box like the bad little boy he's being. Not that there is anything little about Slade Matthews... his size, his hits against the players, his slapshot, or the way the Hawkeyes fans are already going wild for him in the stands.

I head in early this morning to get my morning skate in, knowing that the team was scheduled to get in at the butt crack of dawn. Slade should still be asleep and nowhere near the rink this morning.

I'm surprised when my phone alerts me to an email that comes through my old SkatrGirlPen address. It's not often that I get messages anymore to this email account. I primarily use it when signing up for bill pay or junk mail, like subscriptions.

Most of my email correspondence is in a professional capacity, which means I usually give out my official Hawkeyes work email.

When I open my inbox to see who the sender is, my heart flutters with excitement. It's Win.

I never thought I'd hear from him again, and I'd be lying if I said that I didn't wonder about him occasionally.

Where did he end up?

Why couldn't he email me from there?

Did he get married and start a family?

I have so many questions about the guy that I started tutoring a few weeks into my junior year during fall semester at the University of Washington. The thoughtful and kind soul of a person who seemed to know me so well and knew exactly what to say when I needed it most, even though we never met in person.

Embarrassingly, I had fallen for a guy that I never met in person while corresponding online. I emailed him, asking to meet up in person, but he pushed off the issue, citing finals before graduation, and though I understood, I still remember what the sting of rejection felt like.

Who has a crush on a person they've never even seen at least a picture of?

During the times when Slade was ruining my life, WinForToday067 knew how to bring me back and calm me. He made me feel understood and seen during a dark time for me when rumors were swirling around that Slade Matthews was my unofficial bodyguard and that any male who got close to me would be clobbered on the spot.

I probably gave too much away about my situation at the college, even though we agreed to stay anonymous at the beginning of our tutoring arrangement. I'm sure he figured out who I was. If that's the case, maybe he wasn't attracted to me. Or maybe he didn't want to be associated with me on campus with all the gossip surrounding Slade's threat.

So I didn't push the issue again. Rejection by the entire male skating community and by any athlete who might have had an interest in dating me before was about as much as I could handle.

The thing is, it didn't seem like Win was intimidated by hearing Slade's threat. He only seemed concerned with how I was handling it. Losing him was my last straw and I dropped out of school promptly after.

I've yet to find anyone since then who has ever made me feel like Win did. He made me feel giddy and excited whenever I saw his email in my inbox. I felt safe to share my hopes, dreams, and even the difficult things I was going through at that time with him.

Maybe that's why I have yet to have a lasting relationship. I haven't found anyone who can replace him.

I walk into the locker room with my duffel bag over my shoulder, ready for my morning skate, and look for a place to sit.

I drop my duffel bag to the ground and find a bench near the showers. My hands are almost shaking with anticipation, and I can barely keep the phone still.

A small pang of hesitation rises in me as I remember what he did. He up and left with zero notice and no explanation of why we could no longer correspond via email. I mean, where could you go that you wouldn't have internet for the last four years?

He could have gotten an internship as a polar bear habitat researcher in Antarctica. However, satellite internet has come a long way.

Or maybe he became a fisherman like you see on those Bering Sea tv shows. But even they come to town during the off-season.

The option I hate to think about, but the place my mind can't help but go to, is that maybe he had a serious girlfriend the entire time, and they were getting married and starting a life. Maybe he could sense that I was getting attached and didn't know how to let me down easily, so he made up an excuse to sever the correspondence.

Nothing about our conversations could be construed as inappropriate if one of us had been dating someone else. And it's not as if he led me on. It was the emotional intimacy that drew me closer.

It was the fact that anytime my phone pinged with the sound of a new email coming in, I'd practically drive to my cell to see if it was from him.

I was starting to develop real feelings for him, and I had just gotten up the courage to ask him to meet up when I received his 'Dear John' letter.

If I ever want my answer about what happened, now is the time to find out.

Once and for all.

The moment the email opens, my eyes dart to the sender to double-check and ensure I'm not hallucinating.

From: WinForToday067
To: SkatrGirlPen

Pen,

I hope this is still your email address and that this letter finds you well. I know I disappeared on you after my last email and I'm sorry for that. I want you to know that I haven't stopped thinking about you

> since the day I left and have thought about emailing every day since. But trust me when I say it was better this way.
>
> The reason for my email is to tell you that I'm back in Seattle. And I guess... I just want you to know.

He hopes this email finds me well?

He's thought about me every day since he left but didn't email me?

Does that mean that he did have internet but chose not to reach out to me on purpose?

He wants me to trust that no communication was all for the better?

And what the hell does he mean that he's back in Seattle and just wants me to know?

I want to be excited about this email but how can I be with everything he just said? It doesn't answer a single question that I've had for all these years.

I suppose I was expecting an actual explanation of where the hell he went and why.

Telling me that he witnessed a murder and was in the witness protection program. Or that he's a special forces operative in the military and has been entangled in a deep undercover mission for the last four years with strict guidelines to never correspond with the outside world would have been better than:

Hey Pen, I've thought about you and wanted to get in touch with you... but decided against it and I'm not going to tell you why. Also, I'm back in the same town as you... surprise!

I can't pretend that I'm not happy to hear from him. It gives me some kind of small inkling that he's reaching back out after all these years because I'm not the only one who felt something between us. But on the other hand, if he thinks I can just pretend that he didn't hurt me by leaving like we shared nothing over the short months that I tutored him, he's got another thing coming.

I debate what I'm going to email back to him for a second. The bulleted list of questions I'd like to send would probably be too aggressive right out of the gate. And though I'm not pleased with his lack of explanation, his timing with Slade coming back in the picture means I have someone to talk to who truly understands the situation. I hate to admit this, but I could really use his advice and support right now.

Neither Tessa, Autumn, or Isla were in my life at that time. And it's not as if I wanted to have a heart to heart with my father over the situation either. I think he felt some guilt over the fact that it was one of his players that ruined my Olympic dreams and caused me to drop out of college.

My father doesn't truly understand everything that I felt during that time—loneliness, isolation... a pariah around certain social circles. But Win does.

From: SkatrGirlPen
To:WinForToday067

Win,

I'm not sure how to start this email because the truth is... I have so many unanswered questions. Where did you go? Where have you been? Why didn't you email me if you said you wanted to?

But as your email already stated, you don't have any intention of sharing your reasoning, and so my questions are likely to remain unanswered.

I guess I can only hope that wherever life took you that left you unable or unwilling to continue corresponding with me, you were safe and unharmed.

There is one question, however, that I would like to know. When we were emailing back and forth in college, did you have a girlfriend?

I send off the email, not feeling confident about my response. I don't want to scare him away, but I also need to stand up for myself. I didn't with Slade all those years ago, and if watching Autumn, Tessa, and Isla stand up to get what they want from life hasn't inspired me, then nothing will.

If Win wants to fix what he broke, he needs to work to get back in my good graces.

I'm not asking for a full-out explanation since it doesn't look like I'm going to get it, but a little groveling for my forgiveness would probably fit the bill.

I push my cell phone back into my duffel bag and leave it in the locker room before heading out through the player's tunnel and toward the ice.

After inhaling the cold air of the rink, something comes over me and I end up skating my best performance to date. Maybe my best skate in years, because I finally got the answer to the question I've been asking myself for so many years.

Does WinForToday067 ever still think about me? And now I know... he does.

Slade

I stand in line for Penelope's dirty chai at Serendipity's Coffee Shop after getting home barely four hours ago. I couldn't sleep any longer, knowing she'd be in the stadium skating. It's been three days since the last time I saw her, and I've spent every one of those days watching the old routine I finally found of her and her skating partner's Olympic skating routine. After watching it so many times over my phone, I want to see it in person to make sure she hasn't tweaked it all these years later.

My phone dings with an incoming message. I pull my phone out to find an email response to the one I sent this morning to SkatrGirlPen.

That was fast, but I'm not complaining.

I'm surprised by her email. She does deserve an explanation, but I can't give her the truth without giving myself away as also being Slade Matthews. The same guy she was venting about all those years ago to someone she trusted via email.

If she finds out that I've been lying to her and that Win and I are the same person, she'll never forgive me, and I'll lose her forever.

Her last question, at the end of the email, throws me off. Did I have a girlfriend while she was tutoring me?

The obvious answer is no.

I've never had one nor have I ever wanted one.

Not until I met Pen.

Before her, I never wanted to be tied down to anyone. If my own parent's affections were based on merit alone, how could I expect more from a stranger?

Maybe that's in part because we moved around a lot when I was a kid. I didn't stay in the same school or the same state for that long. My father was always chasing the next big promotion, and as the leading cardiovascular surgeon in the country, he had his pick of hospitals that all wanted him.

It didn't matter that my mother's trust fund was more than enough to live a wealthy lifestyle on. At nearly a hundred-million-dollars, my mother has never had to work a day in her life. My grandfather made sure that neither she nor my aunt or uncle wanted for nothing.

My trust fund is half the value of my mother's and more money than I'll ever need, especially with my newer modest lifestyle that make me happier than I ever was before, spending money with strings.

I've provided for myself just fine since my parents financially cut me off after I took the Hawkeyes farm team contract after college. Now with the biggest contract ever awarded to a player coming out of a farm team in NHL history, I still won't need my trust fund.

That money can rot in a bank account somewhere for all I care. All it ever brought me were requirements and expectations tied to my parents and it used as a way to control me all my life.

But if I turn down the trust fund, the money reverts to my mother, and I won't give my father the satisfaction.

The line moves along with the morning rush and it's finally my turn. I order a breakfast burrito with double protein, a full order of hashbrowns, a yogurt parfait and a sticky bun... and a dirty chai for Penelope. This time, it's not Chloe taking the orders; it's the woman who was making the drinks the first time I bought Penelope her drink while she was in the coffee shop with me. I think her name is Mary.

I don't have to be on alert that she's going to give me a secret message on Penelope's drink like Chloe did.

I walk over to the pick-up window and wait for my order and then I pull up my email to respond back.

From: WinForToday067
To: SkatrGirlPen

Pen,

I know you deserve an explanation, and someday I'll give you one. Just know that breaking off commu-

> **nication with you was one of the hardest things I've ever had to do, and I'm sorry.**
>
> **And no... there's never been anyone else.**
>
> **Only you.**

That last sentence was more than I should have admitted.

There's a significant possibility that what I just admitted is going to blow up in my face, but after holding onto those words for over four years, it feels like a huge weight has been lifted off my shoulders. Even if the person I want her to hear it from is Slade and not Win.

The trouble is, she won't accept those words from the real me... even though, in reality, they're both me.

The fuck-up she knows me as who can't seem to do anything right when she's involved. And the pen pal who's the man I want to be for her.

I'm both.

But when she finds out, will she accept both?

My order number is called, and I grab the items off the pickup window and then head for the stadium.

I get there right as Penelope takes to the ice.

It's almost painful to watch someone with so much talent practically float across the ice with pure elegance . And when I notice the parts in her routine where it's obvious a lift or spin with a partner should be, and she has to skate through the void, the guilt of what I robbed her of is even stronger.

In college, on occasion, I'd catch her out on the ice if I showed up late on weekdays and early for practice. I kept my distance like I was supposed to and she never knew I watched her skate, even back then.

Brent's question comes back to my mind. Why didn't she find someone else to skate with? There had to have been someone she could have found off-campus who hadn't heard the rumors... or maybe someone who just didn't care.

I wonder why she isn't skating with her old partner again. Last I heard, he started skating with a new partner a year after his accident.

I pull out my phone and start recording her routine from start to finish as I polish off the last of my breakfast burrito.

I need to fix what I broke and earn back her trust if I want a shot at her finally forgiving me.

I'll never be good enough to compete in competitions with her. All I can do is try to give her someone to skate with.

It's not a lot but I hope it's enough.

A message from her comes back in response.

From: SkatrGirlPen
To: WinForToday067

Win,
It was only you for me too.

There's the confirmation in black and white on a small cell phone screen.

I had her... once, and I fucked it all up.

Chapter Eight

Slade

It's been a few days since I recorded Penelope's skate routine, and I've been pouring over it diligently, memorizing every movement, going back and forth between the new video I took and the old recording of Penelope and her partner so that I could see his movement too.

We have our first home game tomorrow, and if we win the next three games, we'll be in the playoffs.

I can't believe I'm this close to playing for the NHL championship. It's a dream I've had since I was a kid, and it's all coming true.

Seven invited me in to lift weights with him this morning. Coach Bex moved drills to later this afternoon due to a meeting he couldn't miss with Phil, Sam, and some big-time sponsors.

After our away game, I'm starting to settle into the team. Seven's conversation with me on the plane was the last warning he gave. I think I proved to him out on the ice that I could be a team player, though he gave me plenty of glares from the goalpost every time I ended up in the penalty box.

He didn't like that... and neither did Coach Bex.

"What do you think about the team we're up against tomorrow?" Briggs asks Seven.

"I'm not worried about tomorrow's game. They're a tough team, but as long as we bring our best, we'll dominate. The game I'm concerned about is game three of this week," he says.

"Why are you worried about that game over the first two?" I ask Seven as I spot him on the squat rack.

"They lost the championship last year, but only because of a bad call made by the ref. And this year they look even better," he says, reaching up and gripping his hands around the barbell and then lifting up to do another set.

"Speaking of bad calls, the girls want to do a ladies-only birthday party at the club next Thursday," Briggs says. "The guys are going to head to Oakley's for drinks. You down to shoot some pool?"

Seven finishes his reps, and I help guide the barbell back into position.

He blows out a breath the second the bar falls into place on the rack. His face turning from bright red to a more normal shade quickly.

I thought I could lift a decent amount of weight until today when I saw that Seven has a decade on me but can lift twice my bench weight.

"Yeah, I'll come out," Seven nods.

"How about you, Matthews?" Briggs asks.

I don't know why, but I glance from Briggs to Seven. Seven gives a light nod as if to coach me on how to do it.

I know he wants me to blend in more with the team and buy into the Hawkeyes family way of doing things.

It's foreign to me.

Even the version of what most people consider a family isn't what I know at all.

Having each other backs no matter what. Relying on one another, whether out of the ice or up at Lake and Tessa's penthouse playing poker during home game weeks.

Or whether it's Briggs and Autumn hosting barbecues upstairs in their apartment for no other reason than just to hang out with the players on the team. I'm not used to it.

"Sure. I'll be there. Thanks," I nod to Briggs.

After we finished weights, the guys decide to go for a five-mile run to get in their morning cardio, but I have a check-in with the Hawkeyes physical therapist in an hour, and I want to get something to eat first.

I check my watch and it's just a few minutes before seven in the morning.

At this time in the day, Penelope should have already finished her time on the ice and showered, so there shouldn't be any danger of me walking in on her. Not that it would be an unwelcome sight for me, but I'd never do that without her consent.

I push through the door and the confirmation that the shower isn't running means she must already have finished and be back upstairs in her office.

"Penelope?" I call out in question, just to be sure. "Are you in here?" I ask, but there's no reply.

I head for the showers, listening closely in case she doesn't hear me. From what I know about her schedule, she is usually up at her desk by seven a.m. sharp. She'd be running unusually late if she was still in the shower.

I undress from my sweat-drenched gym clothes, grabbing the three-in-one shampoo, conditioner, and body wash that I keep in my duffel bag. I wrap a towel around my waist and head for the shower.

The shower floors lack evidence that anyone has showered here this morning, but Penelope misses days from time to time when Sam has early morning meetings. She might not have skated and showered here this morning. That is an easy enough explanation.

I dispose of the towel onto the short teak wood table just inside the large tiled locker room showers.

Walking in further, I reach the chrome faucet plumbed into the wall and twist the handle to the hottest setting that the high-end rain showerhead will go. The spray hits me, warming my already hot skin while the high-pressure water pounds against my sore muscles.

The showers in the apartments are nice... but not this nice.

My head falls forward. My chin falls almost to my chest as I let the water do its work to make me feel human again after trying to keep up with Seven this morning. The guy is an animal, and he barely broke a sweat.

I wash every inch of my body with body wash and then suds up my hair before washing it all off. Now the locker room smells like some fragrance that's labeled on the bottle as Misty Forest Beast... whatever the hell that means. But it smelled the least off-putting of all the other fragrances they had for this brand.

I'm fully washed down and feeling partly relaxed when I hear the locker room door swing open.

Maybe Wrenley or Conley decided against the morning run? Or maybe one of the assistant coaches came in early?

Either way, none of them are rushing me out of here. I'd stay in here all morning if I didn't have an appointment with the in-house PT to check out my shoulder.

I lean my head back and let the spray continue to run down the top of my head and over my shoulders.

"What the hell are you doing in here!" I hear Penelope screech.

I pull my chin down and step partly out of the water to find a pissed-off Penelope with her arms crossed over her chest and what looks like a duffle bag over her shoulder.

Fuck she looks beautiful in the morning in a pair of sweats and her hair in a messy blonde pile on the top of her head. I can't deny that my cock notices, too, because it twitches at the sight of her, and if she had been watching, she would have seen it.

I've wanted the woman standing in front of me for too many years, and there's no way to hide how my body reacts to her.

"Taking a shower in the player's locker room," I say with emphasis on the players to remind her that this is still a locker room for the contracted Hawkeyes' hockey team and not the administrative staff. "What are you doing in here?" I ask, not bothering to hide my growing erection.

Her eyes roam over me, and then she takes a deep swallow when she sees how big I get under her wandering eyes.

Penelope

The moment my eyes open and I stare up at the ceiling in my apartment, my stomach turns, and my heart sinks. I don't have to look at the time to know that the alarm on my phone didn't go off this morning and I'm late for work.

I fling off the blankets and race for my duffel bag. I unzip it and then run to my walk-in closet, throwing in the easiest thing I find to make up an outfit: a knee-length spring floral dress, a cardigan, a clean pair of underwear, a bra, and a pair of ballet flats.

With the year well into April, the spring weather isn't as cold, and I've been itching to pull out my dresses.

I grab my bag and sprint for the door to my apartment, heading for the elevator.

Since the stadium is only a couple blocks away, my commute is only a few minutes. Still, since I occasionally run errands or have to drive to pick up lunch for my executives in the office from time to time, I always drive to work instead of walking like most of the players and other Hawkeyes employees who live in The Commons.

Within ten minutes, I push through the doors of the stadium and headed for the locker room.

I don't have time to skate this morning, but I have just enough time for a quick rinse down as long as I don't wash my hair. A professional bun will have to do to at least look presentable for the executives coming into the meeting with my father, Phil, and Coach Bex this morning.

I head for the locker room, taking as long a stride as possible, and push through the doors the moment I reach them. It's still around the time I'd usually be getting ready in the morning, and I already know that no one will be in the locker room for another forty-five minutes, at least.

I head for the showers when I hear the unmistakable sound of them running.

My heart immediately thumps against my chest. Did I make a mistake?

I quickly check the time on my phone, but it's exactly the time I thought it would be. No one else should be in here.

There's only one person who's been lurking around the stadium, leaving dirty chai lattes and watching me skate while I'm too engrossed in my routine to notice.

Slade freaking Matthews!

I glance over to the lockers, and sure enough, only one duffel bag sits on the bench in front of a singular locker.

Matthews #67.

I knew it.

He just poked the bear for the last time and I'm about to give him the worst verbal beating I've ever given a single soul.

I can feel my blood boiling. If I were a cartoon character, I'd have fire blowing out of my ears right now.

The second my eyes connect with the warm-skinned body of the traitor enjoying my hot water, I let out a guttural growl from deep in my chest.

"What the hell are you doing in here!" I yell over the shower water.

Slade's eyes dart open and his head tilts down from where he was pushing back the water that was flowing through his dark tendrils of hair.

My eyes catch on his arms dropping from his hair to his sides as he stares back at me.

He doesn't seem nearly as surprised as I am to find him in here since I already warned him that six am to seven am is my time.

He looks like a model in one of those cologne ads filmed in Greece. His hazel eyes with speckles of green, contrasted against his wet dark hair. He looks gorgeous... like he's photoshopped.

I can't help but notice his barrel chest is thicker than it was in college, and his six-pack and muscular arms flex at my attention. His arms are covered in tattoos when four years ago, he only had a peppering of randoms ink on them.

A large tattoo covers the top of his chest, though I can't make out the design without getting a little closer to study it.

And then something twinkles in the shower lighting... a piercing—a small silver bar through his right nipple.

He stands there, staring back at me and letting me take all of him in.

He's no longer the young, barely over twenty-two-year-old college kid that I'd see only occasionally walking around the college campus.

I can't help myself as my eyes drop down to the growing appendage between his thick thighs.

No, he's not that kid anymore.

Slade Matthews is all man. He's inked up into full sleeves and chest tattoos that reach up to his neck. He's hard as a rock... everywhere. He's dripping wet from his shower and looks like every fantasy I've ever had.

"Taking a shower in the player's locker room. What are you doing in here?" he asks, breaking me from my sex-brained haze.

I realize that I'm ogling the man's impressive cock, and he's witnessing my moment of weakness.

The kind of weakness that you can never show a man like Slade or he'll use it against you.

I raise my eyes to meet his.

I hate that he makes me feel anything towards him at all—especially sexual desires.

"I... I..." the words catch on the clog of desire in my throat.

Think Penelope! With your brain, for God's sake! Not with your clit.

A small smirk emerges in the right corner of his lips. He caught me staring, and there's no denying it, but I will if I have to. I'll deny it to my last breath. I'll never give him the satisfaction of thinking I'm like any of the girls who fall for his stupid good looks and inked-up brawny body.

Not this girl.

Not today... not ever.

"I thought you were already done for the day. But if I'm taking up your shower time, then you're welcome to join me," he says, his eyes hooded slightly and his lips wet and glistening from the shower water.

His tongue darts out to lick his bottom lip, and I just about forget where I am and what my name is.

Thankfully, something deep inside me screams out for self-preservation and I turn instantly, grip the shoulder strap of my duffel bag, and dart back out of the locker room. The sound of my ballet flats slapping against the locker room's wood flooring.

My shaking legs carry me as quickly as possible away from the man who has no business, making my girly parts throb and my nipples twinge as they harden under the gaze of his lustful eyes.

The second I'm free of the locker room doors, and I'm sure he hasn't followed me, I slam my back against the wall of the hallway to regain my composure and process how I could suddenly crave a man I hate so much.

What just happened in there?

What did I just see?

And... does Slade Matthews have a nipple ring?

CHAPTER NINE

Slade

It's the night of my first home game.

Walking into the locker room, everyone seems ready to get out on the ice tonight.

Everything hinges on us winning the next three games before we're officially in the playoffs and have a clear path to the Stanley Cup.

The pressure is high, and so is the energy. These are the nights you live for as a professional athlete. These are games that truly mean something, games where the winner takes all.

If we lose this, we're out for the season, and since I just got here, there's no damn way I'm about to let that happen. I came here to prove that I can compete at this level and failing means that I won't have any reason to come back here and see Penelope every day either.

Everything is on the table, and I'm playing to win.

I walk up to my locker and start getting dressed. Most players are pulling on their gear or are already set and ready to go. Some players perform superstitious gameday rituals, while others seem calm and relaxed.

It's not long before Coach Bex conducts a short and sweet pregame hype, and then we're all headed down the player tunnel.

The stadium lights are off as red, blue, and green strobe lights bounce around the stadium seating, hockey rink, and ceiling.

The large Megatron screen starts to play a PR video designed for the team, and we all watch from below at the end of the player tunnel, waiting for our queue from the announcer.

As the newest recruit on the team, and this being my first home game, the players move around to let me up to the front. My name will be announced first, and I'll open the night for the Hawkeyes as tradition dictates.

The video stops playing, and that's when I hear the announcer's deep rumbling voice.

"And here are your Hawkeyes!" he announces.

The crowd erupts in wild cheering.

It's a packed house tonight, and everyone is waiting anxiously to see if the Hawkeyes will make it into the playoffs.

"Welcome to the ice... the newest member of the Hawkeyes... your center... number 67... Slade Matthews!" he says, drawing out my name. It's the first time I've been announced at a Hawkeyes home game, and I can't help but wonder if my father is watching.

The crowd jumps to their feet as I skate out to center ice.

The rest of it is a blur as each teammate in the starting lineup is announced. After that, the away team is announced, and we all head back to our team benches.

The lights come back on, and Lake, our team captain, skates out for the puck drop.

Before I know it, the game is underway, and we're playing at the top of our ability. Everyone, including the opposing team, brought their best tonight.

In the first period, Lake scores for us, and then the opposition makes a score. In the second period, Briggs takes a shot and misses but then I recover it, shooting it back to him and he takes another shot, scoring another goal for us.

Hearing the crowd go crazy whenever a goal is made has me grinning from ear to ear.

By the time the third period is underway, we're ahead by two points; I'm in the home box when I see Kaenan look up and wave at someone.

I follow his line of sight to find what I assume to be the owner's box. About twenty people stand by the glass on the third floor. I see his little girl, Berkeley, who I've seen him take post-game interviews with on his lap.

Then my eyes shift to a beautiful blonde.

She might be three floors up, but I'd know that silhouette anywhere.

Penelope.

I watch for a moment longer, watching her bounce up and down and cheer as she watches our team skate back and forth, even though I should be keeping my attention on the game.

Right before I stop watching, her eyes shift to mine. She pauses in place as we hold eye contact for a brief second until someone hits me in the arm.

"You're on... go, Matthews!" They yell over the loud music and cheering crowds.

I jump over the sideboards as my alternate replaces me in the box.

I head for center ice and jump into the game. The opposing team has the puck, and everyone is in an all-out mad dash down the rink, headed straight for Seven, guarding the net.

Lake skates in front of the opposition, making him change course at the last second and narrowly missing me to his left. He tries to take the shot but misses, and Lake is in the perfect position to take control of the puck.

He scoops it up and now all of us are skating with everything we have to the other side of the rink.

A defensive player catches up to Lake, but I'm further over to his left.

Lake swivels a look at me and waits until the last second when he knows I'll be free long enough to make the shot. Then he shoots it to me.

I skate down just a little closer, checking all the open spots around the goalie, and I find my opening.

I look around to see if any other player has a better shot, remembering that this isn't about me anymore, it's about the team, but no one is in a better position.

This is my goal.

I take the shot with only seconds on the clock, and the goalie misses blocking the puck. It sinks in, and the horn rings out to call the end of the period.

The game is over, and we won with a two-point lead.

Lake skates full force for me, and then all of our teammates jump over the sideboards and ram into us.

"We did it!" Lake yells.

We won the third to the last game we needed.

With players patting my helmet and smiles forming, this is the first time since my senior year playing college hockey that I have felt like a part of a team again.

My career as a hockey player for the Hawkeyes team seems to be falling into place... but there's one thing I want more than anything, and I feel like I'm further away than I was when I started.

I want back what Pen and Win had, even if all I ever get are emails.

I look back up, still surrounded by players celebrating, to find Penelope staring down at us on the ice with her arms folded and deep in thought. She might be watching our team celebrate, but something tells me she's staring straight at me.

Before post-game media, Tessa, the Hawkeyes PR and media manager, tell me that I would be going in first.

"This is your night to shine. The lion's den wants you. But don't worry; I can tame them if they step out of line. Are you ready?" she asks.

"Bring on the questions," I tell her.

I've never shied away from the spotlight, and public speaking doesn't make me clam up like it does for other players.

With only a limited amount of time per player, it isn't long before all of us are through media and headed to Oakley's.

I pull out my phone and see an email notification.

I click it instantly as I walk the couple of blocks to Oakley's, following Seven, Reeve, and Brett by foot as other players drive.

It's from Penelope, and the time stamp shows that this email was sent right before we went out on the ice. She was sitting above me in the owner's box while she typed this.

From: SkatrGirlPen
To: WinForToday067

Win,

I'm sorry it's taken me several days to respond back. Your emails came out of nowhere and even though I have no idea how I feel about it, I can't deny that they came at a time when I could really use a friend. Someone to give me advice like you did before.

I hit reply and send her an email.

From: WinForToday067
To: SkatrGirlPen

Pen,

You never have to apologize for anything. I deserve your resistance, but I hope to make it up to you and prove that I'm not going anywhere this time.

Tell me what's going on. What advice do you need?

I send it off and then check my text messages. I have over a hundred missed text messages from old buddies in college, my uncle on my mom's side, a few friends I made in Canada and a couple of cousins from my dad's side of the family.

My social media accounts are jam-packed with DM's from people I don't know, including women asking what bar I'll be at tonight. I ignore them all and open the text from my mom. She rarely reaches out unless my dad lets her.

> **Mom: Your father said you won tonight. Congratulations sweetheart. We miss you; come home soon to visit.**

I love my mom, but I know that her allegiance lies with my dad.

I pass over all the congratulations texts and open the only one that I know will make me feel like shit, even after a win.

Dad: OK, you got your win. Are you done making me look like a laughing-stock in front of my colleagues?

Dad: It's time to take this seriously and go to medical school. I already talked to the dean. You don't even have to apply; he'll let you in as a fa-vor to me.

I click into the messages to send off some snarky, spoiled rich kid comment that he's sure to expect... but then an email comes through.

Penelope.

I quickly click out and abandon my father's text in favor of pretending to be someone else to win over a woman who hates me.

I pull up the email.

From: SkatrGirlPen
To: WinForToday067

Win,

The guy who ruined my life in college is back. He now plays for the team I work for and I swear he turns up everywhere.

I wish I could turn the other cheek and let the past be the past, but you know what he did. How can I ever forgive him?

Shit

This is the part that makes me feel guilty, and I almost forgot about it.

She trusted Win even after "he" left her without any good reason, and now I'm using that trust to manipulate her. Maybe even as far as convincing her to forgive the real me.

I can't do it, though.

She has to decide to forgive me, and the real me has to give her a good enough reason to do it.

It has to be her idea if I want her free and clear.

From: WinForToday067
To: SkatrGirlPen

Pen,

I'm sorry he hurt you. I wish there was something I could do to take that pain away from you, but you shouldn't feel wrong for your feelings toward him. What he did to you was inexcusable. If you ever need validation for how you feel about how he treated you, I'm here to offer it.

We continue walking and I lag behind the guys. We cross two crossing walks and we're inching closer to the bar.

I see Oakley's illuminated sign; it looks like the low-key sports bar that the guys have been telling me about. On the opposite side, a small tattoo parlor sits with the open sign still on.

It seems like a good business decision to set up shop as a tattoo artist next to a busy bar—or, at least, it wouldn't hurt business anyway.

I pass by a red Mercedes crossover with someone in the driver's side. The light of their phone illuminated.

I unconsciously look over as we pass by and notice that it's Penelope parked in her car, typing on her phone.

The idea that she and I are less than eight feet from one another as she opens up to me is a reminder of how dangerous this is for me if she finds out that I'm both men and that I've been lying to her this whole time.

> **From: SkatrGirlPen**
> **To: WinForToday067**
>
> **Did you mean what you said in your email last week?**
> **That I was the only one?**

The second I read it, I hang my head.

I need to be honest going forward. It's the only way I might survive this.

With a new instant message application added to the email server that wasn't there when she started 'tutoring' me, I decide to test my luck.

Seven pulls the door open and walks into the bar, Reeve following behind. I keep the door open and check back to see if Penelope has exited her car yet. I don't like the idea of her being out here at night by herself.

I see Lake's truck pull up behind hers, and Tessa gets out of the passenger side, and then Penelope climbs out of her car.

Good, at least Lake and Tessa are out here with her.

Penelope glances over to find me standing with the door to the bar open and the smile she had on fades quickly.

I turn and head into the bar and type an instant message from my email accounts.

Here goes nothing.

Penelope

WinForToday067: I meant it. Did you?

I get a notification from my email instant messenger. I knew we were obviously emailing back in real time but instant messenger makes this feels real.

He's on the other line waiting for my reply as if we're texting instead of emailing.

SkatrGirlPen: Yes I did but why didn't you say anything before?

WinForToday067: You were tutoring me...

> **SkatrGirlPen: So you thought it would be inappropriate because I was tutoring you?**

> **WinForToday067: The only thing inappropriate is what I've wanted to do to you.**

> **WinForToday067: But I didn't want to make you uncomfortable by asking to come to your dorm for an in-person tutoring session when I had no intention of studying.**

Oh!

The nerve endings in my clit tingle the moment I read his response and I readjust on my barstool, taking a quick look around the table to make sure that none of my friends are watching me.

They aren't. They're celebrating with their significant others over the win tonight.

> **SkatrGirlPen: You should have asked. What would you have done if I let you come over?**

I glance across the bar to find Slade sitting on the other side. He's engrossed in his phone as he sits next to Reeve, waiting for Oakley to bring them their drinks.

A few women that I've never seen here before stand nearby, stirring their martinis lazily, sending looks Slade's way. But he either hasn't noticed them or is too busy checking his DMs from wild fans.

Whatever has his undivided attention on that phone must be enthralling because he hasn't looked away once as his finger type feverishly.

Then, I remember my own conversation.

I check my phone, waiting for a response.

What if Win looks like Slade?

That muscular body, those full lips, and those gorgeous hazel eyes.

What if Win has arms covered in tattoos that he could wrap around me?

What if he has Slade's thick, impressive cock dangling between his thighs.

Ever since I saw Slade naked in the shower, with his erection reaching out towards me, an alternate version of what might have happened if I hadn't stormed out has made a regular appearance in my fantasy lately, though I wish I could stop it.

A messenger dings and I break my stare.

> **WinForToday067: I'd be happy to describe it in great detail. But are you sure you want to go down this road?**

My fingers pause for a second, hovering over the keypad. I already know what I'm going to say, but once I've sent it, there's no going back.

> **SkatrGirlPen: Yes, I'm sure.**

I hit send as bubbles of excitement fizzle and pop in my stomach.

I can't believe I'm egging him on... in a public place with all of my friends nearby.

My eyes flash back up to Slade for a moment, and when they do, I see Slade's eyes on me over his shoulder.

Slade's attention cuts back to the bar when Oakley drops off his and Reeve's beers, and judging by the smile on Oakley's face, he must be congratulating Reeve and Slade on the win tonight.

I revert my attention back to my phone, but there's no reply yet.

"Want something to drink? Lake's going up to order a round for our table," Tessa says.

"A glass of wine... sauvignon blanc please. Whatever Oakley already has open is fine, thanks." I tell her.

Usually, I'd take whatever beer Lake is going to get for rounds, but with Win and I's conversation going on, I need something a little different—something to sip slowly and something to calm my nerves a little.

I'll gulp beer down too quickly, trying to keep up with everyone else, and then Lake will end up getting me another, rendering me tipsy and capable of saying God knows what to Win. I want more control than that. I want to feel just a little warm and relaxed, that's all.

> **WinForToday067: Is there a line I should be aware of? I don't want you blocking me after this.**

> **SkatrGirlPen: No line. Tell me anything you want.**

"Here you go," Lake says, dropping off my wine for me.

"Thank you for doing that," I tell him.

He turns back towards the bar to the rest of the drinks,

I take a couple of quick sips as I wait for Win's reply.

> **WinForToday067: First, I would have brought dinner from the small hole-in-the-wall Italian restaurant down the street from my condo.**

We're on the verge of sexting and he's bringing up food?

Who is this guy?

But I can't help but smile at the gesture.

> **SkatrGirlPen: You would have fed me first?**

> **WinForToday067: It would have been the first time we met in person. I would have taken my time feeding you. First, the pasta... then my cock.**

I laugh out loud the second I read his text. Of course, it was coming; I just had to be patient.

> **SkatrGirlPen: Is that how you would have started things? With me giving you oral?**

> **WinForToday067: Jesus, Pen... just seeing you text the words "giving you oral" has me hard. But no, we would have started with me licking a line from your tits to your pussy, and I wouldn't have stopped until you came on my face.**

SkatrGirlPen: You would have gone down on me first?

WinForToday067: I would have devoured you like chicken fettuccini.

I can feel the wetness of my arousal starting to soak my panties. I bite down on my lip as I read it a second time, loving the fantasy. But the more my imagination takes over, the more the man I'm picturing between my thighs is none other than Slade Matthews.

I try to shake the imagery of Slade's long dark strands of hair twisting between my fingers as I grip ahold of his scalp as he licks me.

Stop it, Penelope!

Then I decide to give myself some grace. It's been a while since I've had any. None of the men I've tried dating since Win signed off for good came close to keeping my interest and soon enough, I just gave up. It's been over six months since the last time I was with a man so it's no surprise that I'm easy to rile up right about now.

You're only imagining Slade because you don't know what Win looks like. That's all. Don't beat yourself up about it.

I coach myself out of the little bit of self-loathing I'm starting to feel for having more fantasies about the devil himself sitting at the bar across the room from me.

SkatrGirlPen: And then what?

WinForToday067: I would have wrapped your fingers around my cock

and let you feel how hard you make me.

The memory of Slade's dripping wet cock in the shower comes to mind.

My eyes flutter closed, and I imagine walking into the shower with Slade and sliding my fingers over his smooth erection.

SkatrGirlPen: What would you have done next?

I take a sip of my wine as I wait anxiously, crossing my right leg over the other and squeezing to keep my clit from pulsating.

WinForToday067: I would have asked you if you wanted it from behind while on your knees with your face in the pillow or if you'd prefer riding me, while I fuck you from the bottom.

I practically do a spit take when I read his text, except I inhale it, too.

I choke on the wine as I cough dramatically, gripping the lacquered bar height table with one hand while trying not to pass out from lack of oxygen and keel over the barstool.

My other hand starts to slap my chest to get the liquid out of my lungs.

"Are you ok?" Briggs says, racing over to me from the pool table where he's the closest.

Tessa jumps off her barstool a few chairs down and runs to me. She starts patting my back, thinking that something might be lodged in my throat.

In my peripheral vision, I see Slade rush past the women who are still staying close in case he decides to give them the time of day as he makes a beeline for me with long strides.

"Hey, are you alright?" he asks, his eyes on me and then pinging to my open cell phone.

I hide it quickly, realizing that anyone could have seen it.

"I'm fine! I'm fine!" I tell Tessa, Briggs, Autumn, and Slade, who are all hovering around me, to make sure I'm alright. "I just choked on my wine—no harm done... I promise."

I clear my throat a couple more times.

"Do you need something? I can ask Lake to order you a pretzel and cheese or something. Maybe you need to eat." Tessa says.

I wave her off immediately.

"Really, I'm fine, thanks. But I think I've had enough celebrations for tonight," I say, sliding off my seat. "I'm going to call it a night and head home."

"You want to leave already?" Autumn asks.

"We'll have a whole week of celebration when the guys get us into playoffs; I should reserve my energy," I tell her with a wink.

But really, I'm a little embarrassed that I started sexting with my old online crush and choked on my own wine like a blushing virgin.

Amateur.

Briggs places his hand on my shoulder. "Do you want me to drive you home? I can walk back after I park your car in the parking garage. I haven't touched the beer I ordered yet."

"Thank you but it's fine. I didn't even drink half of my wine. I'll be fine," I tell him.

Briggs looks over to Autumn as if to ask her if he should push harder. She gives him a shake of her head and looks back at me.

"I'll walk you out at least," she says.

I nod in agreement, grabbing my jacket and purse off the floor under the table where I had set it earlier.

"I got her," Slade says over my shoulder to Autumn.

Autumn looks at me, her eyes flaring as she tries not to grin. "Ok, thanks," she tells him.

"Traitor," I grumble under my breath.

I remember that I haven't messaged Win back and I don't want him to think he stepped over the line.

He didn't.

Not in the slightest.

"Let me grab my jacket, and then I'll walk you to your car," he says.

Before I can tell him not to bother, he jogs over to his spot at the bar where he was sitting next to Reeve.

I use Slade's absence as my opening to send off a response to Win.

I type it up and then blow out a breath to gain the courage to send it.

> **SkatrGirlPen: Do you think we should meet in person?**

Sent.

I lock my phone quickly, almost too nervous to see his reply.

Even now... even after what he said, I'm still worried that he'll reject me a second time. And maybe a tiny part of me is worried that the idea of him is far greater than the actual reality of him.

Is it better not to break this spell and keep what we have, even if it's always with a laptop or cell phone between us?

I glance over to see Slade with his jacket in his hand, paused in place as he stares down at his phone... almost frozen in place.

Whatever he just read caught him off guard.

He stares back at his phone, and then, after a few seconds, he tucks the phone into his back pocket.

I try to play it off like I'm not watching him walk over to me when I see one of the three women cut through between the pool tables to stop him.

"Are you leaving?" she asks.

He pauses, not answering her right away, and his eyes flash over to me. I look away, pretending to be interested in Seven and Briggs's game of pool... which, as usual, Seven is dominating.

"I'm just walking someone out," he tells her.

He didn't technically say he's leaving but he also didn't commit to coming back in.

He passes by the pretty brunette with long legs and heads for me.

"Do you have everything?" he asks, searching the table to make sure I'm not leaving anything behind.

"Yeah," I say.

I turn and head for the door as Slade follows close behind.

He reaches out and grabs the bar door just before I can reach it and opens it for me.

I wish he'd stop being chivalrous and pretending to be something I know he's not.

Holding open doors, buying my drink, and surprising me with treats when I show up to work. He's messing with my head and I really wish he would stop trying to jump out of the box I put him in

"Are you sure you don't want to stay a little longer? I know CPR... and I'll give you mouth-to-mouth if you try to suffocate on your wine again," he teases.

"I'd rather die," I say under my breath.

He hears it, though, and his smile fades instantly.

"Come on, don't leave," he tries to convince me one last time as he follows me off the curb and around the front of my car. "Stay at least until you finish your wine."

I hit the unlock button on my key fob and open the door. He reaches for the top edge of the driver's side door and pulls it open for me a little further to allow me to get in while he watches protectively for cars driving by too close.

I stop before I duck into the car when something in the distance catches my attention.

The bar door opens and the leggy brunette who stopped him when he was about to walk me out steps partially out onto the sidewalk looking around the surrounding area. No doubt looking for Slade.

Do they know each other?

Is she a returning conquest?

Or is she just like all the other puck bunnies in town? Just trying to collect all the players, like a set of hockey playing cards.

I have no idea, and just like Chloe, the barista's interested in him, I don't care.

"Don't act like you're going to miss me, Slade. You have more than enough company to keep you entertained tonight."

"Entertained? What are you talking about?"

I nod over to the woman.

He follows my line of sight to find the same woman standing with half her body out in the open and the other half covered behind the door of Oakley's.

He barely looks long enough to register who's waiting at the door for him before he shoots me a look.

"Whoa, hold on. Are you jealous?" he asks.

There's no smile and no smirk across his face as he searches my face for his answer.

"Not in this lifetime, Matthews," I say, sliding into the driver seat and pulling the door shut.

I would have liked to have slammed his fingers in my car door, but he removed them too quickly.

He bends down until we're at eye level, but I don't look over as I hit the automatic start button.

"I'm not taking her home. I'm not taking anyone home," he says.

I hate how my stomach seems to relax for the first time since I saw her walk up to him and ask if he was leaving. Had I really been clenching my abs together at the uncomfortable thought of him taking her home?

I had just been encouraging another man to detail all the dirty things he would have wanted to do to me, less than ten minutes ago.

My feelings towards Slade shouldn't be confusing or complicated. They should be simple. One thing and one thing only—pure hate.

I put the car into drive while Slade takes a step back but still stands in the roadway, watching me drive away.

He can take all three women home tonight for all I care.

Why not call up Chloe too. Make it a real orgy.

As long as I can't hear them, it's not my business. And since I have yet to run into Slade on the elevator or on the seventh level where my apartment is located, his apartment must not be that close to mine.

At least I'll be spared the sound of fake orgasms from the woman only looking to score bragging rights for sleeping with a player.

Then they'll be off chasing some other jersey on the local NFL or MLB teams until we get a new recruit.

No one gets hurt in this scenario. There's no victim to be had. The players get their egos boosted, and the women get what they want, too—a good story to tell their girlfriends over mimosas at Sunday brunch.

All I want to do is go home and wait for Win's text.

Since I haven't heard my phone ding in the last five minutes, I really hope I didn't scare him away.

An hour after I get home and get ready for bed, after checking my phone for Win about a thousand times; I hear my phone ding while sitting on the coffee table.

I run from the kitchen to the living room and dive over the back to the couch to retrieve my phone.

> **WinForToday067: I want to Pen. I really do. But I'm in the middle of a project right now. I need to see this through first.**

I can't pretend I'm not disappointed, especially now with the extra pent-up sexual frustration that his messages caused tonight.

If I don't let out some steam... I might burst.

SkatrGirlPen: I understand. Will you let me know when you're ready?

WinForToday067: I won't make you wait long. I promise.

With that, I head to bed. It's late and we have some elbow rubbing to do with some big wigs coming in for tomorrow's game. Plus this whole emotional roller coaster with both Win and Slade has tuckered me out.

Chapter Ten

Slade

It's Thursday night and Penelope's birthday. She took the day off today so she didn't end up seeing the chai and flowers I dropped off this morning on her desk.

Pink and white Peonies—her favorite. Something I learned as Win when I sent flowers to one of her classes in college.

This morning, Sam eyed me carefully when I dropped them off, but there was not much he could say since several other presents from other Hawkeyes staff members were sitting on her desk. Nothing was as large as the boutique of mixed peonies and daylilies.

DIRTY SCORE   131

I considered taking the flowers to her apartment and knocking on her door, but after that night at the bar, I didn't want to press my luck. She's been avoiding me ever since.

Ducking into someone's office when she sees me walking down the hall, and backing out of any room she walks into when she sees I'm there, too.

A couple of days ago, I beat her to Serendipity's, and the second she walked in the door and saw that I was already in line, she did a one-eighty and left just to avoid me.

Tomorrow, we leave for our first round of playoff games in our conference. The team we're up against gets the home-ice advantage for games one and two. Then we'll be back to play here for games three and four.

I walk into Oakley's just a little after nine pm when all the guys said to meet up.

"Matthews!" Lake yells from across the room, lifting his arm in the air so I can spot him. The bar is busy on a Thursday night.

I weave in and out between other people to get to the eight-top table where Briggs, Lake, Kaenan, Brent, and Reeve are sitting.

"Did Wrenley come out tonight?" I ask, knowing he isn't much for social events.

"Yeah, there's a pool tournament tonight. He wouldn't miss it," Reeve says, pointing to Seven on the far end of the bar with a pool stick in his hand.

"How's he doing?" I ask, searching for the leaderboard.

I see him currently sitting at second.

"He got a rough start, but he's close to the number one spot. I think the guy in first will drop as long as Seven can keep his position and hold it. They haven't played each other yet," Reeve says and then tosses back the rest of his beer.

He must be stewing while watching his current opponent line up for their shot.

I look over to find that Lake is the only one without a beer.

"I'm going to order something. You want a beer?" I ask him.

"Thanks, but I'm on-call as the designated driver if the girls need a ride from the club."

"Got it," I tell him and then head to the bar to order a beer from Oakley.

A few minutes I'm on my way back to our table when I see Lake pick up his phone.

"The club is packed? Well, if she isn't having fun, why don't you all come here?"

The girls might be headed this way, and my first thought is that I get to see Penelope on her birthday. Something that I had originally come to terms with not happening tonight.

"The bar is busy, but we have a big table. You girls can have it; we'll sit at the bar if you still want a girl's night," he says, looking at all of us, and we nod in agreement.

"Do they want us to go get them?" Briggs asks, turning behind him to grab his jacket off the back of the barstool short backs.

Lake shakes his head. "They're already in Penelope's car. None of them have had anything to drink. They just hadn't decided where to go yet," Lake tells Briggs.

"Ok, see you soon. Be safe. Love you, Tessie."

He ends the call and looks over at Kaenan and Briggs.

"The girls are headed here but they're just going to hang with us. I guess some asshole got handsy with Penelope when he heard it was her birthday," Lake says.

I'm just about to get out of my seat and head to the club to teach that asshole a lesson when Kaenan leans in.

"Does she want us to beat the shit out of the guy? We can roll over there now," Kaenan says.

I like his idea.

"No, the last thing you need is another assault charge," Lake says. "They don't want to be there anyway. The club is over-capacity, and the bouncers aren't stopping people from coming in, so they were having a hard time getting beverage service. They'd rather be here in case something like that happens again."

"It won't happen here. Not with the regulars knowing who they belong to," Brett says.

Ten minutes later, we're all watching Seven play for the top spot when Lake's attention veers to the door.

"The girls are here," I hear him announce.

He turns around on the barstool next to mine and waves them over.

Tessa, Autumn, and Isla all head straight for us... and then I see her... at the back of the line of Hawkeyes girlfriends headed this way.

Her long blonde hair is lightly curled at the ends, she has a bright smile, and she's wearing the smallest fucking powder blue mini dress. I won't be taking my eyes off her for the rest of the night, that's for sure.

Tessa smiles at Lake while leading the rest of the women further into the bar and toward our table.

My pulse quickens at the sight of Penelope. No wonder the asshole singled her out. She's always beautiful no matter what she's wearing, but tonight, I'm more surprised she only had to fight off one unwelcome advance in the club.

And with the way every single guy in this bar turns to watch Penelope walk in, I have a feeling I might end up in jail for assault if anyone else tries anything on her.

The girls walk up to us; Tessa takes an open seat next to Lake, and Autumn takes an open spot next to Briggs. Isla walks behind Kaenan and gives him a kiss while Penelope stops just shy of me.

"I didn't know you were coming to Oakley's. I would have brought you something for your birthday," I tell her.

"You don't need to get me anything. I think you've done more than enough for one lifetime," she says, looking away, trying to find someone else to talk to.

She shifts to the right to gain distance from me, but at least she didn't turn back out of the bar the moment she saw me this time. That's an improvement over the last few days.

She didn't get my flowers or chai today and she won't end up getting them until tomorrow. I need to be able to offer her something right now.

I can buy her a drink... but anyone can do that.

I already bought her flowers, and there are no florists nearby open this late.

There's one option I have but I don't know if she's going to like it, or hate me more for it.

"Here, Penelope, sit by Autumn. I'll find another chair," Briggs says, sliding off his barstool next to his finance. "Want a drink, birthday girl?" he asks.

"Yes... please. A blueberry lemon drop, thanks. I couldn't get one at the club. The bar was impenetrable there," she huffs, walking over and hoisting herself up into his spot.

Her birthday is only for a few more hours. If I want something to offer her, it has to be now.

"Isla, sit here," I tell her, sliding off the barstool.

"Oh, I don't want to take your spot," she says.

"It's not a problem. I'm going to step out for a second. I'll be back," I assure her.

She seems to feel better now that I won't need the chair and hops up into the empty spot where I used to sit.

"Where are you going?" Kaenan asks.

"I'll be right back. It shouldn't take long," I say.

I turn and head for the exit.

Pushing through the door of the bar, I hold it open as another couple enters and then I hang a right. The neon sign of the tattoo parlor is still lit up and beckoning me in.

I open the door, and a small bell rings as I walk into the small shop. A loveseat couch sits at the left of the entrance. In front of it sits a coffee table with multiple three-ring binders full of tattoo art that a customer can pick from. But I don't need inspiration... I already know what I want, and it should take any tattoo artist about five minutes to do.

Seven simple letters and two numbers in decent calligraphy.

April 16th.

Today's date.

Penelope's birthday.

"Hey man, can I help you?" a guy in his older years with peppering hair and a greying beard says.

He walks out from behind what I assume to be his office in the back.

"Yeah, I need a tattoo," I roll up the sleeve to my Henley and show him the ice skates. "I need April 16th written on the blank banner."

"That's easy. Take a seat," he says.

He walks up to the chair at his station and spins it around for me to take a seat.

I do as he instructs while he pulls on black latex gloves and gets the ink and his equipment ready to go.

He jots down the date I asked for in nice handwriting on a piece of transfer paper and shows it to me.

"How about this?" He asks to ensure the date is correct and the style I want.

"Looks good," I say.

He goes back to collecting the things he'll need, distributes it all onto a rolling tray, and then pulls it with me towards a backless rolling chair next to mine.

He sits and lays the outline of the date across the banner.

"So... you got a story for this? Looks like a nice tattoo you already have here."

"Thanks. I had a tattoo artist in Canada do it. I just moved back to the States and so I decided to finish it, and I need it done tonight."

"Seems urgent. Do the skates and the dates represent something?" He asks, just making conversation.

Most people who get tattoos do it for a reason all their own. If you don't want people asking about the meaning behind a tattoo, you probably shouldn't put it on the inside of your forearm where people are going to see it.

I should have thought of that when deciding on placement. But I don't mind blowing people off when they ask, especially any woman I've been with since I got it.

They turn green with envy every time they see the tattoo, even though none of them have ever been more than a night to pass the time.

The truth is, I wanted her where I could see her. Every game since I left her four years ago, and before I go out on the ice, I pull up my sleeve, look down at the tattoo, and hope that she's watching, believing that someday I'll find a way to earn back her forgiveness.

I paid my retribution in the form of putting off my NHL career to get back in her father's good graces and prove to her that I'm sorry for what I did, though it's not an eye for an eye. My career was stalled slightly while she lost her chance at the Olympics completely.

"All tattoos have a story, right?"

He just simply nods in response as he pulls the transfer paper off.

"Is this good?" he asks.

I take a look at the placement and nod back in agreement.

"So, the tattoo...?" he asks again.

"The skates are for the girl; the date is for her birthday," I tell him, keeping things simple.

"You don't seem too warm and fuzzy about it all for a guy getting a tattoo for his woman," he says.

"That's because she's not mine."

"Oh, for fuck's sake..." he says, pulling back right before the needle hits my skin. "Please don't tell me she's married, and you're trying to win her back with this birthday tattoo." He grimaces.

My free hand balls into a fist at the thought of Penelope being married to someone else. The idea of losing her for good is a reality I haven't had to face yet. I guess I figured I still have time. But no time is ever assured.

"No... Jesus..." I give a humorless laugh. "She's not married. She's single."

"Thank God because I can't tell you how much money I've lost talking grown men out of grand gesture tattoos that would never have panned out. I'm not a goddamn shrink... though I think I do more of that here than tattoos, some days."

I can imagine what he sees and the stories he hears.

"It's nothing like that," I tell him, staring down at the four-year-old figure skate tattoo.

He puts his head back down and starts the tattoo.

"Ok... so what's it like?" he asks.

The needle touches down against my skin, and I settle into the pain, craving the endorphins that will immediately follow.

"I fucked up four years ago with her. So I left town, got a job in Canada, and got this tattoo the minute I touched down on

Canadian soil. It serves as a reminder of why I left and what I'm coming back for."

"Why did you have to leave to do that?"

"To pay for my sins and earn back the respect I lost from someone who mentored me."

I don't know what came over me to make me spill all of that. I meant to keep it simple and uncomplicated, but maybe I just needed it off my chest... or maybe the guy really did miss his calling and should have been a shrink.

I've never told anyone what the ice skates mean, though I've been asked. As a hockey player, people don't expect figure skates to be tattooed on my forearm.

It's a conversation piece... I'll just leave it as that.

"Did it work?" he asks, wiping away the excess ink on my skin.

"She barely looks at me; if she does, it's with contempt. But I think I'm on my way to earning back my old coach's trust again."

"Then what's this for?" he asks about the date he's tattooing on my arm. "Is this your grand gesture to show her you're serious?"

I wish, but this isn't enough... it's just the start of a long road ahead.

"Not even close. It's just a birthday present."

"A woman hates you, so you tattoo her birthday on your skin forever. Yep... sounds like the right reaction," he says sarcastically.

I know he's just shooting me shit, and I have thick enough skin to take it. You have to when you choose to play a sport for a living. The locker room isn't much different than a frat house and the ice is where some of your competitors are looking to end your career early.

If you can't take it, and dish it back, you won't last in professional sports for very long.

"You know... for a tattoo artist, you have an interesting bedside manner."

He snickers as he starts the number six on my arm.

"I told you... I should have been a therapist."

Chapter Eleven

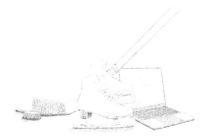

Penelope

I shouldn't be looking over my shoulder at the exit every few minutes, wondering where Slade went and when or if he'll return.

I sip my delicious lemon drop, which Oakley made special just for me. It has a sliced candied lemon on the side and a small metal skewer with three blueberries marinated overnight in some kind of delicious liquor.

Oakley might own a sports/dive bar, but the man has some pretty impressive mad scientist mixology skills, though he won't admit it to anyone.

I want to distract myself with something, so I pull out my email and open the instant messaging. I haven't talked to Win all that much since he told me that he needed to focus on the project he's working on before we can meet in person.

> **SkatrGirlPen: How's your project going?**

I put my phone back on the table, not expecting a response this late at night.

I turn in my seat and join in as we all watch Seven in the last game of pool.

"Are you having a good birthday?" Isla says, walking back from getting a refill on her wine. "We can always head back to Tessa and Lake's penthouse and order a ridiculous amount of takeout and binge-watch the second season of Love Castaway," she offers.

I can see the concern in her eyes as her eyebrows lift in question. She wants me to be having fun, and I am... for the most part.

"Thanks, Isla, but you can't pay for this kind of entertainment. I've never seen Seven with deep concentration frowns. He always looks so calm all the time," I say.

"More like he always looks slightly annoyed to be anywhere with anyone," she adds.

I laugh. "That's true."

I'm glad we left the club and came here to be with our friends. The girl's only night out idea was Tessa's. She worries that I always feel like the third wheel since we spend a lot of time with the guys.

But I really don't, and it's expected that we all spend a lot of time together since we all live and work together. Not to mention that here in a few months, half of our team will leave for the off season, and the guys are gone on away games frequently. It's not as if I could get sick of anyone.

The penthouse idea sounds nice, but with it being as late as it is, I know that we would all end up crashing on the large U-shape couch in Lake and Tessa's place and falling asleep before the food even got to us.

Besides, the guys are leaving tomorrow for a couple of days, playing in Colorado for the first-round Western Conference Playoffs. This means we will have more than enough takeout and Love Castaway nights.

I hear my phone ding, and I twist around to grab it off the barstool.

> **WinForToday067: I hit a snag, but I think I'm working on something right now to get things back on track.**

> **SkatrGirlPen: Good, I'm glad to hear it. If you want any help with the project, I'd be happy to do what I can.**

> **WinForToday067: You are helping just by giving me the incentive to finish this project as quickly as possible.**

I smile at the thought that he considers me an incentive.

I hear the door open to the front door and whip a look to find Slade walking in, tucking his phone in his back pocket.

Was he outside talking to someone?

Something on his forearm catches my eye.

A bandage.

Did he leave because he got cut while in the bar? Did he have an altercation after he walked out of here?

Starting up a conversation with Slade is the last thing on my list of birthday wishes... though curiosity is eating at me.

"Where did you go?" Lake asks.

I'm glad someone asked because I am dying to know how he got that bandage.

"Next door," he says simply, finding an open barstool.

"Next door? At the tattoo parlor?" Tessa asks, her eyebrows stitching together in confusion. "You got a tattoo at eleven o'clock at night?"

"Sure, why not? I have a lot of tattoos—I have to get them somewhere."

"Yeah... sure, why not," she says with a lifted eyebrow and her lips puckered.

Her judgiest expression.

Then she shoots me a look as if to non-verbally say, "Ok, you're right. This fool is crazy."

Told you.

I attempt to tell her with telepathy—my go-to preferred superpower, if I was ever given any.

Although if Tessa, Autumn, Isla, and I all had telepathy, I can only imagine how distracting our interconnected brain waves would be.

I would guess that it would feel like what would happen if four separate interstate highways all merged together, at the same time, into a single lane of traffic.

Absolutely chaos.

"What's the tattoo of?" Isla asks, looking over from her conversation with someone else and seeing Slade's bandage.

"It's a birthday present," he tells her.

"Oh really? Is your birthday coming up?" Isla asks.

"No," he says simply, his hazel-green eyes finding mine.

My heart thumps against my chest.

Did he get a tattoo on his arm for me?

I glance back down at the area where the white material of the bandage is covering it, but it's so large that it takes up half of his forearm. I've seen that forearm with tattoos all over it. Where would he have even found room for another tattoo?

Right next to the tattoo of the 'girl that got away'?

I wish he had asked first. I would have talked him out of inking himself permanently with anything for me.

And if he thinks I'm going to swoon by sharing space next to his ex, he's crazier than I thought.

"Your drink is empty. I'm going to get Kaenan another beer, want something?" Isla asks.

I look at the empty martini glass.

"Actually, I'll go with you," I tell her, looking for an excuse to get some space from him.

I slide off the barstool and follow her into the crowded bar.

This place is usually pretty packed, especially after a winning Hawkeyes game but tonight the bar is full of people coming for the pool tournament, so I don't recognize many of the usuals that come out to celebrate with the team.

I follow closely behind her as we make our way up to the bar.

Oakley walks over with a smile.

"Hi, ladies, what will it be? And happy birthday, Penelope. How did you like the lemon drop?" he asks.

"It was delicious. Can I get another one?"

"You got it. And for you, Isla?"

"Just a refill for Kaenan. Thanks, Oakley," she says.

"Nothing for you?" he asks.

She hesitates for a second and then responds. "Not tonight."

He doesn't push the issue and heads off to get our drinks.

Isla's not drinking?

I want to ask if there's a specific reason for that, but a busy bar is not the place to spill any secrets.

I'll get my chance to ask another time.

One of the regulars that we know starts asking questions about the guys leaving tomorrow for the playoffs when someone behind me grabs my ass.

I jump instantly, not expecting the touch.

"I didn't know they served cotton candy here. Mind giving me a little taste?" a deep male voice that I don't recognize says over my shoulder.

"Excuse me?" I ask, turning around to find the offending hand and who it's attached to.

This is the second time someone has touched my ass without asking tonight, and I'm not happy about it.

The hand in question belongs to a middle-aged man with slightly unkempt hair and glazed-over eyes. He's had too much to drink.

Great, just my luck.

"What did you just say to her?" Isla says, turning around with me glaring at the man in front of us.

In the corner of my eye, I see Slade get up out of his chair and head straight for us.

Oh no... not him.

Anyone but him.

The drunk opens his mouth to speak, "That little blue dress looks delicious, care for a dance?"

"We're having a girl's night, so find someone else to dance with," Isla says.

"And please don't touch me again."

Just as I get out the last word, Slade storms in and grabs him by the collar, lifting him off his feet.

"Did I see you just touch her? Do you have a fucking death wish?" Slade asks.

"Slade... stop it. Put him down," I plead, looking around to see that all eyes in the bar are now on us.

But it doesn't take long before Lake, Brent, and Kaenan are headed for us, too, and Seven and Reeve start walking over from the back corner of the bar where Seven just finished and won the tournament.

"He doesn't get to touch you or speak to you, for that matter," Slade grits out, staring at the guy.

"I barely touched her," the drunk says.

Lake walks up first, rolling his sleeves up, and I know how Lake gets when someone messes with any of us girls.

"What happened over here," Lake asks.

"Nothing, Lake... it's fine," I tell him, not needing any more reinforcements to something that Isla and I had under control.

I hear Oakley walk up behind us at the bar.

"Charley, what the hell are you doing in here? You know you're banned for life. Get out before I call the police again."

"The police aren't the worst of his problems," Slade grits out, pushing Charley sideways towards a dark corner of the bar.

It may be construed as ungrateful by people watching on, but I wasn't in need of saving at that very moment, and Slade has a reputation for being a loose cannon on and off the ice.

"Slade," I say, stepping between him and Charley.

Charley takes the opportunity to slink away when I create a distraction for his escape.

"I don't need your help. I had it under control," I grumble. "Just like I didn't need your unsolicited help with Sean Klein back in college either. Stop butting in where you don't belong."

I look back over Slade's shoulder to see that everyone in the bar is still watching us.

Every time that Slade gets involved, he finds a way to humiliate me in front of my peers.

"God... just leave me alone." I say, turning for the door and speed-walking for the exit.

"Penelope," he calls out, and I can already feel him right on my heels.

Tessa races up to me with my clutch, cell phone, and jacket. "Don't be too mad at him. That guy deserved it," she says quickly as I take my things.

"I just need some air," I tell her over my shoulder as I leave her in the dust.

I'm grateful to have my things so that I don't have to go back in and face the crowd again after that.

I push through the exit and the door doesn't shut as quickly as it should have because Slade pushes through the door right after me.

"We need to talk, Penelope. Please stop running," he says into the spring night air.

"Stop following me, and I'll stop running."

With the street parking too full to find a place, I had to park in the pay-to-park parking lot across the street.

I walk to the end of the sidewalk and check both ways. There are no cars on the road right now. I keep my speed up as I cross the street.

"Just listen to what I have to say, and I'll leave you alone."

I walk past the other side of the sidewalk and into the parking lot, fishing out my key fob and hitting the unlock button a few times to ensure that it's unlocked by the time I get there.

I cross the parking lot to where my car is parked in the third row, with Slade not more than a couple of feet behind me.

"You have nothing to say that will interest me."

I get to the driver's side door and climb in. I hit the lock button the second I'm in, but it's too late, he's too fast, and though I want to be alone, part of me is ready to unload everything on him.

Maybe this is what I need.

Maybe I need to tell him off once and for all

He quickly climbs into the passenger side and closes the door.

"I'm sorry you're mad at me. But you had already been hit on at the club and it's why you were at Oakley's. I wasn't going to let someone else disrespect you like that if I can do something about it."

"You have anger management issues, and you were looking for a fight. Just like you were in college. And with everything you do, the person you end up hurting is me. You ruined my chances at the Olympics... how can I forgive you for that?"

"I know I cost you a lot..." he nods. "But I didn't mean for any of that to happen."

"And then you went and got a tattoo? For what?" I ask my voice on the verge of yelling at him.

"I didn't have a present to give you," he admits.

"What is it of?" I ask, the curiosity starting to get to me.

"You'll have to wait for it to heal."

I have to wait to see the tattoo? Then why bother getting it? This man finds new ways to infuriate me each time I interact with him.

With the blood pumping in my veins and the needs of my body not being met by my vibrator or by Win and the fact that I've had more wet dreams about Slade in the last few weeks than I have had about anyone... ever, I feel like I might combust if I don't let it out somehow.

"You want to give me a present?" I ask, slipping off my heels on the driver's side of my car.

"That's what I was trying to do," he says as he watches me reach under my dress and shimmy my panties down my thighs from my seated position, lifting my butt up to take them all the way off.

"I know what you can give me for my birthday."

The second my nude line-less panties hit the floorboards of my car, I lift myself up over the middle console and straddle Slade's lap in the passenger seat of my car, lifting the hem of my tight-fitted dress up high enough to get my knees on either side of his wide body.

He becomes more alert as his hands hover on either side of my body... not touching me but keeping his hands close in case a slip or fall so he can catch me.

"And what's that?" he asks, his eyes watching me set myself down on his lap.

I know that without underwear on, Slade has a clear view of me bare and clean-shaven under my dress, but I don't care. He's driven me to the point where I don't care at all anymore.

"An orgasm," I say, reaching for the top button of his pants.

My body continues to stay untouched by his hands as I work to undo his pants. Instead, he lays one arm on the middle console of my car and the other on the armrest of the passenger side door.

I'm panty-less on his lap, and he's not going to touch me until I tell him he can?

He just almost spent the night in jail for assaulting someone who touched me inappropriately tonight...

...oh... is that what this is about?

"You want me to give you an orgasm?" he asks as if he might have misheard me.

His eyes break from between my thighs, and when they reach mine, they're hooded and as needy as I am.

"It shouldn't be that big of a deal. I'm just another notch on your bedpost, right? You should have collected plenty by now."

His eyes soften to me for a moment, and I don't like the honesty in them. The concern he's showing in them for me.

"Don't say that. Don't try to cheapen this just to make it fit what you want from me. You're the one that wants this to mean nothing."

Convenient for him, though, isn't it? Slade's not the long-term type, even if it is something I'm mildly interested in.

And I am interested in the long-term, just not with him.

I yank down further on his pants, and his cock breaks free of its confines, standing tall and straight and begging me to sit on it.

I hook my arm around the back of his neck to pull myself closer.

"I don't have a condom," he tells me.

I stop for a second and stare back at him.

I don't usually carry them myself. It seems out of all the things women have to worry about to prevent conception, carrying a condom is the least a man can do.

"Are you clean at least?"

The question almost has me wanting to laugh to myself.

Is Slade clean?

How could he be sure if his reputation is still the same as it was in college?

"I haven't been with anyone in months, and I had to get a full physical, including a full test panel, as part of my contract. I'm clean," he says, his eyes staring back into mine.

"I haven't been with anyone since my last relationship that ended last summer," I admit.

He nods.

"Are you on birth control?" he asks, finally gripping my hips and making me feel weightless as he pulls me closer, anticipating my answer to be yes.

I nod, but I hate how he's starting to take control.

It's my turn to flip his life upside down and take something I want from him for a change.

"Yes, but it won't be necessary because you won't be coming," I tell him, pressing closer to him until I feel his tip glide across my pussy lips and settle right beneath my opening.

The first connection.

My eyelids attempt to flutter closed at the sensation of him, but I won't let them. I won't let him believe he has any effect on me.

"Is this your way of punishing me?" he asks.

"Maybe."

Definitely.

"And after this... am I forgiven?"

"I haven't decided yet."

"You're going to torture me before you forgive me, aren't you?" he asks.

I decide not to answer with my words, and instead, I press down on him, feeling the warm skin of his tip enter me.

We both take a deep inhale at the initial plunge of his head fully inside of me. The stretch is so much more than I anticipated. I misjudged his size, though I know from seeing him in the shower that it's bigger than anything I've taken before. I just didn't realize it was *that* much bigger.

My brain short circuits for a second and becomes temporarily fuzzy, as I lose all thoughts of anything but pleasure.

Having no rubber between us is heaven, and his thick cock that I've been fantasizing about in my dreams doesn't disappoint.

I rock my hips against him with a steady and quick rhythm, working him inside of me, inch by inch.

His eyes jam shut, and I hear his teeth grind as he tries to stave away the urge to come. A guttural sound rumbles through his throat.

I increase my rhythm on top of him as he becomes fully seated inside of me.

The stretch is so good that my body begins to buck more wildly than before... my hips taking over, driving me closer and closer to the edge.

I'm no longer in control of my movements as everything switches to primal need, chasing that orgasm that I've been primed for since I saw Slade naked and dripping wet in the shower.

"Jesus, Penelope... you're so fucking tight," he groans, his hands gripping around my hips.

His hips start to move, matching my thrusts until we're working together to get me off.

I moan out as his cock hits the spot I need as my clit rubs against his pelvis, sparking nerve endings that have my legs beginning to shake.

"You look like you need a little help, baby," Slade whispers below my ear and against my neck. His hot mouth sending more shock waves through my body.

"I'm on top. I'm the one in control," I tell him.

"When you're fucking me, Penelope... you're never the one in control," he says, his hands reaching down and lifting the hem of my dress until it settles around my waist, leaving my butt completely unexposed.

I'm too far gone to care anymore as Slade takes a hand full of each butt cheek and starts to guide my body into a new rhythm that makes his cock plunge even deeper inside of me.

"I could fuck you from the bottom like no one ever has... but this is your birthday present. How do you want it?" he asks, low and sexy.

I demanded that he bend to my will and proclaimed that I was going to punish him, and now I'm releasing all control because I need to know what it feels like to truly be screwed by this man.

I nod, unable to make anything else sound coherent.

With that Slade grips around my waist and starts to thrust up from his seated position, fucking me thoroughly from the bottom position like he said he would.

I grip my arms around his neck and hold on, leaning my head against his as he pulls moans and desperate pleas from my lips.

His movements are so much more aggressive, so much more powerful. He's a professional athlete and it shows in his endurance. I can't match him anymore thrust for thrust so I give into him, letting him take me over.

"Slade," I whimper out.

"See baby, you were never really in control," he says.

"Oh God," I say as he manipulates my body by pulling and pushing me back and forth, making my whole body start to buzz with the impending orgasm.

"Say my name when you come, Penelope. I want to hear what my name sounds like when you come for me."

I can't deny him now, not with him giving me the best birthday present of my entire life.

He pumps into me again and again, his grunts becoming louder and my moans becoming more desperate.

"Kiss me," he demands.

"No," I mutter out.

As stupid as it sounds, that's too intimate.

I can't go there with him.

"Then I won't let you come."

I push back just enough to look into his eyes.

Is he serious?

I'm the one that should be making the demands, not him.

"Kiss me, and I'll finish you," he says.

If he stopped now, I'd be in agony from not getting off. I can't risk that he's bluffing.

I lean in, wrapping my hands around the back of his neck and press my mouth to his.

He releases one of my ass cheeks and thrusts his hand into my hair to keep my mouth pressed to his.

A burst of colors like fireworks electrifies behind my eyelids the second our lips touch.

His tongue slides across my lips, demanding entry into my mouth and I open for him with a moan.

Our tongues tangle together as I feel my body racing to the edge of the cliff.

I've dreamed about these lips and now they're against mine.

I can feel my body tightening around him, squeezing as it prepares for release.

"Is that the spot? Do you like it right there?" he asks against my mouth.

"Yes," I say as he repeatedly hits the same place that has my toes curling.

It only takes a couple more thrusts, and then my body breaks loose, and I free-fall into the hardest orgasm of my life.

"Slade," I call out as I grip around his shoulders, panting as my body spirals out of control.

Slade pulls me closer, kissing me more tenderly than the feverish way we were taking each other's mouths before.

"I've got you. Just relax," he says, his fingers lightly brushing strokes down the back of my neck as I regain the feeling in my legs.

After about a minute, I'm starting to feel my toes again, and I open my eyes to find Slade watching me.

"That was..." I try to come up with something adequate, but mind-blowing is the closest thing, and that seems too tame for what just happened.

"I'm glad I could give you what you really wanted for your birthday, but you have about three seconds to dismount, or I won't be able to stop myself from coming inside you," he says, eyeing me carefully.

"You wouldn't. I told you that you couldn't."

He shakes his head and swallows hard. I can see the almost physical pain in his eyes as he tries to hold back.

"I don't have any control over this. I've held off as long as physically possible, but goddamn it, you're beautiful, and I'm bare inside you," he says.

"One..." He starts the countdown, and panic sets in.

Do I get off, or do I stay on?

Am I really considering staying on? What the hell is wrong with me?

"Get off, Penelope, or this won't end the way you want."

"You better not. You don't deserve it after what you cost me."

He ignores my warning as he continues his counting.

"Two... I'm serious," he threatens as his jaw tightens again, trying not to come.

"Slade, don't you dare—"

"Three," he says and then squeezes my hips and pulls me down hard against his lap.

I grip around his shoulders as he pumps harder into me.

"Fuck..." he growls as he releases inside of me, emptying himself deep as his cock twitches while his orgasm rips through his body.

I don't know what possessed me not to climb off his lap when I had the chance, but I couldn't get myself to move.

The painful look on his face subsides into relief as he finishes.

His breathing labors as his eyes stare back at me, his nostrils flaring. "I warned you,' he says.

A knock on the glass of the passenger side of my car makes us both jump.

"Ready to walk home?" I hear a muffled voice on the other side of the door.

We both whip a look over to find Tessa.

The moment she sees the wide-eyed look of panic on my face, she realizes what she just walked up on.

"Oh my God!" she says, shielding her eyes and jogging away from the car.

Shit!

"Penelope..." he says as I watch my friend run from my car.

I push open the door of the car to get away from Slade as fast as possible. I can't think straight when it comes to him. He's like a radio frequency disruptor that makes my brain waves turn to static air.

"I hate you," I tell him, more because I'm finding it harder and harder to stay away.

"I know," he says back.

The look of defeat on his face and the smell of sex all around us leaves me feeling a little guilty for saying it. This was my idea, not his, and I knew better than to give into a moment of weakness and his close proximity.

I climb off his lap and grab my clutch with my phone and key fob in it. Then I step out onto the parking lot asphalt barefoot, keeping the door close to shield me while I pull my dress back down over my hips.

This parking lot has security, so my car will be safe here overnight. I didn't have a lot to drink, but there was no point in risking it when we always had plans to walk back as a group anyway.

I yank down my dress to cover up my exposed skin and decide to leave the underwear. I can't take one more second with him.

"I didn't drink. I can drive you home," he offers.

"I'd rather walk," I say.

"I can drive your car to the apartment then so that you have it in the morning."

I nod, barely looking at the man I just took bare while his cock is still hard and sticking out of his pants. Slade quickly fumbles around to grab my shoes off the driver's side floorboards.

I would have left without them. It's all cement sidewalk from here to the apartment building. But without shoes, there will be more questions.

"Here," he says, reaching for my jacket in the back seat.

I slip on my shoes and then my jacket.

"Are you going to get into the driver's seat?" I ask.

He looks down at his erection, which hasn't gone limp in the slightest.

"I'll need another minute," he says.

"Slade! Penelope! Let's go," I hear Lake's voice in the distance.

I look to find our whole crew waiting on me, minus Brent, Kaenan, and Isla, who live in the suburbs and have already left.

I pull out the key fob in my clutch and toss it to him.

He catches it, and then I head towards the group waiting for me.

A text comes through my phone as I walk to join the group.

Isla: Sorry your birthday ended with that creep touching you. I hope you're ok. Thank God Slade was there to step in.

I shoot off a quick text back.

Penelope: It would have been fine without Slade. All he did was make a scene.

Isla: Go easy on Slade. I was there, and the drunk didn't seem to get the hint. Plus, Lake wasn't far behind and he wouldn't have held back like Slade did.

Isla: Kaenan said if he had seen what happened before Slade did, he would have put that dunk in a choke hold within the first second for touching you and thrown him out of the bar.

I know that Lake, Kaenan or any of the other players in the bar would have stepped in too. But they don't have a history of overstepping like Slade does.

A few minutes later, my red Mercedes drives by us.

"Is Slade driving your car back to the apartments?" Lake asks, walking arm in arm with Tessa directly in front of me, with Seven and Brent behind, bringing up the rear of our group.

"Yeah," I say simply.

Tessa watches the car as it passes us and then pulls her arm out of Lake's and hangs back to link arms with me. She slows down our pace until Seven and Brent move past us and join Lake, bringing him in on their conversation.

We walk closely behind as Lake checks back every once in a while to make sure we're close.

"So... how was it?" she asks softly enough that the guys in front of us won't hear.

"I don't want to talk about it."

"That good, huh?" she snickers.

"I hate him, remember?"

"Hate sex is the best kind, I should know. But makeup sex with Lake is pretty damn good too. Maybe you should try that next and give him a pass on shoving the drunk."

First Isla, now her too with forgiving Slade?

"He just keeps poking his nose where it doesn't belong," I tell her.

"Ok... you're right. If you didn't want him to get involved, then he shouldn't have. But did he really get a tattoo for you?" she asks.

I whip a look over at her.

Did he tell our friends that he got a tattoo for me?

Does everyone know?

"Did he tell you that?" I ask.

"No, Isla did. He told her that the tattoo was for a birthday, but it isn't his birthday. Then she said he looked at you like you were his next meal. She didn't have to be Sherlock Holmes to unravel the mystery."

It was at that moment that I realized that he didn't show me the tattoo he got because he said it needed to heal.

"I guess," I say.

"What is the tattoo of? Please tell me it's a heart with an arrow shot through it," she says with a teasing chuckle, gripping around my arm tighter as she pulls me closer.

"I have no idea," I tell her honestly.

And now I'll be up all night trying to figure out how Slade can turn my body into jello... and what tattoo he got for me.

CHAPTER TWELVE

Penelope

It's been four days since my birthday and the incident where I inexplicably tripped over the middle console of my car and fell on Slade's dick while I hate-screwed him to scratch an itch that doesn't feel any more satisfied than before.

Not because it wasn't good...

God, it was too good.

But now my body is craving Slade's monster cock, and no amount of Serendipity's delicious sticky buns are going to curb my appetite for another round with him.

I woke up the following morning to a bouquet of mixed flowers, including gorgeous peonies, and my car keys sitting outside my apartment door.

He must have asked one of the guys on the team what my apartment number is because I never told him. My heart warmed to see my favorite flowers sitting on my apartment doorstep. How did he know they're my favorite? I bet he just picked whatever the florist told him to get.

First, the chai lattes, sticky buns..., and now stunning flowers at my door?

I hate how my heart wants to forgive him.

This is a real problem.

One that I have to fix.

I picked up the flowers and put them near my apartment window so they could get some sun, and then I internet searched the words Stockholm Syndrome just to be sure.

The results were inconclusive...

1. **Doing things that are out of character for yourself.**

Having unprotected sex with the man I hate... check.

2. Feelings of depression or helplessness.

I feel helpless in avoiding me jumping him again. Does that count?

3. Behavior that leads to self-harm.

I had sex with Slade Matthews in a parking lot... actions of self-harm? 100%!

4. Feelings that others might not understand your relationship.

If the look on Tessa's face when she caught us in the car says anything... I think she's a bit confused. But the person who most certainly doesn't get this sexual frustration I have with Slade... is me.

5. Feelings of anxiety or shame.

I don't feel either of those. Though a little bit of guilt rose up the following day when I thought about how I was waiting for Win to be ready to meet up but screwed someone else a few nights ago.

Not that Win and I have any agreement or have discussed exclusivity. I mean, we haven't even met in person yet. And he did drop me out of the blue one day and disappeared for four years. There's no guarantee that he won't just do it again.

Besides, Win could have been doing the same thing that night with some woman he met at the bar in the passenger side of her car, too. It's certainly possible.

Still, it doesn't change the fact that I have feelings for Win, and at the same time, something I can't explain is happening between Slade and I.

It's silly to consider that I have to pick between two men. Win has always been there for me—the shelter during the worst storm, and Slade... well, he's not even a contender. Not that he's asked to be one. He's just there—showing up around every corner with his sexy finger-swept hair, chiseled jawline, and piercing hazel green eyes.

And those lips.

God, I can't forget about those lips.

No wonder the rumors about girls getting addicted in college and stalking him started circulating. I can see how it could happen to any unsuspecting woman who doesn't know him like I do.

The team left for their first round of playoff games in Colorado the morning after the night at the bar, which has spared me from the inevitably awkward interaction with Slade in the halls of the Hawkeyes' stadium for the last few days. After tonight's game in Denver, they'll be on a flight back home for the next two playoff games, and I won't be able to avoid him then.

My phone dings with an instant message from Win as I set my phone down in the kitchen to start the BBQ wings I'm making for the girls, who should be showing up any minute for the puck drop starting in thirty minutes.

> **WinForToday067: I'm headed into a meeting, but I just wanted to check in with you today. Yesterday you said your birthday sucked, but you didn't say why. Anything you want to talk about? I have a couple of minutes before I have to silence my phone.**

He's going to a meeting at seven o'clock in the evening.

It seems odd, but I still have no idea what he does. Maybe he's a computer programmer who works for a foreign country on a different time schedule than us. That's plausible, right?

I stare down at my phone as I drop the chicken wings in a bowl and dump a whole container of BBQ sauce on them, stirring them around until everything is well coated.

Do I want to tell Win what happened the night of my birthday?

Not particularly.

But he's the one I usually go to when I'm having Slade Matthews problems. His advice is always solid, too.

> **SkatrGirlPen: I had a run-in with my nemesis at the bar, and it didn't go over well.**

Using tongs to pull out each BBQ wing, I place them each on a baking sheet and then open the oven door, placing the pan and wings in to cook while I wait for Win's reply.

> **WinForToday067: What did he do this time?**

It's only six words in a simple text, but the way Win instantly takes my side and assumes that it's Slade's fault, always makes me feel instantly supported.

> **SkatrGirlPen: He picked a fight with some drunk guy who touched my ass at the bar. I had it under control, but instead, he jumped in like the watchdog he keeps thinking I need. He just about beat the guy to a pulp. I was humiliated yet again while the entire bar watched Slade make a spectacle of the situation.**

From Isla and Tessa's perspective, I should be happy that a big guy like Slade was there to tell the guy to get lost. But they weren't there the last time that Slade "came to my rescue" and ruined everything for me.

SkatrGirlPen: I could have handled it quietly myself, you know? My friends think he was being protective. Am I overreacting because of our history?

WinForToday067: No matter his intentions, he should respect your boundaries. Have you considered having a conversation with him about this? Maybe it's time you two talked this out.

SkatrGirlPen: Talk it out? I told him that I want him to leave me alone. Isn't that enough?

I can't help but feel a little weird talking about the man I slept with four days ago to the man I'm waiting for to be available to meet up so we can see if there is something more between us.

Not that Win and I have any sort of relationship or understanding. And for all I know, he was banging his way through the greater part of Europe.

And for God's sake, I haven't even met the man.

WinForToday067: You two will be working together for the foreseeable future. Don't you think it would help to lay it all out for him and maybe hear his side of what happened? Maybe there's more to the story? Avoidance doesn't seem to be working. Maybe at least you could agree on a ceasefire?

> **SkatrGirlPen: It's more like I need to challenge him to a duel. At least in the end, there will be a resolution one of us can live with.**

Ok, that was dramatic. I'd erase it so Win doesn't think I'm an unhinge crazy person, but I already sent it.

> **WinForToday067: I'm sorry he ruined your birthday, Pen. I'll make it up to you someday, I swear. I have to go, though. Goodnight.**

> **SkatrGirlPen: Thanks for hearing me out and letting me vent. I don't know what I would do without you.**

Slade

I stare down at her last message, reading it a couple more times even though the rest of the team is grabbing their gear from the locker room and heading out for our away game tonight.

"I don't know what I would do without you."

Fuck, I'm so screwed.

She's going to hate me when she finds out.

Hearing her say that I ruined her birthday hurts. Because for me, minus our fight in the bar, it was the best damn night of my life.

And it wasn't solely because of the sex.

For the first time in four years, I finally got to touch her skin, kiss her lips, and run my hands through her hair. Our bodies were connected, and maybe for just a split second, I thought she'd see what I saw. That this thing between us is something worth fighting for, even if it means we're fighting each other.

If she gave me the choice, I'd take fighting with her every day over not having her at all.

"Let's go, hustle, hustle, we have a championship to win," I hear Coach Bex say to all of us in the locker room.

I tuck my phone into my duffel bag and grab my gear.

I can only tackle one fight at a time, and tonight's fight is beating Denver.

Then tomorrow, I offer Penelope the only thing I can to attempt to make up for what I cost her. It won't be the Olympic-level partner she deserves, but it's the best I can do.

A practice partner.

CHAPTER THIRTEEN

Penelope

It's six am, and I love the sound of the silence in the rink with the lights dimmed around the stadium and only lighting on the ice.

I sent my phone down, pairing the phone to the Bluetooth speaker and hit play.

The music starts to play through the speakers, and just as I'm about to push off, imagining Toby next to me, starting our program, an arm reaches around me where Toby's should be, and the other hand takes mine that should be outstretching into Toby's.

My head whips around to find Slade pushing us through the ice in the exact position my partner used to be in.

What is happening?

Slade's powerful movement pushes us across the ice, giving me the moment I'll need for the spin ahead.

I'm in shock as I stare back at him, my body going into autopilot to skate the same routine that Toby and I created so many years ago.

How does he know the routine?

We get to the part of the routine where he spins me twice and then releases me to finish out the spin on my own.

The second my spin ends, I don't rejoin him like I'm sup-posed to— skating in tandem with some synchronized foot-work. I just stop dead in my tracks and stare back at him with his hand outstretched towards me, waiting for me to take it to continue the routine.

"What are you doing?" I ask.

"Skating with you. You need a partner."

"You're not my partner. I don't have one because of you."

"I know. That's what I'm trying to make up for."

I stare back at him blankly.

"I retired from competitive skating. I'm not sure what you're trying to accomplish here."

"Why did you retire? Why didn't you try skating singles?" he asks, staring back at me in a t-shirt and Hawkeyes warmup pants.

I retired because I gave up trying to find someone to skate with from the University, and trying to find someone living states away who didn't know about Slade would have taken too long. The Olympics had only been weeks away, and even if I had found someone who already knew the routine, which only Toby and my coach knew, it takes years to learn to skate in perfect harmony with a partner.

Now he wants to have a conversation about why I didn't skate singles.

How about because I was heartbroken over losing Toby as my partner due to injury, having not a single male ice skater willing to compete with me because of him, and then watching my Olympic dreams slip through my fingers with no way to stop it from happening?

I couldn't even look at an ice rink for three months, let alone skate on one.

The only thing that got me back out here was that I got a job with the Hawkeyes right after and I was forced back into proximity of a rink. I owe Phil Carlton so much for offering me this job.

This job saved me from letting my love for ice skating die. And since Phil and Coach Bex let me use the ice when the players don't need it, it feels like the best consolation prize I could hope for.

Is that what he wants to hear? That I almost gave up ice skating for life because of what he did?

"I lost my chance Slade, and starting over in the singles world at twenty-one years old wasn't exactly all that appealing. Is that a good enough answer for you?" I ask.

The figure skating world is highly competitive, with new talent coming up the ranks every year.

"Why not try again? The Olympic tryouts are coming up again this year, and I've watched you out on the ice. You're just as good as you've ever been... maybe better. I can condition with you until we can find you a suitable partner."

"Slade, I'm too old to try now. And someone already skating at an Olympic level isn't going to want to skate with someone who's been out of the game for so long."

"Fine, I still think you should try again, but if you won't skate professionally, then at least skate with me."

"No offense but you have no business in competitive figure skating even if I was interested. Plus, you could get injured and lose your hockey contract."

"Let me worry about what happens if I get hurt. And I'm not suggesting that we compete professionally. Just skate with me here in the mornings like you do now. Just do it with me," he says.

Is he crazy?

The skates are different—the technique is different.

Where hockey requires brute strength, ability to change direction in seconds, and hand-eye coordination, figure skating requires fluid and graceful movement, impeccable timing and body awareness with your partner, and the longevity for programs spanning longer than a hockey player is out on the ice at any given one time.

They're both demanding sports but require different skill sets. I can't teach him everything he needs to know in a morning crash course. However, the idea of having a partner even just to practice in the mornings with again is tempting. And I've seen

Slade's ability to lift and his endurance while in the passenger seat of my car.

I don't doubt that he's strong enough for lifts and spins, but is it worth letting Slade get close just to have someone to skate with?

"How do you know the routine? We never skated it professionally," I say.

"Your coach uploaded short videos of it. I've studied most of it, but there are some missing pieces that I've been trying to fill in by watching you."

"You've been watching me skate? Like... in the stands? Without telling me you're here?" I ask, my eyebrows furrowing at the thought of Slade standing around watching me.

"Would you have skated that freely if you knew I was watching?" he asks.

I ignore his question because honestly... I'm not sure.

And I'm not exactly thrilled that he's been watching me without me knowing. But on the other hand, coming to watch me skate and scouring the internet to find ancient videos of my coach posted in order to become a partner for me to skate with is... oddly, sweet.

"Can I think about it?" I ask.

"Sure," he says, the disappointment in his frown showing through. "I leave tomorrow for Denver. We'll talk when I get back?"

"Yeah. I'll see you when you get back. Good luck tomorrow."

"Thanks. I'll let you get back to skating," he says, then turns to skate out of the rink.

"Hey," I say before he reaches the player's tunnel opening. "Are you going to hide out and lurk around, watching me in the shadows?" I ask.

He stops and looks over his shoulder. "Not this time. The stadium is yours."

He steps out off the ice and then turns one last time.

"Want a sticky bun with your chai today?"

I bite down on my lips trying hard not to smile as wide as I want to.

"Sure, that would be great. Thanks."

He nods and then turns back to leave.

A part of me wants to call him back and agree to skate with him, but I don't. I stand there and watch him until he disappears down the tunnel.

Agreeing to this means spending not only a lot more time with him but also this is a highly emotional program. It's about a couple in love who face their own demons through the program and end up in each other's arms.

It's hard for me not to feel emotions while skating. It's a part of who I am. I give my routine everything I have.

Since Toby's preferences are for men and not women, we were able to act the part without our emotions ever getting entangled.

It was a great partnership since so many amazing pair skaters have ended up breaking up when one or both develop feelings for their partner, and then it all falls apart.

Slade and I have had sex.

We have history and baggage from our past together. Can we really keep that off the ice?

And if we can't... what kind of mess could we be unleashing if feelings get complicated?

He's already so damn sexy in full hockey gear, skating expertly on the ice. How am I going to resist him when we're skating together, and his hands are all over me?

What I do know is that I'm really craving a sticky bun right now.

Slade

Walking up the stairs of the jet the day after, Penelope said she'd consider skating with me. My phone dings with an incoming message.

> **SkatrGirlPen: He wants to skate with me.**

> **WinForToday067: Who?**

I already know it's me but she doesn't know that I know.

> **SkatrGirlPen: Slade Matthews. The man responsible for me not having a partner to begin with.**

> **WinForToday067: Do you want a partner?**

I crest the top of the staircase and then find my way to the back of the aircraft, setting my phone on vibrate.

This team shares gossip quicker than a park bench full of old ladies on a warm Sunday afternoon.

If anyone finds out that I'm talking to some pen pal I've had since college... or worse, that it's Penelope, this jet will be humming with something new to talk about.

For the last couple of away games, Seven hasn't sat in the same row as me, but he does sit in the row in front. Since we both sit in the window seat, we're even closer than if he sat in the aisle seat in the same row, but whatever, I don't mind it.

Though I've gotten to know the guys on the team a little more each week, I spend the most time in the gym with Seven. Since we're roommates on out-of-town games, I spend the most time with him, too.

I get along with everyone on the team now, but I probably care more about his opinion than I do anyone else's.

I take my usual spot, and he's already seated, his Bluetooth earbuds already secured, and he looks to have fallen asleep.

Figures.

I stow my things and then check to see if Penelope has messaged back yet.

She has.

> **SkatrGirlPen: I guess it would be nice. There's no question that he's strong enough to lift me but I'm going to have to coach him into the partner I want. Is that worth the effort? And will letting him into the one last thing that's still a part of my old life ruin it for me?**

WinForToday067: Is there something you're worried about happening if you skate together?

I'm curious to see what she'll tell Win. She never told 'him' that she and I slept together. If she's worried that it might happen again, would she tell him?

I doubt it.

SkatrGirlPen: Yes. What if we fight like we do whenever we're near each other?

We don't fight every time we're near each other. It's more like, every time we're in the same room, she does everything she can to avoid me.

That's the difference.

WinForToday067: I understand that the guy can be a dick sometimes. Maybe this would be good for you? Maybe this is what you need to bury the hatchet. It sounds like he's trying to make it up to you. And on the bright side, he won't come with any bad habits from old partners or have any competing opinions about how a move should be done.

I know I'm using my influence against her right now and I'll probably go to hell for this, but I have to take my shot.

SkatrGirlPen: Slade… not opinionated. That's funny.

> **WinForToday067:** Ok, but it sounds like he's willing to do whatever he needs to make up for your missing partner. Isn't it worth a shot?

She doesn't answer right away and when I hear the jets fire up for departure, I know I'm about to lose cell reception to get the answer I've been waiting for.

> **SkatrGirlPen:** I think it might be.

Relief hits me.

It's not exactly an answer, but it's something.

> **WinForToday067:** I've got to go. I'll talk to you soon.

Then, as I stow all of my gear away for takeoff, a text message comes through my phone.

> **Unknown Number:** Hey, it's Penelope. I got your number from Tessa.

> **Slade:** Hey, we're about to take off. What's up?

I instantly program her number into my phone so I have it.

> **Pen:** If you're still available, I'd like to try skating together. We'll start with one practice. Let's see how that goes.

It's not the vote of confidence I was looking for but it's a start.

Slade: I'll be home tomorrow morning. I'll see you at the stadium.

Pen: Ok. Good luck tonight.

Slade: Thanks.

CHAPTER FOURTEEN

Penelope

I skate onto the center ice, my legs almost jittery with anticipation as I wait for Slade to walk up the player's tunnel to join me on the ice.

Last night I stayed up late watching old videos of me and Toby skating while I thought about what Slade said about me competing again.

God, that was a fun part of my life.

I haven't skated with a partner in over four years, and I'm feeling a little nervous about being rusty.

I texted Slade last night and told him not to worry about coming in to skate this morning since the team was probably going to party all night.

They won their fourth game in Denver, putting them at 4-1. They won the first round of playoffs and now they are on to round two. Their first game will be in three days in Alberta.

He texted back and said that he wasn't going to drink and would try to sleep on the plane to be fresh for the day.

He's taking this seriously and I guess so should I.

"I'm here, coach. Tell me what to do," I hear Slade's voice echo through the stadium.

I turn my head to find Slade skating towards me in black men's figure skates.

"You got new skates?" I ask, smiling at how different his feet look in them compared to his usual hockey skates.

"I had to look the part, though they're not broke in, so we'll see how well I skate in them. Do you like them?"

"I think having the right equipment will help, yes."

He smirks down at me and I know he thought out something dirty he would love to say out loud, but he holds back.

Progress, I think.

"I'm glad you approve. I know I'm on probation at this point. I figured a few brownie points wouldn't hurt."

"Always looking for an edge, aren't you, Matthews?"

"With you, it seems I always need one."

I smirk up at him, happy to know he doesn't consider me a push over.

His lips widen into that drop-dead gorgeous pearly-white smile of his, and I remind myself that I'm not interested in anything but his skating abilities.

"OK, so you know some of the routine?" I ask, skating over to the ledge where I left my phone.

"Yeah, I think I have most of it," he says as I queue up Beyonce – Halo. I haven't updated the music since Toby and I skated this routine, and the tempo and mood still match.

"Let's just start from the beginning since you already seem to know part of it judging from what you showed me a few days ago."

He nods with his hands on his hips as he waits for me to skate back.

The song starts, and I don't have to give him any starting queue. He follows Toby's movements perfectly as if he and I have skated this for years.

He skates with me through the ice, our movement far more in tune than I expected, considering we've never skated together before a few days ago when he took me by surprise. Our awareness of one another surprises me, too. If that night in the car is anything to go on, it seems we have some chemistry in that department.

He sends me into my spin and then skates around me, grabbing my hand just slightly late, but it's nothing we can't tighten up later. We begin building up momentum as we skate toward the turn.

I look over at him to see how he handles the fancy footwork that Toby and I choreographed methodically.

Slade's movements and toe kicks aren't perfect and a little clunky, but I expect that from a hockey player not trained in figure skating. The biggest thing is that he's still managing his momentum at the same time to make sure he keeps up with me.

The triple-twist lift is coming up next. This move took Toby and I months to perfect. And we put it in the beginning of the routine when were fresh because it took everything Toby and I both had to pull this off.

In a split second, I know it's a bad idea to suggest we can do this without at least testing it out in the gym first. It's a difficult lift for trained professionals, but at least Slade's strong enough that if he can just use my momentum when I jump to toss me up high enough and at the right angle, we might have a shot at it.

When I look over at Slade as we skate into it, I can already see it in his eyes...he's anticipating it.

I guess we're going for it.

I skate out in front of him as he places his hands on my hips and I jump as high as I can. He lifts up but at an awkward angle, and instead of spinning into a twist, I come crashing down on top of him.

He wraps his arms around me protectively as we both fall towards the ground. At the last second, Slade twists so that I come down on top of him, his back colliding with the hard ice below us.

I hear the wind get knocked out of him the second we hit the ice, but he still manages to wrap his arms around me.

We slide for a second and then stop.

"Are you ok?" he asks in a grunt.

That must have hurt him so much more than me. He keeps his head lifted off the ice as his eyes dart around every inch of my body he can see from his position under me to make sure I'm ok.

"I should be asking you that question. I fell on a human; you fell on ice."

He makes a sigh that sounds like relief and then finally allows his head to lay gently against the ice rink under him, staring up at the stadium ceiling.

"I'm fine. I'm used to falling. Actually, it's the least painful thing that can happen to me during a game."

We both let our racing hearts slow down a little from the workout.

"You didn't need to take that hit for me. You're still a professional athlete in contract with the Hawkeyes and you getting hurt could cost us the Stanley Cup."

Not to mention that if my father finds out that I let Slade try that move during the playoffs, he'd probably send me to Canada next to work for the farm team.

"I'll never let you hit the ground. Not as long as I can help it."

He pushes a strand of hair that came loose during our practice and tucks it behind my ear. The resolve in Slade's eye, staring back in mine, tells me that I can trust him to take care of me.

I've fallen plenty when Toby and I practiced tough stunts. It's part of the process, though Toby didn't drop me often. He was a great partner and was incredibly protective.

He wouldn't let us try a move until we had perfected it in the gym first. Then, he felt safe to try it on the ice.

I shouldn't have let Slade attempt that just now. I can't let the Hawkeyes down by injuring their starting center just for me to have someone to skate with.

"Let's table the lifts until tomorrow. Maybe we can use the padded gym space to practice those before we try them on the ice," I tell him as my hands push off his chest until I'm on my knee on the ice.

He sits up and pushes to his feet quicker than me. He outstretched his hand to help me stand.

"Are you calling off practice?" he asks, a little defeated.

"We'll try again tomorrow. I need to think through the steps of how Toby and I would start working through a routine instead of just tossing you into one with zero experience. That was reckless on my part. I'm just a little out of practice on how we used to prepare for this. It's been a long time."

"Ok. However, you want to do this," he nods, though I can see he's not happy about cutting things short.

"How about a bagel breakfast sandwich at Serendipity's? I'm starving." I offer.

"I can always eat."

And now that smile of his is back and I have to remind myself that I'm supposed to be waiting for Win. I can't fall for Slade even though everything he's doing is making it so hard not to.

"I bet it takes a lot to feed that body," I say, giving his long torso a once-over.

And then I realize what I just did.

I commented on his body like a pervert and then totally checked him out.

Oh my God.

He chuckles. "It takes a lot of expended energy to play hockey, that's true. Unfortunately, my body would revolt against me if I tried to live off a breakfast of dirty chai's and sticky buns, but you make it look damn good."

I bite down on my lip to keep from blushing.

Slade in flirt mode is hard to resist but I have to keep this as professional as possible, or we'll end up in the passenger side of my car again.

And though nothing is technically happening with us, I feel like maybe I should tell him that there is someone else.

"Slade... I—" I start, picking at my fingernail.

Why do I not want to tell him about Win.

That's wrong, isn't it?

He shakes off the Slade charm quickly and shifts his weight from one side to the other.

"Come on. Let's go before you change your mind and don't want to be seen with me in public."

I laugh and then we both start to skate for the exit.

CHAPTER
FIFTEEN

Slade

Penelope and I make it right before the morning rush and get our order placed.

I grab the plastic number off the counter that she hands me and then follow Penelope to a small table in the corner.

We both take a seat, waiting for our food and her drink to come out.

"Thanks for buying... again. You should have let me pay this time. You did break my fall this morning and you've spent a fair amount on my latte habit already," Penelope says.

She pulled out her card the second after we ordered and slid it to Mary, but I intercepted the transfer and slid the card back. Then pulled out my wallet and handed Mary my card.

It wouldn't matter what I make; I'd never let Penelope pay for a meal. Not because I don't think she's capable of providing for herself and covering my order as well, but because I want to take care of anything she wants or needs.

Not to mention that I make far more than I'll ever spend with my Hawkeyes contract, even without the inheritance that kicks in here in a month from now.

"I'm happy to pay. I still have a lot to make up for," I say. "But I will take an exchange of information if you'd like to give it of your own free will."

"What do you want to know?"

"Anything you want to tell me. Maybe your childhood? How growing up with Sam Roberts as a father would make for good breakfast conversation."

She smiles. "Sure, I can tell you about my childhood, but then I want to know about yours."

My smile drops at her request.

Now, I wish I would have asked for something else.

I don't like telling people that I was raised with a silver spoon and that I don't get along with my parents. People assume I'm just another spoiled rich kid who's ungrateful for everything I was given.

Nor do I like pointing out that my father considers me a massive disappointment and thinks that a hockey career is beneath our family.

"I grew up in Michigan," Penelope says. "My parents met during my dad's rookie year there and married pretty quickly after. As a kid, I remember my dad traveling often and watching his games whenever they were televised. When my dad got traded to Seattle, my parents divorced."

I knew this part.

Or at least I knew that Sam was divorced when I started skating my freshman year of college, but he never spoke about his ex-wife. I just remember walking into his office and seeing a picture of a beautiful young blonde in her high school cap and gown on his desk—Penelope's high school graduation picture.

I should have recognized her at that frat house party the minute I saw her, but she was several years older than in the picture and no longer wearing braces, a cap, and a gown.

She didn't look like Sam's daughter.

She looked like... mine.

I never believed in love at first sight. And even when I first laid eyes on Penelope in that loud, overcrowded party, I didn't realize it then, either. But now I recognize it for what it is. I fell for Penelope the minute our eyes met, and she smiled at me but getting to know her as Pen over those six months is what sealed it for me.

"Your mom didn't want to move to Seattle?" I ask.

"It wasn't the move that made her file. When I got older she told me that my father only had room for two loves in his life. Hockey being number one and then her. But when I was born, I took the number one spot and hockey took second. She was no longer on the starting lineup."

"Shit, that's sad. Was she bitter after that?" I ask.

"No, she told me that she's just happy that something else finally came before hockey for once in his life and that if he only had room for one, she's happy that his love for his daughter outweighs it all."

"Your mom loves you," I say, not as a question.

Penelope's mom chose to let the love of her daughter outshine her.

My mom always picks my dad over me, no questions asked.

I know what it feels like on the other side of what could have happened to Penelope.

It's not that my mother doesn't love me. But like Penelope's mom... I'm not on the starting lineup.

"She does," Penelope's smile widens. "But I think she was wrong about my dad. I think she crushed him with those divorce papers, and since he had to leave for work, he didn't think he had a fighting chance. He doesn't exactly wear his emotions on his sleeve, you know?"

"I know exactly what you mean."

I've looked up to Sam Roberts since the day he pulled me aside on that college campus rink my freshman year when I was ready to prove I could outskate and outscore all of my teammates. He told me that if I wasn't going to be a team player, then I could exit the same way I walked into his stadium.

He's never given up on me since that day, even when he sent me to Canada.

"He never remarried," she says, picking at the pink nail polish on her thumb. He never had a serious girlfriend, either. And my parents never fought over me. He paid child support diligently, and my mom invited him to every Thanksgiving, Easter,

Christmas, and birthday party to make sure that I felt as little of
the divorce as possible. I spent the summer in Seattle with him
during his offseason."

"What about your mom? Did she remarry?"

"She's been married two other times, but they've all ended in
divorce. I think she gave up the only man she ever loved."

"Do you think they'll ever figure it out?"

"No, it's been too many years. I think their love is more of a
friendship now."

I nod, but the sinking feeling that I'm going to miss my shot
and end up as Penelope's friend has my palms almost sweating.

"What else should I know about you?" I ask.

"I've finished my online degree at the University of Washington. Phil encouraged me and even offered to pay when I took
the job here."

"You did?" I ask, my eyebrows lifting in surprise.

I'm glad she accomplished that for herself after I caused her
to drop out.

"Yep, and I'm taking night classes to get my Sports Management Degree."

I stare back at her. She's full of surprises today.

"What do you want to do with it?" I ask.

Her eyes dip back down to her nails like she's embarrassed to
admit it.

"I don't want to be an administrative assistant forever."

"You can do anything you want."

And I believe that. Penelope is smart, charismatic and not
afraid of hard work.

"Even be the GM for a hockey franchise?" she asks, her eyes lifting to mine.

There's a vulnerability to them that she's never shown me. She cares about my opinion on what I think she's capable of and maybe this is the moment that I'm no longer the outsider begging for a chance that she'll open the door and let me in.

"If you want to be a GM, you'll be the best in the NHL. I have no doubt."

"You'd work under a woman?" she asks.

I lean in a little closer and lock my eyes with her.

"I would happily work under you for the rest of my days if you'd let me."

A pink flush hits her cheeks, but she doesn't look away.

"I have your food," Mary says, walking up to our table, breaking the moment.

Damn it, now I wish I hadn't ordered anything, even though my stomach is starting to protest, and the smell of the food Mary has is making my mouth water.

"Thank you, Mary," Penelope says, watching her breakfast sandwich get lowered in front of her, along with her Chai latte.

After all of our food is laid out, mine taking up most of the table, Penelope pulls her sandwich up to her mouth and then asks the question I've been dreading before taking a bite.

"So tell me about your childhood. Where did you grow up?"

I squeeze a dollop of ketchup on my plate for my hashbrowns and then take a quick bite of the potatoes before answering.

"My dad is a surgeon, my mom is a trophy wife, and I moved more times than a military brat. Hockey was the only constant thing in my life. The rules never change; the rink looks identical from one state to the next, and I've always been better than most of my peers because I wanted it more. And that's about it."

She blinks twice, her eyebrows downturned, as she takes a sip of her drink.

"That's it?" she says finally with a chuckle and then licks her bottom lips from the foam of her drink.

Fuck, do I wish I could be her lip right now.

I swallow my last bite and then pull my eyes from her perfect heart-shaped lips.

"It's a quick rundown, but there's nothing more important to share. My dad and I don't get along. He thinks I'm wasting my life playing the game I love, and my mom is his shadow—my life in a nutshell."

"I'm sure he doesn't think that."

I pull up my phone and show her the last text my dad sent me... last night after we won our first round in the Western Conference.

Penelope leans forward to read it.

> **Dad: Enjoy it while you can. Your hockey lifespan is about up by now. You can't outrun it. You should have been a doctor.**

I see the minute she finishes the text. Her eyes lose their crystal blue when she reads my father's inspirational congratulations.

She pushes back into her chair and there's a short moment of silence that falls between us.

"He's wrong, you know. You're a talented hockey player and you have a lot of playing years ahead. Your career just started," she says.

"Maybe."

I take a bite of my food not wanting to further the conversation about my father any longer. I don't want to waste a second on him when I have Penelope giving me the time of day for once.

"When do you want to start practice tomorrow?"

"Same time? But in the gym?" she asks.

"Sounds good. I have to meet Seven in twenty minutes for weights."

"Do you need to leave now? We can get to-go boxes," she says, eyeing the small table by the register where to-go boxes sit.

"No, I still have time. Tell me about how you got into ice skating."

Her face lights back up, and now we're back on track.

"My dad took me ice skating when I was two, and my mom said she's never been able to get me off the ice since."

"That sounds like you," I say.

For the next fifteen minutes, Penelope tells me all about her career in ice skating. Every competition she's won, when she and Toby became partners... and I eat up every moment of it, watching her smile at me like she did that day at the frat house.

She might not be smiling because of me but I'm just happy to be in proximity of it again.

CHAPTER SIXTEEN

Slade

I walk into the stadium for training with Penelope when my phone dings.

I'm not expecting anyone to be messaging me this early in the morning, but maybe Seven or Briggs need to change our meet-up time this morning.

> **SkatrGirlPen: How's that project coming? Any closer to finishing.**

Shit, I knew she'd ask again. I just need more time.

I guess I'd been holding out hope that she would forget about wanting to meet Win the closer her and I got and maybe even forget him altogether. But that's wishful thinking.

I can't show up to a meeting spot and out myself until there's a really good shot that she'll forgive me for lying to her all this time.

> **WinForToday067: I'm getting closer, I promise. I just need a little more time.**

I just need more time with you.

I could feel her walls coming down yesterday when we skated together and the look in her eyes when I broke her fall after the failed attempt at that lift.

I saw it again when she told me about her family over breakfast.

Seeing the pity written on her face when I told her about my dad wasn't fun though, but I had to open up to her if I want her to continue to do the same.

> **SkatrGirlPen: Ok. Going to practice with Slade. Wish me luck... and no broken bones.**

> **WinForToday067: Are you worried he'll drop you?**

I don't like the idea of Penelope thinking I'd ever drop her; on purpose or on accident, but I still haven't established trust with her.

Something I'm trying to rectify now.

> **SkatrGirlPen:** The funny thing is... no, I'm not worried that he'll drop me, though I've been dropped before. It's part of the risk.

Relief hits me that she at least believes I won't let her hit the ground.

> **WinForToday067:** How was skating with him yesterday?

I stop short of the gym.

I'm sure she's already inside, and it's fucked up that I'm right outside messaging her as a different guy. I know I just need to come clean.

> **SkatrGirlPen:** Shockingly not terrible. He's not as graceful as Toby but I can't expect a lifetime of training like Toby had to show up in a hockey player overnight. You might be right about us burying the hatchet. I don't have to be ok with what happened in our past to move on and be civil with him. Trying to avoid Slade around the stadium was only giving me unnecessary anxiety, worrying about the unexpected moment I might be caught in a hallway at the same time... awkwardly passing by.

> **SkatrGirlPen:** Thanks for the advice. You always know what to do.

WinForToday067: I'm here for you. Always. No matter what happens in the future. I'm not going anywhere this time.

I mean that as Slade, but the truth is that I'm both, and I want to believe I know that given the chance, I can give her both.

SkatrGirlPen: Thank you. I believe you.

I put my phone on silent, drop it in my duffel bag slung over my shoulder, and then take the last few steps towards the gym door.

The second I do, Penelope jumps a little.

She was expecting me... right?

"Morning," I say.

"Hi, good morning," she says, pulling her hand from her chest.

I walk over to the corner where I usually drop my duffel bag and pull the black nylon strap from my chest and drop the bag on the ground.

"Did you come prepared to work?" she asks, a playful smile across her lips.

"How hard could it be," I tease back.

"I'm going to make you eat those words," she says with a lifted brow.

"I'll eat anything you tell me to."

I prepare myself for an eye roll, but all I get is a lifted brow, and then she turns towards a Bluetooth speaker in the corner of the gym is usually streaming music or a podcast while we work out.

"Good boy," she mutters to herself, but it's loud enough for me to hear.

My cock heard it too and twitches in my grey sweats as I watch her hips sway side to side and her long blonde ponytail swish with her movement as she makes it across the room.

She reaches the speaker, taps a few things on her phone, and then the song from yesterday starts to play through the system.

She turns back and heads for me.

I didn't expect that lift from yesterday looking as tough as it ended up being. Now, thinking back to college, I remember seeing figure skaters practicing their lifts on the gym floor before they tested it out on the ice. They look exhausted after practice.

If I know Penelope, she's going to make me work for my position as her partner, and there is no better position than getting an excuse to keep my hands glued to her body for the next hour of practice before I have to lift weights with the guys.

She can work me as hard as she wants... she'll never hear me complain.

"Ok, how about if we start by moving through the steps from the beginning to the end. We'll go through the entire routine first without any lifts. Once we have that down, we'll start working on one lift at a time."

I like her idea of working through the routine methodically. First, we'll get me familiar with the steps, and then we'll tackle the harder portions.

We awkwardly dance/walk a few times through the routine since there's no way to really mimic ice skating.

Since I couldn't find the routine in its entirety with every one of Toby's movements, Penelope had to help me fill in the missing pieces.

"I think I'm getting it," I say as soon as we finish the third attempt at the complete routine with very few errors.

I've always been a fast learner, but this is a different world, and I wasn't sure if I could keep up.

"You're picking it up quickly. I'm impressed."

A smile widens across my lips just before I take a drink from the metal water bottle I left on the gym floor by my duffel bag.

"Is that a compliment?" I ask.

"You don't totally suck... is that better?"

I chuckle. That's more of what I'm used to with her.

"The first one was better. I like it when you're nice to me."

I set my water bottle back on the floor and then head back towards her, eating up the distance between us to meet her back by the full-length mirrors.

"Are you ready to try the twist lift again?" she asks.

"I still have a few minutes before the guys get here to work out. Let's give it a go."

"Let's just start with a single twist," she says, walking over to me and giving me her back.

I put my hand around her waist, relishing the heat of her body against my fingertips, my eyes glued to her perky ass only a few inches from my cock and then I remember that I need to focus. I can't let her get hurt during this stunt.

She places her hands over mine.

"On the count of three, I'm going to jump as high as I can. Use my momentum to toss me up into a twist."

"Got it."

"Are you ready?" she asks, listening over her shoulder for my response.

"Ready."

She starts counting, bending at her knees with each count, my hands following along with her hips.

"One. Two. Three."

She jumps, and I hoist her up into a twist, but when she comes down, it's at an awkward angle.

I reach out to pull her against me but she's further out front than I realize, and I grab onto whatever I'm able to stop her momentum from hitting the floor.

It's not pretty as I grab onto her waist and a wrist. As we fall, my left arm pulls her tight to me, and my right braces us since Penelope is going to hit the ground first.

This time, I can't twist her on top of me like I did on the ice.

We're going to hit the padded ground but it's not soft enough to make it pleasant.

My right hand connects with the ground first, and I hear a pop from my shoulder. Pain immediately radiates through my shoulder and down my arm.

We crash against the gym floor mats, though my outstretched arm slowed us down.

"Oh my God, Slade, are you ok?" she asks with me lying on her. "I heard a pop."

"I'm fine," I grimace as I pull the arm that took the hit back from under her. That's going to fucking hurt tomorrow, but nothing's broken or dislocated, so an ice pack overnight and seeing the physical therapist during office hours across from the locker room is on my immediate agenda for tonight.

She reaches for my shoulder and soothes her hand over it gently.

"Are you sure? That didn't sound good. Should we take you to the hospital to get it checked out?" she asks, her eyes glossy with concern.

The pain in my shoulder is worth the way she's looking at me right now.

"It'll be fine, I promise. I've suffered a hell of a lot worse," I tell her honestly.

"You could have broken your arm falling on it like that. You should have let me fall."

I stare back at those eyes full of concern for my well-being, something I don't think she would have felt for me even two days ago. If she only knew how many times I'd break her fall if she just kept looking at me like that.

"Penelope, I would break every bone in my body before I'd let you get a scratch. And if you don't believe me, ask me to prove it again."

I can't help it.

I can't stop it.

"Why do I believe you?" she asks.

"Because you know it's true."

Protecting her comes even more naturally to me than breathing. And the more she lets me in, the more I know that there is nothing she could ask me for that I won't deliver on.

Anything but leaving her alone.

Unless it's truly what she wants.

Though I think walking away a second time might kill me.

Her eyes search between mine for a moment and then she does something I'd never expect.

Her eyes dip down to my mouth—her tongue darts out to wet that full bottom lip... and I'm fucking gone.

"Penelope?" I ask softly.

"Yes?" she asks in barely a whisper.

Her crystal blue eyes settle back on mine.

"Can I kiss you?"

She doesn't say a word.

Instead, she lifts her hand up between us and wraps her hand behind my neck. I can feel her heart beating faster against my chest as her eyes lock with mine.

Her pink lips, full and glistening from her wetting them.

I bend down, hoping I'm reading this right, and I press my lips to hers.

The taste of her peppermint toothpaste clings to my lips, and the smell of vanilla fills my nostrils.

I breathe her in, feeling her body under me as her chest fills with oxygen, and then she lets out a sound that's a mix of a blissful sigh and a moan.

My cock begins to stiffen at the sound and the warmth of her body under me.

She wraps her other arm around my neck and pulls me closer.

My tongue darts out to lick her bottom lip. I don't demand entry; I just want a taste, but her lips part for me on their own volition.

This isn't a frantic, crazed-in-the-moment kiss like we had in her car. This is softer... slower... me showing her how I can take care of her if she lets me.

The door to the gym screeches open and Penelope yips under me in surprise, pulling her mouth from me immediately and then tries to hide herself under me.

My best guess is that she doesn't want to be caught stuck under me with my tongue down her throat in her place of employment. That doesn't surprise me.

I'm the dirty secret she doesn't want anyone to know about.

I cover her body with mine as much as possible and then look over my shoulder towards the door to see who just walked in.

"Morning, Matthews," Seven says.

He doesn't make eye contact as he walks in with his duffel bag slung over his shoulder.

He just stares directly ahead and walks towards the small gym locker room.

It's a quarter of the size of the locker room attached to the rink but it's better than walking across the stadium to use the bathroom or shower on the other end of the massive building.

"Hey, Wrenley," I say back.

"I'll be out in a second," he says, walking calmly to the back of the gym.

"Ok."

There's a moment of silence right before he gets to the door.

"Morning, Penelope."

Penelope's eyes clamp shut, and her nose wrinkles for a second.

We've been caught but damn she's cute about it.

"Morning, Wrenley," she says back, her eyes opening back on me and her cheeks warming red.

She's blushing, and I swear to God I fell a little harder for her just now.

As if it's possible to fall anymore.

He walks through the door, and right before it closes behind him, he says, "Conley just parked. You've got less than ten seconds."

And then the door closes firmly behind him.

I scramble to my feet and then pull her off the ground with my uninjured arm.

I know that Wrenley won't say a damn word, but Conley... I don't know him well yet.

And though Penelope and I haven't talked about it, I'm guessing she doesn't want all the players on the roster, or Sam, to know we were making out on the mats of the Hawkeyes' gym.

If Sam's going to find out about anything going on between us, I want to be the one to tell him. He needs to hear it straight from me.

First, I need to make sure that something is actually happening between us, because based on the message earlier with Win... I still have direct competition.

With myself.

Penelope

I speed walk out of the gym and towards the parking lot, distancing myself as quickly as I can before Briggs sees me.

Not that he would suspect something with both Seven and Slade in the gym now, but I'm not going to chance a run-in and find out.

With my gym bag in hand, I head for the employee parking lot. With Slade loose in the building, and that kiss still fresh on my lips, I don't trust either one of us in a locker room shower. Best to be safe and shower at home.

With my father's first appointment not until later today, I have plenty of time to go home, shower, and get myself right again.

Walking through the hallway of the stadium that leads to the main building to the gym, I see Briggs headed in my direction.

Be natural.

He doesn't know a thing.

Don't look guilty.

"Hi, Penelope. Good morning," he says.

"It really is, isn't it? Good to see you," I say, picking up speed and walking faster than I ever have past him.

"Where's the fire? Is Autumn meeting you for a fifty percent off sale on day-old sticky buns at Seredipity's Coffee Shop, again?" he asks as I wiz past him.

We did that like one time, but somehow, he's never let us live it down.

"Delicious pastries wait for no man," I call over my shoulder to him. "Bye, Briggs."

I don't listen for his reply as I make it out of the side exit and almost home free as I step out into the employee parking lot.

I get to my car door, open it and then shut it as quickly as possible.

I take a quick sigh of relief.

Until I hear a knock on my window.

I scream bloody murder as I whip a look at the person at my window and grab my chest with my right hand.

Tessa.

She's never here this early.

I roll down my window.

"Hi," I say, I wasn't expecting you.

"You literally screamed like that last blonde alive in a slasher movie. What is going on? Are you ok?"

I take a deep breath and let it out.

"Yes, I'm fine. I just wasn't expecting you. You startled me."

"I'm sorry. I didn't mean to freak you out. I'm meeting Shawnie and Juliet here early to review party plans before Juliet drives back home to Vancouver."

I just nod far too much for the information given to me.

"Are you sure you're ok? I'm a little early. We can make some coffee in the breakroom and chat before the girls get here," she offers.

The last thing I need is to tell her that Slade and I kissed.

I told her that sex with him was a one-time thing, and now that we ripped off the band-aid, I wouldn't be going near him again. If I admitted to kissing him again, she would give me that Tessa grin that always means she knows more than I do about what's about to happen.

"Yeah, I'm golden... just a little jumpy this morning. I killed a spider on my desk and thought he might be back for vengeance," I say, pulling up the most bizarre excuse.

She just nods, understanding exactly what I mean.

"Ok, well, I'll be here when you come back for work. Come find me later if you want to get lunch and talk, ok?"

I nod again and then press the push start button on my car.

"Thanks. I'm just going to take a shower, and then I'll be back."

She doesn't ask why I'm not just showering here since I usually always do. She's being merciful and letting me go.

I watch her walk towards the side entrance and disappear inside, and then I pull out of my parking spot and head for The Commons.

I park in the parking garage and then take the elevator up to my apartment.

Walking into my bathroom, the shower is a welcome sight. I push open the curtain and turn on the shower water but the shower head only drips water.

What the hell?

I try turning the faucet handle on and off again but nothing comes out. I try the bathroom sink but it's running fine.

Great, just great.

Now, I don't even get a shower.

I call the apartment management company for this building. There's only one maintenance guy for this building but he's usually quick to come by and check on things.

"Pacific North Management, how can I help you?" a woman answers.

"Hi, yes, this is Penelope Roberts. My shower isn't working, but the bathroom sink is. I think there's something wrong with the shower head. Can you send the maintenance guy to my apartment at The Commons, apartment 718?"

"I'm sorry, Penelope but the usual maintenance personnel for that building is on vacation. I will call the maintenance personnel from one of our other buildings and ask him to stop in and see what he can do," she says.

"Ok, that would be great, thank you."

"No problem. I know he's pretty backed up with his work-load, but he has 72 hours to see to a non-emergency situation."

"Seventy-two hours? You're kidding, right? My shower doesn't work! How am I supposed to get ready for work every morning?"

She doesn't know that I can use the stadium where I work at to shower because that's not the point. I should have a working shower.

"I'm sorry about the issues you are experiencing, Ms. Roberts. Our maintenance personnel will be there as quickly as possible. However, he has to take emergency calls first, and then he'll get to the other calls in order of when they were placed, and we've had a lot of calls this week."

"Wait, hold on a second..."

I'm about to tell her that this is unacceptable and that the Hawkeyes spend a lot of money putting players up in this apartment building because of me, but before I can, she speaks again.

"I have another call coming in. Have a lovely day," And then she hangs up.

I check my phone to make sure she actually hung up on me and I see that the call has ended.

"That little…"

I want to call her back and give her a piece of my mind, but there's no point in pissing her off. She could move me further down the list if she wanted to.

I'd better not chance it.

At least I have a place to shower… just not today.

Damn it.

CHAPTER

SEVENTEEN

Penelope

It's been a couple of days since Slade and I went to the gym for practice, and my shower still needs fixing.

The good news is that the guys won the first game of the Western Conference 2nd round.

They play tonight and then they'll be home late tonight or early in the morning depending on how late media goes and when the jet gets in.

A text comes in from Isla.

> **Isla: Sunny offered to take Berkeley tonight, so it will only be me. I'm go-**

ing to drop her off at Sunny and Marc's new house and then head over to your apartment. What can I bring to eat for the game?

Sunny, Isla's future mother-in-law, is a doll and loves having Berkeley whenever she can. Ever since Kaenan won full custody of Berkely, Sunny has been dating Kaenan's lawyer, Marc Salinger. She's been spending more time in Seattle, and she takes Berkeley as often as Kaenan and Isla are willing to part with her.

Penelope: Chips and dip?

I'd ask her to get the alcohol, but after declining a drink at Oakley's for my birthday almost two weeks ago and then not drinking one of the limited edition tangerine hard ciders that Tessa brought from our favorite brewery two nights ago... it has me wondering.

I didn't want to call her out in front of the girls when everyone was here a couple of nights ago, but if she doesn't drink anything tonight, I won't be able to hold my silence.

Isla: Perfect! See you soon.

Thirty minutes later, all of us girls are standing around the kitchen getting our food ready before the game starts.

Autumn reaches into her grocery bag to pull out the ingredients she brought for cheesecake dip to go with the fruit tray when I hear her gasp.

I look over to find Autumn pulling out a box of pregnancy tests.

"Oh my God, Autumn, are you..."

The other girls both look over immediately, but Autumn shakes her head, "These aren't mine, I must have reached in the wrong bag."

We all start darting and look at each other until Isla confesses.

"I brought them—they're mine. I didn't want to take them at home alone while Kaenan's out of town and with everything going on with the playoffs... I don't want to stress him out."

"Stress him out? Hasn't he suggested having a baby before Berkeley is too old?" Autumn asks.

"Yes, he wants more kids, but I'm on birth control... this wasn't planned. We were going to have a wedding first," she says a little shy about the conversation.

"Come on," Tessa beams over at Isla. "Let's do this before the game. We have to know if the Hawkeyes are getting a new baby."

Autumn and I squeal with excitement and I walk over to Isla, wrapping an arm around her shoulders, pulling her with me towards my master bathroom while Autumn looks in the bag and finds a second box of pregnancy tests.

"How many tests do we need?" Autumn teases.

"I was nervous and didn't know how many I should test. I've never taken one before," Isla says, the middle between her eyebrows scrunching up with nerves.

I'm glad she decided to do this with us so that we can support her.

We're all excited as we head down the hall towards my bedroom.

Well, all of us except Isla, who seems still a little stiff in between my arm and shoulder.

Autumn and Tessa busily open up the boxes and get every-thing organized while I head back to my kitchen and grab a disposable red solo cup.

When I return, I hand Isla the cup.

"Here. Pee in this."

None of us exit as Isla pulls down her pants and sits on the toilet, attempting to steady the cup in the toilet as she holds it in place to pee.

Of course, we don't watch her... because we're not total weirdos.

She finishes and places the cup on the counter.

Tessa adds all six of the pregnancy tests that Isla brought, and Autumn starts the timer on her cell phone.

"In three minutes, we're going to know," Autumn says, bouncing with glee.

We chat about Isla and Kaenan's wedding plans, Berkeley as a big sister, and how Isla is going to tell Kaenan if the tests come back positive.

Is she going low-key, telling him over a nice quiet dinner? Or make a huge banner out in the yard for when he pulls up to the house tonight.

Each one of us thinks of something more outlandish than the last, until finally the beeper goes off.

We all gather around the cup, mushing in with each other as Tessa carefully pulls out the first one.

Pregnant.

Clear as day.

"You're going to be a momma!" Tessa yells.

We all hoot and holler as Isla's chest and cheeks redden instantly, but the biggest smile stretches across her face. She's always told us that she wants kids, and now there's going to be another brown, curly-haired Altman running around the stadium in another couple of years, and I can barely wait.

Autumn and I jump up and down, hugging the poor girl who just got the surprise of her life but she doesn't look even the slightest bit disappointed.

She looks overwhelmingly happy.

I wish I could be a fly on the wall when she tells Kaenan. He loves Isla more than life, and I know he'll be thrilled when he finds out.

Tessa double-checks them all.

"Six positives, momma, congratulations... we're having a baby!" Tessa yells and then we all start jumping up and down again, wrapping our arms around Isla while she giggles to our excitement.

A couple of hours later, our boys lose the second game, but the good news is that they still have the two home games coming up and the best-of-seven if they need it.

Watching Slade out there, I can see that he's sharing the puck like the team player I know he can be. And he even spent less time in the penalty box than usual— all huge improvements.

Everyone packs up their things and Isla heads to the bathroom to collect the pregnancy tests to show Kaenan when he gets home tonight.

We all agree to Serendipity's lunch the next day so that Isla can tell us how Kaenan takes the news, though none of us but

Isla have any doubt that Altman worships the ground Isla walks on.

I close the door as everyone leaves. Autumn and Tessa take the elevators to their apartment level, and Isla heads to Sunny's to pick up Berkeley.

A text message lights up on my phone that I left on silent.

> **Slade: I'm taking a red eye tonight to Chicago to meet my uncle and sign some paperwork. Then I'll be back first thing in the morning. I'll miss our practice, just to let you know.**

> **Penelope: Okay, that's fine. The maintenance guy is supposed to be by my apartment today to fix the shower.**

> **Slade: You're having issues with your shower?**

> **Penelope: Yeah, for a few days now but no one's fixed it.**

> **Slade: Go to work and leave your key with Seven. I'll tell him you're going to drop it off. I'll fix the shower.**

He's going to fix my shower?

> **Penelope: How are you going to do that?**

> **Slade: I learned a lot in Canada.**

His answer only provided me with more questions. For example, did he go to trade school to be a plumber during his four years over there, and I didn't know?

I guess there's a lot about Slade that I don't know.

Penelope: Ok, thanks.

Slade: Not a problem. Seven has my spare key for emergencies. You can use my place to shower until I get yours fixed. It might take a day or two if I have to order parts.

I could ask to use Autumn and Tessa's places inside the apartment building, too, but it's nice that he offered.

I finish loading the dishwasher and then turn off the lights in the kitchen, and head to bed.

The following day I head up to Seven's to drop off my key and get Slade's so I can take a shower before work.

I knock on Seven's door and hear his loud footsteps as he approaches. The door creaks open, and Seven is in full workout gear, probably about to head to the gym. The guy's work ethic is ridiculous.

"Hey, Slade said you have a backup key to his apartment."

"Yeah, right... he said you'd be coming by," Seven says as he pushes the door open a little wider for me to come in and then disappears into his apartment as I wait inside the door, keeping it from closing.

"Here," he says, handing me Slade's apartment key, and then I hand him a copy of mine.

"Thanks. Not having a shower sucks," I tell him.

I turn to head back out the door, not expecting Seven to want to chitchat, when I hear him clear his voice.

"Penelope…uh… you doing ok?" he asks awkwardly.

I turn around, already knowing what he's hinting at.

"Is this your "Seven" way of asking if Slade and I are dating?" I grin.

Seven would probably rather step on red-hot coals a mile long than discuss my love life with a player… or lack thereof, in this case, so I know this is coming from a place of care and concern. Something I know Seven is capable of but doesn't like to show much, though I don't know the backstory on it.

Shockingly, he's not exactly an open book.

"It's just that I've seen you two interact. It seems that you have history, and none of it is good. But then I walk in and…"

"Find us making out on the floor of the gym?"

I can't believe I just said that out loud, but it's not like he didn't catch us in the act. We might as well put it out in the open between us instead of beating around the bush.

He nods.

"Right."

"Nothing is going on between us. He hurt me years ago, and I'm barely learning to trust him again. He offered to help me train, and that's all. Things might have gone a little further than they should have that day."

He puts his hand on the door handle to hold it open so that I no longer have to.

"You sure it's nothing?" he asks carefully.

I cross my arms over my chest, not loving that it seems Seven is sensing something between Slade and me. Something that I'm trying to avoid.

"I think he has a thing for you, and I don't want to see him get hurt. I don't know his whole story, but enough to know that he's a loner by default, not by choice."

"You forget that I'm just an ice skater... he's the player, and we attended the same college. I've heard enough rumors to know that Slade wasn't alone all that much."

His eyes glance down at the key in my hand.

"I don't know who he was in college, and the last thing I'm going to do is put my neck out on the line for a guy I'm still getting to know. Plus, I think Sam might kill me for encouraging you towards a player on the team, but I don't think he's the same guy he was then. We room together on the road, and besides a drink or two at the hotel bar on occasion after a win, he and I are both in our rooms by curfew. I haven't seen him show interest to a single woman in the time he's been playing for us... and trust me, there is no shortage of woman shooting their shot with the new center."

I stare back at him and purse my lips.

I'm not shocked that Slade has women all over him. I've seen his cheering section at the home games and the women who rubber neck whenever we're in public together. I've seen puck bunnies at Oakley's trying to garner his attention with low tops and short skirts.

But hearing that he's that way out of town, too, surprises me a little. I still don't know why Seven thinks this information means anything to me. He also has no idea what happened between Slade and I years ago. And although I wouldn't be against spilling my guts to Seven since the guy is a damn vault, keeping Ryker and Juliet's secret, I don't want him to see Slade any different.

"How do you figure that Slade not sleeping with puck bunnies has anything to do with me?"

He looks at me for a second like he knows he's saying too much but he's in too far now.

"Have you seen his tattoo on his left forearm?" he asks.

"The ice skates?"

He nods.

"What about them?" I ask.

"Have you seen the revision since your birthday?"

"Revision? He told me he got a tattoo for me for my birthday. Those skates are for someone else."

"Are you sure about that?"

Behind me, I hear a set of footsteps coming down the hall, and then, within seconds, I feel someone behind me.

"Oh, hey, Penelope," I hear Reeve's voice.

I turn to find Reeve in full running gear.

"Hi, Aisa."

"You ready for our run? Briggs is meeting us in the lobby," Reeve says over my shoulder to Seven.

"I was just leaving," I say, turning back to Seven. "Thanks for the key."

"Sure," Seven nods.

I turn and Reeve gives me room to pass by.

"Good to see you," he says.

"You too."

I travel down the hall towards the elevator and the only thing I can think about is Slade's tattoo.

Did he revise the figure skating tattoo for me?

That doesn't make sense.

Would he really alter a tattoo he got for the woman who got away and call it my birthday present?

For a guy who gets tattoos with significant meaning behind them, it seems sacrilegious to multipurpose his ink.

Something isn't adding up, and now I'm going to think about it all day until I see him again and can see the revision for myself.

Slade

With my uncle having a last-minute out-of-town meeting he had to take to meet with a supplier, I ended up meeting with the family's lawyers on my own and signing the documents that will give me full access to my inheritance.

There's still another month until my birthday but my uncle likes to button up things as early as possible. With the ink dried on his signature early this morning before he left town, and now on mine, there isn't anything anyone can do to stop the funds. Not even my uncle.

I had them wire it into a trust account, one that I have no intention of touching. If I ever have kids, they can have the money.

I already had to pay for the strings attached to my inheritance with pre-med courses, but my kids never will. I'll never hold it against them for chasing a goal in life, and I'll never hold my good opinion or love hostage from them, either.

It's a little after eleven in the morning when my flight returns to Seattle, and the rideshare drops me off in front of the apartment. I get the key from Seven for Penelope's apartment and head down immediately.

I slide the key through her door, and it opens.

Walking through her apartment, the smell of vanilla hits me first. Then I look around to find a well-kept, clean apartment.

Bookshelves are stacked from top to bottom, with romance novels and vein plants scattered throughout. Picture frames of her from when she was a kid are displayed, as are more recent photos of her and Tessa, Autumn, and Isla posing together at parties and Hawkeyes games.

I head for the bathroom, not wanting to waste too much time. If I get this done quickly and efficiently, I might earn myself her first call when she needs something fixed again next time.

I walk through the bathroom and turn on the shower faucets. Sure enough, there are only drips coming from the shower head.

I check the bathroom sink and water gushes out without an issue. Then I check under the sink, pulling out the trash to see underneath.

I barely glance at the trash but then do a double-take when something catches my eye. I instantaneously stop, my eyes gluing to the plastic applicator in the waste bin.

Eight little letters jump out at me and my heart thumps hard against my chest.

"Pregnant"

A positive pregnancy test is sitting in Penelope's trash.

What the fuck?

A dozen questions stream through my mind in a flash.

Penelope's pregnant?

Is it mine?

Why didn't she tell me she thought she might be?

Did she take this test all alone?

Do her friends know? Does Sam know?

Then I think back to her birthday and the lack of protection we used, though she said she was on birth control.

I've heard it happens.

Birth control is only 91% effective.

We wouldn't be the first to get pregnant while on birth control, and I doubt we'll be the last.

Holy fuck... Penelope's pregnant.

My panic and concern move through me like an emotional roller coaster in a matter of seconds until I'm up on my feet, and I've settled on an emotion that has me wondering where I can find her right now.

I'm fucking happy... and mildly relieved.

A smile stretches across my face. I wish she would have told me right away. I wouldn't have gone to Chicago last night. I would have come straight home to be here for her.

I need to see her and I need to see her now.

I need to tell her that she can count on me.

No more fuck ups.

I'm going to be the man and the father she needs me to be, even if it's not mine.

Eighteen years.

I just lucked into eighteen years to prove to her that I'm the one who's going to show up every single day and take care of her and this baby.

I grab the pregnancy test out of the trash and bolt out of the bathroom, making a beeline for the door.

I'm not sure if Penelope will accept me, even with a baby on the way, but I have to try.

CHAPTER EIGHTEEN

Penelope

The door to my office swings open with great force and the moment my eyes flash up, I see a heated Slade headed straight for me.

"Slade, what's wrong?" I ask.

I jump out of my seat instantly, my flowy dress swishing around me as I move quickly. He takes significant strides into the office towards me.

"You're pregnant?" he says, his eyes wide, his breathing labored, and his hair windswept like he ran here.

"What? Why would you think that?" I ask, scurrying around out of my spot to meet him at the front of my desk.

We're both lucky that my father is out of the office today and isn't hearing the commotion.

There's no way he wouldn't hear Slade's demanding voice on the other side of his office door.

My ass hits my desk as he squares up to me. Not because I'm scared of him but because whenever we get too close, it seems I end up in his arms.

He lifts the positive pregnancy test to show me.

It's Isla's.

I feel a little relief that there isn't some rumor going around that I'm pregnant. Slade just mistook the test for mine.

"You left it on the top of the trash can in the bathroom. Were you going to tell me if I hadn't found it?" he asks a little hurt showing in his downturned eyebrows. "I know I've fucked up over and over again, but I won't fuck up anymore. I swear."

My heart almost breaks at the desperation in his voice.

"Slade, it's not what you think—I can explain," I say quickly, eyeing the pregnancy test, understanding how this might look to him.

"Is it mine? Please say it's mine," he says, leaning in closer, his chest heaving as he tries to catch his breath.

His baby?

Slade thinks I'm pregnant with his baby and I can see how he came to that conclusion. We had unprotected sex two weeks ago and now I have a positive pregnancy test in my bathroom.

"Slade, you have this wrong."

But I can see it in his eyes that he's not listening.

"Shit, I don't care if it's mine or not. Just let me take care of you—both of you," he says, stepping forward

His hazel eyes lock onto mine, practically pleading for a chance, and then his mouth drops down to meet mine, and I welcome it. Butterflies erupt in my belly the moment our mouths connect. He kisses me, adding pressure against my lips and I kiss back.

His hand wraps around the back of my neck, taking our kiss deeper, and then he wraps his other arm around my waist and hoists me up, planting my ass on my desk.

"We'll get you the best OBGYN in the country. I don't care what it costs," he says between our kisses.

"Slade..." I try again to interject to tell him the truth, but it's only half-hearted because being in his arms again turns my whole body to jello.

I wrap my own arms around his neck, encouraging him closer.

"I'll buy you and our baby a house in the suburbs near Kaenan and Isla. Any house you want. We'll build a family—I'll take care of you—I want to take care of both of you."

I know I shouldn't let him continue like this. I'm not pregnant, and he's making promises he shouldn't.

I shouldn't let him keep believing that I'm carrying his baby, but I've never seen this side of Slade... I didn't know he had one, and it's unexpectedly intoxicating.

"I can explain," I attempt again but I'm so drunk on his kiss that the words come out as barely a whisper.

"You won't want for anything, I promise you. I'll spend every last penny of my trust fund and my contract salary to give our baby everything," he says as his kiss starts to travel down my neck.

"You don't have to do that..." I try again, but the more he says, the more I melt into him.

Pulling him closer.

"I want to, Penelope. I'll do everything right this time. I won't let you down. Please just let me stay close. You can make the rules, and I'll live by them."

My legs intuitively open for him, and he walks between, pushing my thighs wider to accommodate his larger body.

He presses his pelvis against my center, and an unmistakable bulge rubs against me.

I moan at the feeling of him between them again.

I don't think before my hand reaches down between us, and my fingertips grip around his hard cock behind his jeans.

He growls the moment I squeeze his shaft.

"You're hard," I say.

The idea of him running down two blocks to get to me with his indecent size visible to anyone he would have passed by has me relishing that he came here for me.

Slade Matthews is so big that he isn't suitable for public consumption when erect.

"I thought that the night you straddled me in your car was the hardest I've ever been in my life." He says as his kiss travels down over my collarbone, headed for my breasts. My head falls back for a second as I let his mouth kiss and lick anything he wants.

"But getting you pregnant..." he breaks off in a groan as if getting me pregnant is the most erotic thing he's ever done.

"Fuck, I've never been this hard before. It hurts how bad I want you."

I can't wait another second to feel how hard he is for me.

I sneak behind the waistband of his pants, gripping around his cock and then sliding up and down to feel his full length in my hand for the first time.

Something I didn't get to experience that night in the passenger seat of my car.

"Jesus, Penelope," he groans.

Why is it that every time I think I know him, he morphs into something else, narrowly escaping my ability to pin it down in place and label him as the man who hurt me and doesn't deserve another chance?

It doesn't seem fair since Win hurt me, too, and it took me less than a day to let him back in. However, he didn't cost me the Olympics or cause me to drop out of school due to the embarrassment of the rumor he helped create.

I still don't understand why he went so far as to threaten all jocks in the entire school, but my body can't resist him any longer.

I crave to know what it feels like to be with him again.

Once wasn't enough to satisfy me.

I pull my hand out of his pants, and even with the possibility of getting caught, my fingers scramble for the button on his jeans.

I need to feel more of him.

I need to witness him in the light of day.

He looks between us the second his button pops free and his eyes flash to mine. We stare back at one another as my fingers pull down on the metal tab of his zipper and the metal teeth let loose.

He keeps his left hand low on my waist as his right-hand dips down beneath his underwear and pulls his cock free. The length, girth, and I suspect, heavy weight of him forces his boxer briefs down lower, giving me a full view of what filled me so full the night of my birthday.

I knew from the way my body barely took him that night that he was bigger than anyone I'd had before. But seeing the evidence makes me wonder how I took him at all.

He pumps his cock twice as he studies my reaction to him. I watch his hand's movement and the bead of precum that glistens over his tip. I lick my lips unconsciously at the thought of how delicious that would feel pushing inside of me.

"You fucking wreck me. Did you know that?" he asks, releasing his cock to bob between us and then reaches out, ducking his hand under my dress.

My body bucks towards him giving him better access as his finger glides over my wet panties. My body advances towards him before I can make a conscious decision. Our eyes lock as the look of realization flashes in his eyes that he does the same thing for me that I do for him.

"Are we doing this? Do you want me to fuck you in this office?" he asks.

"Yes," I nod.

His eyes hood and darken at my answer.

"Do we need a condom?" he asks carefully, without making any movement forward.

He's letting me make the call, just like he did the night of my birthday.

He thinks I'm pregnant and, therefore, can't get pregnant again, but I know better.

Isla said she was on birth control when she got pregnant, so it's just as easy as I could, too, but being bare with him was the best sex I've ever had.

I don't want anything between us.

"You're the only one I'm with," he assures me when I don't answer.

"No condom," I confirm, though I know it's reckless.

His lips crash back down on mine. Our hands gripping onto any part of each other we can get.

I should stop this and tell him that we shouldn't have sex at my place of employment. And on my desk, of all places.

I should tell him that I'm not pregnant and that he can take back his promises.

But I don't do any of those things. Instead, I take his kiss and revel in being in Slade's arms once more.

Being with Slade makes me want that dirty side. A side of me I've never felt or wanted with anyone else.

I want to live on the edge a little—feel a little wild and untamed.

The kind of girl that would warrant Slade's attention.

Not that I've ever wanted it before he showed up to the Hawkeyes stadium, looking even more gorgeous than ever.

I reach down and grip around his cock, guiding him gently to bring his tip against my entrance.

He groans as his tip notches at my wet opening and my arousal coats his head. He leans me back, his arm keeping me secure. His other hand gripping himself at the base of his cock as he presses into me.

I moan out as his head pushes through me, and he kisses me harder to muffle my sounds so no one hears us.

The walls are thick in this office. Soundproofed during the renovation of the office recently, but he doesn't know it, and I like that he thinks we might get caught but isn't stopping anyway.

With every thrust he makes, he advances into me further.

I can feel every inch of him as he stretches me to accommodate his size.

My ass wiggles against the desk as he takes me.

"Lay back," he instructs. "So, I can hit that spot that made your eyes roll back last time."

More hot, wet arousal from my body coats Slade until he's sliding in me with ease.

His hand secures behind me, helping me to lay back with my back flat on my desk.

Folders and paperwork needing to be filed lay behind me but I couldn't care less.

"I need you deeper," I beg him, my legs shaking as Slade bends over me, his left hand bracing himself up by the side of my head and his right hand holding my hip in place as he rails into me harder and harder.

"Agree to let me take care of you, and I'll give you whatever you want every night."

Why am I so tempted to say yes?

But his offer was made with haste and designed with the idea that we would have a baby to raise together.

"Say yes, Penelope," he says, lifting one leg at a time until both of my legs above me, bent over his shoulders.

He grips my hips and yanks me hard against his cocks.

"Slade," I whimper out at how deep he is now.

His thumb comes up over me and begins to rub against my clit.

"Goddamn it... you're like a vice around my cock... so close, I can feel it."

He's right, I am.

I'm right on the edge.

"You look so good laid out for me. Next time, I want you naked in my bed so I can take my time tasting you," he says.

He keeps up his same rhythm until finally, the floodgates break open, and I come hard against his cock, moaning out his name. My body rings out my climax as my body shakes from the magnitude of an orgasm that only Slade can give me.

"Can I come inside you?" he asks.

I know he can't hold back his own orgasm much longer. He already said that he's painfully hard and he has to be ready to burst. And I want him to do that inside of me.

I nod.

This time, I'm not trying to punish him. I want him to feel as good as I do.

This time, I'm not fighting it.

I want it all.

"Come inside me," I tell him.

His hands grip my hips even tighter until I hear him groan and empty himself inside me, thrusting a few more times until he releases every drop as deep as he can.

We stay just the way we are for a moment, panting and staring back at each other. I know that even though he's still deep inside of me, I have to tell him what I've been trying to say since the second he flew through my door.

"I need to tell you something."

"Ok," he says, seeing the look in my eyes.

He slowly pulls my legs down over his shoulders and then helps me to sit up towards him.

Only then does he begin to pull out and then tuck his erection back in his underwear, though the tip still peaks out of the top.

My dress bunches around me, still hiked up but covering most of everything.

"I'm not pregnant. That test was for a friend. She took it last night," I tell him, trying not to give Isla away.

It's not my news to share and it's certainly not information that Slade needs before Isla tells Kaenan, though I imagine she told him last night.

"You're not pregnant?" he asks.

The disappointment in his eyes is unmistakable.

"No."

"Are you sure?"

"Yes. I told you; a friend took it—"

"I know but... are you... late?" he asks, trying to find a delicate way to ask such a personal question.

A question that I never thought Slade Matthews of all men would ask me. The problem is, I can't say no to his inquiry because... I am a couple of days late.

"I should have started two days ago," I tell him honestly. "But that's not unusual for me. I'm sure it's coming," I say quickly to assure him that being a day or two late means nothing.

"Then you still could be pregnant?"

His eyes anxiously searching mine as if he's hoping I'll agree to that possibility.

"I'm on birth control, so I can't be," I say, unsure if I'm trying to convince him or me.

Though with Isla's surprise, it has the doubt festering in the back of my mind. Maybe stopping at the market down the road to get my own pregnancy test on my way home wouldn't be the worst idea.

Giving myself peace of mind while I wait for my period to start will keep me from tossing and turning tonight wondering if I'll wake to my period or if I'll wake to another day of an unanswered question.

Am I pregnant with Slade Matthews's baby?

At the same time, not working myself up and just giving it a couple more days would be better.

Slade's question about whether or not I would consider completing in the Olympics could turn out to be no longer plausible anyway if I'm pregnant.

The door to reception opens, and Slade quickly lunges forward to cover me, not that there is much to see.

"Hey, do you want to get lunch at Seredipity's—oh my God, you guys!" Tessa says, shielding her eyes quickly when she sees that I'm sitting on my desk with my dress still hiked up and Slade's pants down at the ankles.

She turns quickly and slams the door closed behind her.

"Do I need to wear a damn cowbell so you two can hear me coming or what?" her sarcastic voice muffled behind the door.

"I'll meet you at Serendipity's in fifteen minutes," I yell to her.

"Good, you have a lot of explaining to do." She says, and then I hear her footsteps becoming fainter as she stomps back down the hall.

"Fifteen minutes? Don't you think we should talk?" he asks as I lay my hand against his chest to push him back.

He goes without much effort on my part, taking a couple of steps away from me to allow me to slip off my desk.

"Talk about what?" I say.

"About how we keep finding ourselves fucking in unusual places. Maybe we should take this to an apartment bedroom next time. One of ours, preferably."

"Or maybe we've gotten this out of our system, and we should stop," I say, though I already know that a second time hasn't cured my appetite for him.

Each time only makes me want him more.

But it's just a sex thing, right?

We can't build a relationship on that. Not like the relationship that Win and I could build.

Comparing them doesn't feel fair but it's the only way to know if I'm making the right decision.

He pulls up his pants and secures the button while I step down from the desk and then pull my dress into place.

He walks over to a box of tissues and pulls three sheets from it

"Here," he says, handing them to me.

"What's this for?" I ask, taking the tissues from him.

"For your underwear. I was really turned on. There's going to be... a lot."

As much as I don't love a bunch of tissues in my panties, I don't need Slade's cum dripping down my leg at the coffee shop while I try to convince Tessa that nothing is happening between us.

I place the tissues where they need to go, though I wish I could take a few minutes to wash them off in the bathroom. Leaving Tessa to wait any longer will only make this worse.

"Also, I'll have to order a new showerhead. The one in your shower is clogged. It should be here in a couple of days, and then I'll install it," he says.

"Thank you for doing that. If you know what I owe you for the part, I'll reimburse you."

"Don't worry about the money. I'll take care of it."

"Thank you," I say, after putting the tissues in place, and then reach over and grab my purse and cell phone to head to Serendipity. "I should go."

He nods and I slip past him towards the door.

I'll give myself another day or two before I buy a test because I'm not sure if I can handle the results right now.

Positive or negative.

CHAPTER NINETEEN

Penelope

Walking into Serendipity's, I spot Tessa sitting at our usual table. She's already wearing her "I told you so smirk," so I know I'm in for it.

She let me off too easy the first time, but twice in two weeks? There's no way she won't demand information about what's going on between Slade and I.

The birthday hate-sex excuse won't work twice in a row. And she barely believed me the first time.

With the long lunch line already forming, I stop at the back of the line to order before I face the firing squad of one sitting at the table. Tessa Tomlin, my executioner of truth, and when she aims, she rarely misses.

"Nice try but I already ordered your usual," she calls out the busy coffee shop. "Now get your butt over here."

I head her way, practically dragging my feet as I go to buy myself more time.

How am I going to explain this one?

I hook my purse to the side of the wooden chair and then plop down in it.

She pours a packet of sugar into her coffee and then stirs slowly, not unlike the villain in old movies who sits in their chair petting their cat menacingly.

"Save whatever excuse you've conjured up during your walk over. I know you too well to know that you don't screw men in the middle of an open parking lot in your car. And sex on your desk in the same office that your father or Phil Carlton could have walked in on at any moment without at least locking the door? That's ballsy, even for Lake and I, and we love finding new places to do it."

She's right. I wouldn't do that.

I hang my head a little in embarrassment.

"I know... I know, it's just—"

"I'm so proud of you," she beams.

Huh?

"Uh... come again? You're proud of me?" I ask cocking an eyebrow and straightening my spine now that it seems I won't be getting a lecture today.

"You're branching out—you're taking risks. Albeit a little bigger risks than I would, but beggars can't be choosers over here, so I'll take it." She smiles. "I knew you had it in you, but I've never seen it. The old Penelope would never do this, even though this is exactly what you've pushed Autumn, Isla, and me to do, and we all ended up with the right guy. I was wondering when you would do the same thing for yourself."

This isn't exactly the "I told you" I was expecting.

And the right guy?

Slade isn't the right guy... not even close.

"You act like I live in a convent and never date."

"Oh please..." Tessa says, testing out her coffee by taking a small sip off the white paper to-go cup. "You've been playing it safe since we met."

"I don't date safe guys," I argue, but I didn't even convince myself.

"For a girl who reads on the kinky side of the bookstore, replacing the dust covers on her dirty books when she goes on vacation with her dad, and has a password combination to her reading tablet that's harder to crack than the damn nuclear missile launch code, you sure date some squares."

My jaw drops, and my eyebrows furrow as I let out a dramatic gasp. Mostly for theatrics, but Tessa gives me a lifted brow in return as if to tell me to prove her wrong.

I can't believe she's calling me out about my dating choices and suggesting that having sex with Slade, the man who single-handedly ended my dreams in public places, is within the realm of sane.

"The guys I've dated over the last couple of years have been nice," I tell her.

"The damn kiss of death," she mutters against her coffee cup and then takes another small sip.

"What?"

"Nice... you said nice. There is no guy on this planet that wants to hear that he's "nice". You might as well tell him that his pecker is tiny. He might actually survive that humiliation."

Ok, now she's just plain not making any sense.

"So, you want me to date jerks instead? And, by the way, Slade and I are the furthest things from dating."

She chuckles as if I'm an adorable little toddler who just mispronounces the word ketchup to catsup.

"No, honey, *you and I* are the furthest thing from dating. Though if I were a dude, you'd probably be my type. I have a thing for blondes with blue eyes," she teases after describing Lake Powers, her fiancé.

"Yeah, well, I'm not six foot four."

"Good point. I like them tall. You wouldn't make the cut."

"Hey, that's mean," I shoot back, though I'm not insulted in the least.

I like my men tall, too.

"Hypothetically speaking... of course. Now explain to me how you ended up going from wanting Slade dead to screwing him on every surface in your office. Not that I don't already know how this story goes since I've lived it."

She has a point.

She and Lake had history, too, but not like I have with Slade.

Lake cost her a vacation with a guy she was settling for anyway. Slade cost me my childhood dream.

It's not exactly like looking in the mirror.

"He was in my apartment fixing my shower when he found a pregnancy test that Isla left behind. He thought it was mine and that I was pregnant."

Tessa's jaw drops.

"What did you tell him?" she asks, her eyes widening, gripping her coffee, and leaning in like I'm about to tell the most epic story of all time.

"He stormed into my office with a pregnancy test and told me he'd buy me any house I want," I tell her, cutting out all the parts where he made my heart pound and my knees go weak at how he reacted to thinking I was pregnant and pleading to be allowed to take care of us.

I hate to admit it, but a little part of me wanted to be pregnant because of how excited he was.

The day that I tell someone I'm pregnant, I hope that they react with that much enthusiasm, begging me to tell them that the baby is theirs and offering to be a supportive partner.

"And then what? You told him that you're not pregnant, so he decided to finish the job on top of your desk?" she asks with a smirk.

"No. He barged in with his pants on fire and didn't listen to me when I tried to tell him that the pregnancy test wasn't mine. Then he made all of these promises and begged me to let him take care of us. And then..."

"And then you totally had sex with him in your father's executive office reception area because he's crazy about you?" she asks.

But it's not a question; she is trying to lead the witness.

"Oh my God," I say, leaning my elbows against the table, smashing my face in my hands. "I can't believe I did that."

The more time we spend together, and he shows me all these sides of him that I didn't know existed, the harder it is to write him off completely.

What the hell am I going to do if I'm falling for both Win and Slade simultaneously?

Or have I already fallen for both?

"What's really going on between you two? There has to be something I'm missing. You don't just jump a player on the team that you work for and have hated for years for no reason."

I see one of the usual cooks walk out from behind the counter with our order.

They're so busy today, and with Mary training a new person because Chloe didn't end up working out, Mary's a little short-handed up front today.

"Thanks," we tell him.

He lays down both plates of food and then takes the plastic number from our table.

"Nothing is going on between us... he's just—"

"Gorgeous?" Tessa interjects.

"No."

But that's a lie because he is.

"Good in bed?" she asks.

"No," I say.

Another lie.

Though we technically haven't done it in a bed.

"Has natural protective instincts and a killer slapshot? I thought for sure that he was going to beat up the drunk at Oakley's who grabbed your ass."

"Are you just going to keep going if I say no?"

"Probably, so just give me the answers to the questions I want to know, and we can stop this charade. Why aren't you interested in Slade?"

I open my mouth to speak, but she holds up a finger to stop me.

"And don't tell me that it's because of whatever happened half a lifetime ago. I know what he did sucked, but if you still harbored as much resentment towards him as you claim that you do, I wouldn't have caught him sinking his puck in your goal twice in two weeks."

"Ok, fine," I relent. "He's gorgeous, he's great with his..." I stop myself before uttering the word "cock" in a family-friendly coffee shop. "... hockey stick, and yes, he's protective and as of recently, he's been showing me a different side of him that has me wondering which Slade is the real one."

"Could he have changed since college? Maybe he feels bad for what he did, and he's reformed? Have you talked to him about everything since he moved back?"

He does seem different from the guy he was in college.

"Sort of, but not in detail. He knows that I'm still upset about everything that he cost me, and he's apologized on numerous occasions but what do I do with his sorry? Do I just accept what happened, forgive him, and move on?"

"I don't know... can you forgive him and move on?"

I think about it for a second, lifting a french fry from my plate and crunching on it for a second.

"If you had asked me a week ago, I would have said no, but he's been trying to make it up to me by coming in to work on my old routine with me, so I have a skating partner... and now I—"

Tessa jumps in before I can finish my sentence.

"You two are skating together now? As in, he's figure skating with you before his own grueling practice to make up for the fact that he scared away your prospects years ago?"

I nod, hearing her say it out loud. I already know how she's going to react.

"Well shit, I'd fuck the guy too."

"Tessa!" I say, my eyes widening at her to use better language while out in public.

A group of Girl Scouts and their moms just sat down a couple of tables over.

"What? This could be free education. If they listen a little longer, they might earn their birds and bees badge today. It's a win-win for everyone."

I know she's kidding, so I shake my head and grin, picking up another fry. Tessa picks up her sandwich and takes a bite.

We both chew for a second and then she starts back up.

"Ok, so let's recap to ensure I have all the details. Slade screwed up royally in college, is now back after serving penance for his crimes against you, has apologized profusely for what happened, has now taken up a second form of stringent practice to make you happy, and you two have been running around Seattle boinking like bunny rabbits. Did I miss anything?" she asks, pulling her sandwich back up to her face to take another bite.

"There's someone else," I blurt out. "The guy I've been talking to online."

I've mentioned Win as my pen pal buddy before, but I never really explained that I have feelings for him.

She pauses mid-bite and puts her sandwich back down.

"The tutoring guy that just came back from the dead and started emailing you again randomly? That guy?" she asks as if I must be joking.

"That's the one. And he didn't come back from the dead. He told me he was leaving and wouldn't be able to email back and forth anymore. He gave me a heads up, at least."

I know I'm making an excuse for him, but it's true. He didn't ghost me... he gave me notice. Though I never thought he'd resurface.

"Have you two met in person yet?" she asks, but I can already see the sharp downturn of her brow.

She is skeptical, and I get it.

"Not yet. He said that he wants to meet up but he has a big project that he's trying to finish. We're going to meet up when he's done."

"He's putting off meeting you for a work project? Really? Does he know that you're seeing someone else?"

"I'm not seeing anyone else," I tell her, though I know she won't let me get away with that.

Her head tilts to the side, and she sighs. She thinks I'm being difficult, but I'm simply telling the truth.

Slade and I are not dating.

But it's not as if I haven't considered telling Win that Slade and I have done more than skate during practice.

The thing is, Win and I have no agreement not to see other people. Will my admission lead to him feeling compelled to tell me about all of his conquests since we started talking again?

I'm not sure if I can handle that.

"Are you holding yourself back from seeing if there is something between you and Slade just because of a guy you haven't met in person?"

"That's not exactly it..." I say, but I'm not a good liar, and she sees right through it.

"Oh my God, it is! Penelope," she says, adjusting her seat to lean in across the table a little closer. "This email guy disappeared on you for four years and then just showed back up out of the blue with no explanation as to where he's been, what he was doing, or why he stopped talking to you. And now, after all these years, he thinks you should do more waiting before meeting up so he can complete a work project?"

She makes a good point.

What project could be so important that meeting up with me would derail that?

"Maybe you're right," I say.

I don't know what he does for a living or what this project could be about, but there isn't any project I've ever done that would keep me from wanting to meet him finally after all these years.

"If Lake and I had spent four years apart and had just emerged from some hole in the world where the internet couldn't reach me, nothing would prevent me from seeing him. I think you should demand to see him."

I hate it when she's right, but she's right again.

> **SkatrGirlPen: I think we should meet now.**

WinForToday067: I'm still working on something. What's the rush?

> **SkatrGirlPen: Slade and I kissed, and I need to know if there is something between you and I.**

A kiss doesn't quite convey the full picture but I think he'll get the point.

WinForToday067: Do you have feelings for him? Is that what this is about?

> **SkatrGirlPen: This is about you and me. Four years is long enough to have waited. I need to know once and for all if we have a future. Don't you want to know too?**

There's a long pause, and I held my breath, worried he might say no.

WinForToday067: I already know that I want you, Pen. I have no doubts. Just tell me when and where.

The second I read his responses, I exhaled the oxygen from my lungs, instantly feeling lightheaded from not breathing.

> **SkatrGirlPen: Can you meet in two days at the public ice rink in the city? Do you skate?**

> **WinForToday067: Yeah, I can skate. I'll meet you there. What time?**

He agreed to meet me.

Finally!

And now the nerves of what that means settle in.

I'm about to meet the man who I thought I lost after all these years.

> **SkatrGirlPen: How about seven, after work?**

I'll want to go home after work and freshen up before we meet.

> **SkatrGirlPen: Will you be carrying something? How will I know it's you?**

The rink could be busy that day and I don't want to drive myself crazy by thinking every guy inside could be him. I want to know the minute I see him that it's Win.

> **WinForToday067: How about pink peonies?**

My heart flutters at how he remembers my favorite flower.

> **SkatrGirlPen: That's perfect.**

WinForToday067: I'll see you then.

This is right.

Being with Win is right.

I don't know why I ever questioned it.

And once we meet, my confusing feelings for Slade will fade away because I'll finally be with the right one.

CHAPTER TWENTY

Slade

I got the message from Penelope yesterday that Win has run out of time. I'm unsure about my chances with her when I show up and she finds out it's been me this whole time, but I know they aren't good.

With our meeting set for tomorrow, I know that today is my last day to make her fall for me if I want a chance for forgiveness.

I walk into the gym around our usual six am practice time to find Penelope already standing by the speaker with her head down, scrolling through her phone.

"Morning," I say, pushing through the door of the gym.

She looks over her shoulder at me but looks more or less uninterested in my company.

Where is this coming from?

"Are you ready for another morning of practice? I think we should focus on the first lift," she says.

"Sure am. Let's nail this thing."

I walk over to the corner of the gym where I usually set my things and drop my duffel bag against the wall. Then I turn back around and walk closer to where we usually start our practice.

New music streams through the speakers. She must have picked a random playlist since we're just working on this one lift.

"Let's just stick with you tossing me up and catching me. If we can get that, then we'll add the spin. Sound good?" she asks.

Her eyes barely make eye contact with mine and then she turns, giving me her back for the lift.

I get into position with my hands on her hips, hating the idea that this might be the last time I touch her. Her hands come up to her hips and cover mine.

"I'll count off," she instructs.

"Got it."

"One...Two..." She counts down with each bounce she makes, preparing to jump up as hard as possible. "...three."

She leaps up, and I use her momentum to toss her into the air.

She twists in the air just enough to face me as she comes back down.

I get my hands on her, catching her from falling this time, though setting her back to the ground ends up a little abrupt, and she just about twists her ankle.

"Oof," she says, gripping my shoulders as she lands.

She rights herself quickly and then shakes off her ankle.

"Are you ok? Did you sprain it?" I ask quickly. "Maybe you should sit down?"

"No…" she shakes her head. "I'm fine. Let's try it again. Just a little lighter transition to set me down, if you can."

Again, she barely looks at me as she turns around and gives me her back. We repeat the same movement three more times, each a little better than the last, until I finally set her back down gracefully.

The second she touches down, a smile widens across her lips, and her eyes dart up from watching her feet touch the ground up to mine.

"That was perfect," she beams.

"Yeah, it felt smoother. I think I can handle a twist if you're up for it."

"You think so?" she asks, a glimmer of excitement in her eyes.

"There's only way to find out."

She nods and then turns again to give me her back.

I lean in over her shoulder right before she starts counting.

"Give the twist as many rotations as you want. I'll catch you—I promise."

"I know you will," she says softly.

I wasn't expecting that response, but it feels a lot like a break-through.

Then she starts counting again.

On the count of three, Penelope jumps, and I toss her up higher than before.

She does a full triple twist, completing the rotation.

I hold up my arms, ready for her to come back down, coaching myself over and over not to drop her.

And then I catch her, gently guiding her back down until her feet hit the ground.

We did it.

We fucking did it.

"Oh my God!" She says, her eyes reaching up to mine.

Her eyes widen and her bright smile beams up at me.

She starts bouncing up and down, her hands on my shoulders.

"You caught me. We nailed the triple twist lift!" she says.

She wraps her arms around my neck, and I fold my arms around her back. She lifts up while I spin us around once.

She giggles and I can feel the vibration through my arms.

I set her feet back on the ground, though I'd prefer not to put her down at all... ever, but she doesn't remove her arms. They still hang around my neck—her full breasts pressed to the bottom of my rib cage.

"I knew you could do it," she says.

"Did you?" I ask with a lifted brow, not believing her completely.

"Of course I did. I knew you wouldn't give up until we got it."

"How did you figure that out?" I ask.

"Because you're not the quitting type."

And there it is.

It's not just the single best compliment that anyone has ever bestowed on me, but it's also the only thing that keeps me fighting for her.

Does she understand that her compliment is the reason why I'm here? That quitting the farm team wasn't an option because the one thing I can't quit, no matter how hard I've tried, is her.

"Thank you," I say, my hands still around her back, holding her against me.

If she's not going to make an attempt to push away, then I won't let go.

"For what?" she asks.

"For seeing me."

Her crystal blue eyes don't leave mine as her fingers brush up the back of my neck, almost to soothe me.

My eyes drop to her full lips as they part. And just as I start leaning in to find out if she'll accept my kiss, her arms come back around and drop to her side. She steps out of my arms and bites down on her lower lip. Her cheeks pinken just a little, like she knows that I was about to kiss her.

Though I would do anything to keep her in my arms, I won't force it.

I release her, too.

Regretfully.

"I think our time is up, and the guys should be here soon for morning skate. I should go. The girls and I have a lot to plan for the final round of playoffs this week. All of the sponsors are coming in."

She's right. We all need to stay focused this week.

"I have a lot to do, too. I got the new showerhead in my mailbox. I can replace it today before you're off work if you want?"

"That was fast. Thanks," she says, turning toward the speaker to turn off her music.

I watch as she walks away, pulling her phone from off the top of the speaker and grabs her duffel bag off the floor next to it.

"I'll see you tomorrow morning at practice. Maybe we can start back on the ice?" she asks, yanking the duffel bag strap over her shoulder and starts for the exit.

I nod, "See you tomorrow in the rink."

She gives me a once over, but she's not checking me out—she's considering something. And I have a feeling I know what it is.

Is she going to miss me when she gives me up for Win?

Penelope

I started out this morning deciding that I would be the picture of professionalism with Slade during practice.

If I'm going to meet Win tomorrow and we're going to start dating, I need to be able to be in the same room as Slade without acting on my attraction to him.

I have to believe that my attraction for Slade will vanish once Win and I finally meet. Otherwise, I'll have to put more space between us.

I took a quick shower in the locker room before the guys all showed up for skating drills. Then, I went to my office and answered a few emails before my meeting with Tessa and Autumn about the list of people who need to be invited from the media outlets and sponsors who will need VIP arrangements when they fly in for the playoffs happening at home.

I head to one of the smaller conference rooms that we decided to meet in. By the time I walk in, Tess and Autumn are already seated with their tablets for note taking and coffees they made from the break room.

They smile at me as they continue a conversation they must have started right before I walked in.

"If we win, will you travel with Lake to the Stanely Cup away games? Briggs is asking me to come," Autumn tells Tessa.

"Lake asked me too. I think we should, don't you? Any work we need to do, we can do on the road."

"And I'll be here if you guys need me to do anything," I chime in as I pull out a chair and take a seat.

"You should come with us if we win the final. How often do the Hawkeyes make it to the Stanley Cup."

"The last time was when Bex played for us," Tessa says, though we all know the Hawkeyes history pretty well... it's been a while.

"Yeah, but with Phil and my dad away at the games, someone needs to be here who has access to both of them if questions or concerns come up."

They nod in understanding.

"You didn't get your chai this morning? It seems like you never miss these days," Autumn says.

I haven't told anyone that Slade brings me one daily, and I'm not about to tell them now.

"Practice went a little longer than I planned. It's fine, though. I'll get one at lunch. Are we ready to start?" I ask.

"Sure, should we start going over the list of executives coming in? I think it would be nice to have gift baskets sent to each of their suites at the hotel," Autumn suggests.

"I like that idea. I'll reach out to Juliet and Shawnie about that restaurant that catered for the alumni brunch. That food was so good. I'll ask Shawnie to order some baskets and have them delivered to the hotel."

"That's a great. I know they are doing a big display in the lobby for all of the home games, but what about asking them to decorate the owner's suit—"

A knock on the conference door interrupts Autumn as Tessa and I are making notes.

"Come in," I call out.

The door opens, and the second my eyes settle on the tall man walking through the door, my belly flutters with wild butter-flies.

Damn, I hate when it does that.

Slade.

Armed with a coffee to-go cup. I don't have to wonder what the contents are, and a pink cardboard box from Serendipity's Coffee Shop.

"Slade, hi," Autumn smiles.

"What a surprise," Tessa says, tossing a smirk my way and then smiles up at him next.

"I hope I didn't interrupt. I was at Serendipity's getting breakfast and thought you might need some sugar for your meeting," he says, walking in.

"You got that for us?" Autumn asks as she eyes the box of hidden goodies.

"I don't know what they gave me. I told Mary to fill it with whatever she thought the three of you would like."

He drops the box on the conference table. Neither Tessa nor Autumn waits for a second to push out of the chairs and walk over.

They open the box and "oh and aw" at the contents, each selecting a pastry.

"And this is for you," he says, walking over and placing the to-go cup next to me on the other side of the conference table.

"Thanks," I say, seeing Tessa and Autumn grinning at me in my peripheral.

"No problem. I have a PT appointment downstairs, and then I'll head over to your place to fix the shower."

I nod, and then Slade turns to head out.

"Have a good meeting, ladies," he says, giving Autumn and Tessa a quick wave.

They each thank him for the snacks and then he disappears past the conference door, closing it behind him.

"Want one?" Autumn asks.

"No thanks," I say, pulling my tablet closer and start jotting down more notes.

"Are you sure? There are a couple of sticky buns in here—your favorite," Autumn says.

"I'm not hungry, but thanks."

I don't want to give in to Slade's sweet gesture.

Why is he making it so hard to push him aside? Especially now that I'm meeting Win tomorrow.

"You're turning down a sticky bun? Aren't you on your period? You're usually a week behind me," Tessa says.

Shit!

With everything going on, I totally forgot that I was going to give myself another day or two to see if my period started before testing. Now I'm four days late. That's still not unheard of for me but it's not common either.

I can feel the blood drain from my face instantly.

"You don't look so good. Are you getting sick?" Autumn asks.

"Actually, I think you might be right. I don't feel very well all of a sudden," I say, rising from my chair.

"Don't worry about the meeting. We can handle everything—just go home," Tessa says.

I nod, grabbing my tablet and my chai off the table.

"I'll go lay down for a little bit and see if I feel better," I tell them as I head for the door.

More like, I'm going to go home, take a pregnancy test, and if everything checks out, I'll come back to work.

If it's positive, I'll have to think of a way to tell Win that I'm pregnant. Will he still want to meet me?

I already know how Slade will react to finding out I'm pregnant, and it can only be his.

This just got so messy.

CHAPTER TWENTY-ONE

Penelope

I burst through my apartment door with a brown paper bag in one hand and my heart pounding in my ears.

I race to my master bathroom, yanking the box out of the bag and practically ripping the box apart.

Pulling all three tests out, I sit down on the toilet, doing my best to aim as well as I can on each test while leaving enough liquid in my bladder to pee enough on each.

Stacking up a pile of toilet paper and laying it on the countertop, I drop each test on top and check the time on my phone. In three minutes, I'll know the results.

I stare down at my phone, trying to determine who I'll call first to tell them the news.

Then I hear someone walking into my bedroom.

I'm instantly startled until I peek out of my bathroom and see Slade heading straight for me.

He stops in his tracks the second he sees I'm here. He looks as surprised as I am.

"I didn't know you'd be here. That was a quick meeting," he says, continuing towards me.

I quickly eye the pregnancy tests sitting on the counter but there's no way I have enough time to stash them because he's already walking up to me with a small box in his hand and a wrench to reinstall the shower head that he already told me he would install while I was at work.

Damn it.

"I wasn't feeling well, so I came home to lie down," I say, facing him and blocking his entry into the bathroom, not that he won't be able to see over me.

"You're sick?" he lifts his palm up to my forehead to feel how warm I am. "I don't think you have a fever, but you do look a little pale. Have you eaten anything today?" he says.

"Not much," I tell him.

"I can go down to the soup place a block away and get you something to eat when I'm done—"

Then, I watch as Slade's attention catches on the layers of toilet paper and pregnancy tests lying side by side on the counter over my shoulder. There's no other reason for his immediate silence.

"Do you know the results?" he asks, still staring at them from the distance of the doorway.

"No, not yet. I just took them."

I step aside and let him enter. It's too late to hide whatever the results are. We might as well know together now.

He walks in closer and looks down at the results, but I'm too far away to read them from here.

It only takes a minute for him to stare down at all three of them. Finally, he blinks and turns his head back towards the shower, taking the last steps until he pushes back the shower curtain.

His reaction is so much different than his reaction the first time he thought I was pregnant. Why does that instantly disappoint me?

It shouldn't.

This is closer to the reaction you would expect from a man that you've had casual/hate sex with only a couple of times.

"You'll be happy," he says with his back to me.

He reaches up to unscrew the old shower head.

How can he be sure I'll be happy with the results?

The anticipation of finally knowing the answer is eating at me so I take a deep breath as I walk into the bathroom and peer over the test.

Three little white applicators share the same result.

Not Pregnant.

This should be the moment when relief washes over me. I should feel free of being shackled to Slade for not just eighteen years, as Slade said, but for our entire lives.

Birthdays, Christmases, graduations, their wedding..., and grandkids. Slade and I would spend our entire lives seeing each other for one event or another until one of us kicks the bucket.

These pregnancy tests tell of a different ending. One where I am free to spend all those years sharing those memories with someone else.

I should be overjoyed.

I won't have to start a new relationship with Win carrying another man's baby.

Win won't have to consider whether he's willing to be a stepdad to Slade's child.

But instead of feeling the weight of a possible accidental pregnancy lifting off my shoulders, I'm torn. I'm not completely relieved to not be pregnant, and I'm not fully disappointed by the negative results.

I'm somewhere in the middle and that might be more confusing than anything.

How can I want for both?

How did I let my emotions get so entangled with two men that I want to have it all?

I hear the sound of the cardboard box Slade had in his hand earlier dropping to the ground. I look up to find Slade screwing on the new showerhead and then tightening it up with the wrench.

He reaches down and turns the shower handle. A full-pressure stream of water sprays out from the shower head.

He fixed it, and now he has no reason to come back to my apartment.

He picks up the box off the ground and then plops the old showerhead into it for later disposal.

"You're ready to go. You can call off the maintenance guy who never showed up," he says, turning to me.

"I'd still like to reimburse you for the shower head," I tell him.

"You don't owe me anything. I'm glad I could take care of this for you. Let me know if it acts up for you again."

I nod and then turn back to stare at the pregnancy tests as if, somehow, they might change.

He starts walking out of the bathroom and then stops directly behind me.

"You knew you weren't sick when I walked in. You were just pale because the idea that you could be pregnant with my baby made you sick. Didn't it?"

I can't even begin to explain to him the mixed emotions I've had about possibly being pregnant since I bolted from the Hawkeyes stadium less than an hour ago. Mostly because I can't even explain them to myself.

"How do I look now?" I ask, lifting my eyes from the tests to the mirror so he can see my reflection.

I wonder how quickly he'll see that I'm struggling with the results.

I catch him staring back in the mirror as his eyes dart around my face in an attempt to read my emotions.

"Like the most beautiful woman I've seen," he says.

He's not going to call out the fact that if I was truly happy not to be pregnant, I'd be smiling. Or at least not sulking.

I glance back down to the negative tests. It's odd that I'm having such a hard time looking away from them.

"How am I supposed to feel about this?" I ask, needing some kind of direction.

I feel Slade's hand pulling my hair gently off of my shoulder and over to the other side, clearing the hair from around the right side of my neck.

He bends down, his pillow soft lips lay a gentle kiss against the apex between my neck and shoulder.

My eyelids flutter closed, and I bend my head further out of the way instinctively to give him more access, but he doesn't kiss me again like my body is craving. Instead, he lifts his head, his mouth close to my ear, and his right hand snakes around to the front of my flat belly where no baby bump is growing.

"I can't tell you how to feel, Penelope. But I can tell you that when I thought you were pregnant, I ran full speed from the apartment building to your office because I had to see you. That brief hour that I thought we had made a baby together was the happiest I've ever been in my life."

I spin around in his arm and he keeps it secured around me.

"The best day of your life?" I ask. "And how would you have felt if these tests were positive?"

He was so sure of what he wanted that day when he found the pregnancy test, thinking they were mine.

He wanted that baby, and he wanted it with me.

"If you're asking if I wish those tests were positive, the answer is yes. And the answer will always be yes because I know what I want... I want you."

His hazel green eyes stare back into mine.

With every passing moment, he makes it harder and harder to pick Win—the one that got away.

Win is steady and sure, while Slade is wild and fearless. But being with Win feels safe, and being with Slade feels like I might end up learning my mother's lesson all over again.

Falling for a hockey player who will love hockey more than me. Do I even have a shot at being on Slade's starting lineup?

Being with Win is the safest decision and that's the choice I should stick with.

Then I remember the tattoo on his left arm and the conversation that Seven and I had about it. I remember seeing the bandage and Slade saying I couldn't see it because it was healing.

I turn to look at the inside of his forearm and there it is in all its glory. The banner is now filled with my birthday—April 16th.

"You put my birthday on the other woman's tattoo?" I ask.

"There is no other woman," he says.

"Yes, there is. You said she's the one that got away," I tell him, recalling the conversation vividly because we were stuck in a copier closet together.

"You're the one that got away, Penelope. There's no one else. There's never been anyone else."

"But I... that can't be true. You said you got that when you landed in Canada. I hated you then... my father banished you. You couldn't have gotten that for me," I argue.

"Banished is a little strong. I'd say that he highly encouraged it. And did you not see the initials on the blade when you saw it in the copier room?" he asks.

I study the tattoo closer, and then I see it, shaded in the blade. It's hard to read, but it matches the older ink from the rest of the tattoo. It's not new like my birthday date; it's part of the original tattoo.

"P.R.," I whisper out loud.

"Penelope Roberts. The girl that got away. I got the tattoo as a promise to myself that someday I'd find a way to redemption and earn your trust again."

I turn back to him, locking my eyes with his, waiting for him to tell me he's kidding. But he doesn't. He just stares back, waiting for all the information that I just received to sink in.

"Will I ever be more than you're dirty secret? The guy you don't want to tell your friends about?"

There's a sadness in the way he's looking at me, but I think I see hope in there, too.

I have to be honest and tell him the truth.

"Slade, I need to tell you something," I say, unsure of how to word this after everything he just confessed. I don't want to hurt him but he needs to know about Win. "There's someone else."

"I know," he says simply.

He does?

"How could you know that? I've never brought him up before."

"I can see it in your eyes right when I think you're about to give me a shot. I can feel it when we start getting closer, and you pull away."

The brightness in his eyes dims a little.

"I'm meeting him tomorrow to find out if there's something between us and I think it's only fair that I tell you."

I see his Adam's apple bob as he swallows hard.

I know I'm crushing him.

There was a time that I would have reviled in making him hurt to get back at him for what he did to me, but so much has changed now.

"Is there anything I can do to convince you not to see him and give me a chance instead?"

I shake my head.

"I can't wonder, "what if" for the rest of my life. I have to meet him to know for sure."

"Then, can I ask for one thing?"

"What is it?"

"Can I have you one last time? We can use a condom," he says, his hand coming up to glide over my jaw. "No more pregnancy scares, just one last time and then I won't fight you anymore. I'll let you go. I want you to be happy, and though I've tried, I know I'm not the one you want."

Tears begin to well in my eyes but I won't let them fall. I'm the one making the decision to give Win a shot over Slade because he's not the wild hockey player. I don't get to cry over it.

I know I shouldn't agree to this.

Giving into what I want too... one last time.

I nod and Slade steps in closer, his hands lifting and coming along either of my neck, the ends of his fingers lacing through my hair. He pulls me in as his lips drop down against mine.

There's something so different about this kiss. It's not the rushed, angsty kisses of our last few times together.

Slade's taking his time.

We're not in danger of being caught in my bedroom and this isn't a scratch that we're both trying to itch.

This is the last time.

The one I want to remember.

The what-if that will never be, but at least this once, Slade and I have come to an understanding.

I kiss him back, gripping his shirt as I pull myself closer to him, pressing my breasts against his chest. He takes a step forward, guiding me back until my ass hits the bathroom countertop as he presses himself against me harder.

I dip my tongue into his mouth and his chest rumbles against mine in a growl.

I want to pretend that his body against mine has no effect, but my dampening panties tell another story.

My body tingles everywhere that his touches mine. I've never felt this physical need for someone like I need Slade.

I reach my arms around his neck and that's the moment that he pulls me up his body.

This isn't going to turn into just a goodbye. This will be the night that I'll never forget... with the man I chose to give up.

Slade

I hold Penelope closer to me, her body beginning to meld against mine.

She agreed to one last time, and I have no intention of rushing through it.

"The bed," she whispers against my lips.

I lift her into my arms, and she comes willingly, wrapping her legs around my waist as I carry her out of the master bathroom and into her bedroom. I won't argue with her request.

I turn and walk towards her king-sized bed with a grey tufted headboard on the other side of the large, well-decorated room.

I walk towards her nightstand and set her down on the bed near her headboard.

I watch as she pulls off her dress and discards it to the floor. She doesn't wait for instruction as she reaches behind her and unclasps her bra, dropping the material on the ground of her bedroom.

My erection thickens at the sight of her full pear-shaped breasts. Her nipples, a dark shade of peach, pebbling into tight buds and making my mouth water. She doesn't shy away from my view of her. Instead, her bright blue eyes lock onto mine challenging me to look away.

That's a game I'll lose because she's fucking stunning, and I can't take my eyes off of her.

She hooks her thumbs into the side of her panties and pulls her thong down over her perfect ass and then down her thighs until they drop to the floor. She toes them off next to her bra and then sits back down where I set her.

I've never seen Penelope completely naked before.

Each time we've had sex, it's been a rushed moment in time. But now we're in her bedroom without the possibility of some-one walking in on us.

The reality of her is far better than the fantasies she's played a starring role in for the last four years.

The light from the afternoon sun streams through the slats in the window blinds, giving me the light I need to see every inch of her clearly.

I take a step closer, wanting to touch her.

For just tonight, Penelope's mine.

I reach into my back pocket and pull out my wallet. My fingers grip the foil wrapper of the condom I put inside of it yesterday, just in case she ever gave me another chance to be with her. As much as I wanted her to be pregnant when I stormed into that office days ago, the last thing I want is for her to feel trapped. And though she doesn't believe it, I still think she has the talent to compete.

I won't let an accidental pregnancy keep her from trying for the Olympics. She's too talented, and I don't want to hold her back.

I toss the condom onto her nightstand, and she watches as it lands. A look of disappointment spreads across her face as a corner of her lip turns down and her jaw tightens. She stares at the golden packaging, but reading into her reaction won't help me anymore.

She's made her choice.

And she didn't choose me.

Her attention falls back on me as I pull off my shirt, discarding it to the side of the bed, and then my pants and boxer briefs follow next as I kick them to the side.

She takes her time taking in every inch of me and bites down on her lip when she finally reaches my hard-on.

I take a step closer, and she reaches out, wrapping her fingers around my cock.

I groan the moment her soft, warm hands tighten around my throbbing erection.

She lowers her head down against me and wraps her lips around my tip.

"Fucking hell... Penelope," I say, my fists tightening at my side, fighting the urge to slide my finger in her hair and fuck her hot wet mouth.

Her tongue glides over my tip, causing my cock to pulsate and my balls to tighten. I feel her tongue lap up the small amount of precum from my tip and now I'm fucking gone.

If I don't slow this down, this last time with her will end in seconds. No amount of reciting the pledge of allegiance in my head will stop me from coming too early.

"Whoa... hold on," I say, carefully pushing her shoulder back.

If this is the last time I get to touch her, I want to be inside of her, bringing her to orgasm when I come.

She pulls back, and her eyes dart up to mine like she did something wrong.

"I'm sorry, did you not like—"

"Jesus... no. Your mouth is fucking amazing, but that's not what I want."

She seems surprised and I don't blame her.

If we had a lifetime together, I wouldn't stop her... but we don't.

I only get this one moment, and then tomorrow, she'll find out I lied.

"What do you want?" she asks.

"The same thing I always want... you."

I watch as her eyes dilate.

She was turned on before, but now I'm sure that for the brief time we have together, Penelope Roberts belongs to me and I belong to her.

"Then take me," she says.

My lips drop to hers, and I hook my hands under her bare ass, lifting her off the bed. I pull her against me and revel in the feeling of her wetness between her thighs against my stomach. Knowing that I get her soaking without touching her makes me painfully hard.

I drop us onto the memory foam, making sure that I don't hurt her as I come down on top. I'm already settled between her thighs as we lay horizontally on the bed. Reaching down to adjust myself, my length presses firmly against her dripping wet center.

She feels so goddamn good that I have to stop myself from pushing in bare like we've done every time before.

"Don't stop, please," she begs.

And fuck me if the sound of Penelope begging isn't the best thing I've ever heard in my life.

"I won't stop until your legs are so tired from coming that you have to call in sick tomorrow."

She takes a shallow breath and stares up at me, her eyes glazed over with need.

"Now, Slade, I need it now," she says, reaching between us and gripping my cock.

I reach back and grab the condom off the nightstand, ripping the wrapper with my teeth, and pull the condom from the package.

I slide the condom on quickly, double-checking before I line up against her again.

The moment I push into her, my eyelids clamp shut to keep myself under control, and I see stars. Not even a condom can stop the sensation of entering her heat and tight channel that wraps around me like we were made to fit together.

A whimper breaks through her lips as I push further into her. I bury myself inside, inch by inch. She grips around my shoulders to hold on, her sharp nails digging into my back.

I hope to God she marks me. I want her fingernail scratches like a tattoo forever on my skin— never letting me forget she was there.

I want the evidence that this wasn't a dream when tomorrow comes, and she no longer belongs to me.

I bend down and kiss her, inhaling all her sounds.

My lips travel down her neck and over her chest until I reach her breasts.

I've been waiting too long to taste her and won't wait another second. I suck her nipple into my mouth and she arches her back in response with a desperate moan and slides her hands into my hair to pull me tighter against her. I love the way she responds to me and shows me how much she wants it. So, I reward her with more.

I swirl my tongue around her perfect nub as my thrusts increase in pressure, driving in harder. I flick her hard nipple gently with my tongue. Her pussy squeezes me tighter as more wet arousal coats my cock.

"Oh..." she whimpers.

I angle myself so that I'm hitting right where she wants it, and I can feel her body begin to shake under me. I'm taking her to the edge of what her body can handle, and I know it. I've memorized the strokes she likes and the spot my cock hits that make her eyes roll.

"This might be the last time for us, but you're never going to forget the way I fuck you. You'll be lying in his bed wishing he were me."

She shakes her head as if she doesn't want that to be true... but we both know it is.

It won't be Win, though. Tomorrow, he'll lose her too, when I'm the one who shows up in his place, and then the truth will come out. I won't even bother to hope that she'll find a way to forgive me... it won't happen.

No, some other fucker down the road will get my girl, and there is nothing I can do about it except make sure she never forgets how I make her come.

Her body clenches around me, and I thrust in and out of her, pulling more whimpers from her. I know she's primed for a release.

I bend down and take her other nipple into my mouth, making sure to taste them both. I swirl my tongue once as her thighs squeeze against me, and then I gently scrape my teeth over her nipple as she comes, calling out my name like a song, her body pulsates around my cock like a fucking vice.

I hold back as long as I can while helping her chase her orgasm to the end.

I wish I could hold back longer, but watching her fall apart under me and calling out my name because she knows exactly who makes her feel this good, is all I can take. I come hard, white heat spilling out of me as I fill the condom deep inside of her.

My cock spasms over and over like a shock wave in the aftermath of my orgasm.

"I love you," I say.

The words slip from my mouth of their own volition. I didn't mean to speak them out loud. There's barely anything worse I could have admitted at this moment. But I won't take the words back because they're not a lie.

I do love her.

She doesn't say anything back. Instead, she pulls me down and seals our lips together. We stay like that for a while until I finally get up to discard the condom and bring her something to wipe up with.

I should be on cloud nine with how hard we both came... but instead, the orgasm high dies off quickly when I know that soon this will be over, and I'll have no excuse to get to stay.

CHAPTER TWENTY-TWO

Penelope

Laying in my bed facing Slade with his right arm under my neck and our legs entangled together, I trace the tattoos on his chest lazily as he uses his other hand to brush my hair back out of my face in gentle strokes.

I glance down at the metal bar through his nipple and flick at it lightly.

He doesn't even flinch as he watches me.

"How bad did that hurt?" I ask.

"Not any worse than taking a puck to the groin."

I chuckle at his comparison.

"Don't you wear pads and a cup?"

"Yeah, but a puck can travel at over 100 mph. It still hurts like a mother fucker," he says, rubbing his free hand over my bare hip.

"Do you have plans for any other piercings?" I ask.

"No, I got it on a dare one drunk night after we won our state college championship. We got back late for curfew, and your dad was so mad that he made us do laps around the hotel in the pouring rain at 3 am."

"That sounds like him," I smile at the thought of Slade giving my dad grief. I lived back in Michigan during the school year, but my dad called me every night, rain or shine, game or no game, just to hear how my day went. And I remember the first time I heard Slade's name. My dad would tell me stories about the last stupid thing Slade did that week, but there was a difference in his voice when he spoke about him compared to other players. That's why I knew it hurt my father to punish Slade.

Slade was more to my dad than just a player. In some ways, Slade and my father are a lot alike. And maybe he saw a younger him in Slade. I'm not really sure. But I felt like I was missing out on something every time I heard the next crazy story.

So, when I told my mother that I wanted to move out to Washington and live with Dad for my junior and senior year of college, she didn't hold me back.

"Why didn't you take it out and let it heal then? I'm sure it wouldn't have taken long."

He shakes his head.

"A dare is a dare. And besides, it reminds me of the second-best time in my life. Playing for your dad and the University of Washington is an experience I'd live over a second time if I could."

"If that's the second best... what's the first best time in your life?" I ask.

"Anytime I'm with you."

His honest eyes catch on mine, and though a part of me wants to look away, I know that if I want any answers to the questions I have about our past, now might be the last chance I'll get it.

"What would have happened at the frat party if I hadn't been the coach's daughter?"

He blinks for a second, and I can see he's debating his words.

"I would have walked into the kitchen and introduced myself."

"And then?" I ask.

"Then I would have used my basic aquatic knowledge to impress you with meaningless facts."

I chuckle.

"Like what?" I ask, feeling myself inch closer.

"Like..." he says, thinking about it for a second. "Did you know that flamingos are pink because their diet is made up mostly of shrimp?" or "Did you know that a blind goby fish depends entirely on a ghost shrimp digging a hole for them both to live in for protection."

"Those aren't pick-up lines. And where did you learn that?"

"My dad only let me watch the Discovery Channel growing up. He thought cartoons would rot my brain. He expected me to be a doctor, remember? Plus, you're too smart to fall for a pickup line. I would have tried to make you laugh instead."

A warmth spreads over my body and an ache forms in my chest. Our start could have been so different.

"What would you have done after you got me laughing?"

"I would have asked you for a date and your number."

"You wouldn't have tried to take me back to your condo?" I ask, knowing full well that Slade Matthews did very little actual dating back then.

His reputation suggests he worked quicker than that.

"No. I would have taken you on a date, and then when I dropped you off, I would have asked if I could kiss you good-night. Then I would have asked for a second date."

I lift an eyebrow in challenge.

"And then you would have asked to come up to my dorm?"

He shakes his head.

"I would have walked you to the entry to your dorm building to make sure you got in ok and then I would have spent the entire drive home wondering how many dates I would have to take you on before I could propose."

My stomach flips and I get a little lightheaded at what he just said.

Before I can say anything back in response, his phone rings.

He bends over me, reaching for his pants and pulls his phone out of his pocket.

"Shit... Wrenley. I forgot that I was supposed to meet him ten minutes ago," he says and then answers.

"Hey man—yeah, no, I lost track of time. I got the part for Penelope's shower yesterday; I'm at the apartment... I'll be five minutes— OK, bye."

He hangs it up and drops the phone on the bed, falling back down on the mattress, sliding his finger over his forehead to soothe whatever emotions he's going through right now.

"Fuck..."

"You forgot that you were going to meet him?" I ask, but I know it must be something because he said he'd be there in five minutes.

"Yeah, and there's no one else there to spot him. I can't blow him off," he turns to look at me.

He's going to leave, and given the weight of what our history could have looked like instead of what happened, it's probably better this way. The longer he stays, the less sure I am about my decision, but maybe that's just due to proximity.

I can touch Slade—see him—feel him—skate with him.

But with Win, his silhouette is still fuzzy when I imagine a future together.

"You should go then," I reassure him.

He pulls me closer and presses his lips to mine to give me one last kiss.

Then he pulls his arm from under me and starts getting dressed. I slide off the bed, too, and head to the bathroom to get my fluffy bathrobe and his wrench.

He's made record time getting dressed as soon as I come out.

He grabs his phone off my bed, and then I give him the wrench.

"I'll walk you out," I tell him.

He nods.

We walk down the hall in silence until we reach the door.

There's one other thing that I have to do that I really don't want to, but I know that if Win and I are going to have a chance to make this work, I need to put more space between Slade and me.

Slade opens the front door and turns back to me.

"I think we should stop skating together," I tell him.

His eyebrows furrow instantly in confusion.

"Are you cutting me out completely?"

"If I want to make this work with Win, I can't have you this close."

"Why? Because you know you should be with me?"

He says, his fingers reaching for the terrycloth tie of my robe, rubbing his fingers over the material.

"Slade, please don't make this harder than it is."

He drops the tie but steps closer to me and back out of the doorway. "Don't you think picking the right person should be easy?"

I cross my arms over my chest protectively.

I don't know how easy it would be for him to change my mind, so I won't let him try.

"Don't come to practice tomorrow," I say.

He stares back at me for a moment.

"I'll see you around Pen."

Pen.

No one calls me Pen.

No one but...

"What did you just call me?" I ask, but he's already turned and out the door, his long legs eating up the hallway.

I close the door behind me and realize that the only thing that can make me feel better is a movie marathon, a fluffy robe, and a tub of ice cream that I don't have to share with anyone.

After tomorrow, everything will make more sense. I have to trust my decision.

Slade

Getting on the elevator to head to the stadium, I shake my head.

There's a part of her that wants to pick me—I know it. But she doesn't want to admit it.

I fucked up.

I never should have brought Win back from whatever Siberian hell hole in the universe I sent him to.

I brought him back to help wiggle my way back in and it blew up in my face... again.

You'd think I would have known better, but I had no idea that her feelings for Win were that strong back in college. If I had known that I brought back my own competition, I wouldn't have done it, but I felt desperate and I made a bad call.

A decision that now means I lose it all.

Tomorrow, when she sees me at the rink, I'll be lucky to make it out of there without an ice pick to the throat.

I open my phone and do an internet search:

Jenny McPhearson, figure skating coach.

Her number is listed as an instructor, and I click on her call information.

I put the phone up to my ear, hoping not to get her voicemail.

"This is Jenny."

"Hi, Jenny. You don't know me but my name is Slade Matthews, and I—"

"Slade Matthews? The same Slade Matthews that played hockey for the University of Washington four years ago."

"Yeah, that's me," I say, surprised she remembers me.

"The same Slade Matthews who cost my most talented student her chance at the Olympics?"

Oh... shit...

"The same guy," I say, preparing for an ear-lashing of how I ruined Penelope's life.

If anyone knows the amount of damage I caused firsthand, it's Jenny.

"Well, this is a surprise. What exactly can I do for you, Mr. Matthews?"

"I'm playing for the Hawkeyes now and I want to fix what I fucked up," I say, realizing I just cursed over the phone. "I was hoping I could get Toby's number from you... if you're still in contact with him."

"You want Toby's number?"

I can hear the confusion in her voice.

"I heard he was skating singles now, and I think Penelope could use a partner. She seems to think her career is over and that her best days are behind her... but I've seen her skate. I'm not a trained professional and might be biased, but I think she's as good or better than ever."

There's a short pause on the other line.

"That's interesting, Mr. Matthews. Tell me more..."

I fill Jenny in on Penelope and her skating. I even admit to her that I tried skating with her, and Jenny just about laughs me off the phone.

By the end of the call, I got what I needed... Toby's number.

CHAPTER TWENTY-THREE

Penelope

As I walked into the men's locker room this morning, bright and early, I couldn't help but feel a little sad that I know Slade won't be meeting me on the ice for our practice.

All I can hope is that it will all be worth it after tonight and I'll have confirmation that pushing Slade away is the right move.

I drop my duffel bag in the locker room by the showers and then head out to the ice.

The cold air cuts through my lungs and I take a deeper inhale until it almost stings.

I love the ice rink anytime of the day but when the lights are dimmed in the stands, it feels like my own world.

I stand on center ice, taking a moment to determine what to do with myself now that I don't have a partner.

I loud clang sounds, as if a door just closed and I look around all over the stadium to see where the noise came from.

It doesn't take long before there's movement coming from the player's tunnel.

A tall male walks toward the rink, still cloaked in the dim lighting. I can't see who it is and my heart gallops thinking that maybe Slade is refusing to stay away.

A part of me hopes it is.

But then the figure comes closer into the light and the moment I recognize the face, I shriek with excitement.

"Toby!" I yell as I skate full force towards the tunnel opening.

His big five-foot-eleven stature and boyish grin flashes over at me.

"What the hell? Why didn't you tell me you were skating again? I had to hear it from Jenny," he says.

He skates out to me, and we embrace instantly.

He grips around my middle and spins me around like he used to when we would play around on the ice.

"I'm not exactly skating. Not like you, anyway. I heard you've been medaling in every competition all around the country?"

"Well, I had to do something with my time. My skating partner quit competitive ice skating before I could get healthy again. Now you're skating in the Hawkeyes stadium with Slade Matthews? There better be a juicy story to go along with this, or otherwise, I took a redeye here for nothing," he teases.

Slade Matthews? How does he know that we've been skating together?

"You owe me information first. How did you find out that I'm skating again, and how are you here at six in the morning."

This is one of the best surprises I've ever had, but there is a huge piece of information missing. Toby didn't just stumble out of bed in North Carolina and end up in Seattle before the sun is even up to come skate with me, especially since we've lost touch over the years.

"I got a call out of the blue from Jenny yesterday. She said that you were skating again but that you didn't have a partner. She wanted to know if I would be interested in training with you again. Then, I got a call from none other than Slade Matthews, the man we love to hate. He told me that he was booking me a flight with all expenses paid trip to Seattle for a week to come try skating with you again."

Slade called him?

"You talked to Slade?"

"Yep."

"And he bought you a ticket?"

"Yep, and put me up in a rental condo that's walking distance to the stadium. It must have cost him a fortune but I'm not complaining."

I have more questions than my brain can keep up with.

"I don't get it, why?"

"I was hoping you could shed light on that. He told me not to call you either. He wanted it to be a surprise this morning. Are you surprised?" he asks with jazz fingers.

I laugh.

"I have never been more surprised in my life. I'm so happy you're here! And I'm getting you the whole week? Your husband won't mind?"

"He's the first chair on some major deposition with his firm this week, so he won't even know I'm gone. Plus, I couldn't pass this up! He's going to come out the following week for a little vacation. We've been talking about moving back to Seattle. So, who knows, you might get to keep me," Toby winks.

"You're kidding?" I squeal again.

"Let's see how this week goes. What should we do first?"

Toby and I spent the rest of the morning discussing our week of practice. The smile I had the moment I saw him walk through the tunnel stays plastered on my face the entire time we practice together.

I tell him about Win's sudden return and how I'm going to meet him for the first time tonight. Then we part ways so I can get showered and head to work. I have no idea how I will focus on work while I watch the clock tick down to seven.

After I get up to my office, there's a chai waiting and a sticky note.

"You two looked good out there."

Slade was here this morning.

And he called Toby and spent God knows what to make this happen for me.

The only thing I can ask myself is...

Did you pick the wrong guy?

It's just after six-thirty, and I've tried on everything in my closet.

"You look gorgeous in everything you've tried on," Tessa says.

"But nothing feels right," I tell her, spinning side to side to look at the violet blouse I've already tried on three times. Not that it matters since I'll be wearing a rain jacket.

"Do you want to go upstairs to my place? You can try on anything you want. Harmony and Chelsea keep sending me new samples for the summer line coming out, to see what I like best before they make their big order for the boutique. I bet they sent me stuff you would look amazing in."

Her offer is tempting but I need to just settle on something.

"Thanks, but I know I'm just overthinking it, and I want to get there before him and skate for a few minutes to settle my nerves. I'm just going to wear this and call it good."

I know it's not the clothes that have me concerned. I'm not even worried he won't find me attractive because he knows who I am. But I guess I just want this to have a fairy tale ending, as cheesy and unrealistic as that might seem. I've spent so many years crushing on this guy, and it could turn out that the magic was always in the mystery of it all.

"Then you need to go if you want to be early because parking downtown is a pain."

I nod, taking one last look at myself in the mirror, and then shrug.

This will do.

Tessa walks me out to my door and she exits the apartment first.

"Call me the minute you can. Or at least send me a happy face or sad face text so that I know if you're riding off into the sunset or if I need to assemble the troops immediately for an impromptu girls' night sleepover," she offers. "I can kick Lake out to sleep downstairs at Autumn and Briggs's and we can have the penthouse to ourselves."

Oh God, I hope I'm not sending a sad face.

But it's nice to know that if it all goes to shit, I have friends that won't let me sleep alone tonight.

"You don't have to kick Lake out just for me," I tell her.

"Oh, don't worry about him. He says that Autumn buys Briggs better snacks," she says, rolling her eyes playfully.

"Let's hope it's the sunset tonight," I say.

"It will be. I have a good feeling that this guy is the one. Just be open to whoever walks through that door, Ok?" she says, rubbing my shoulder quickly. "Give the guy a chance."

I nod. "I will. I'll give you an indicator soon."

"Ok, good luck."

Tessa turns right towards the staircase at the end of the hall since she only lives up one flight of stairs, and I head left towards the elevators.

Twenty minutes later, I found a parking spot in the parking garage across the street and I'm walking towards the outdoor skating rink. The weather said there was a chance for rain, and though the clouds look menacing, I think we might beat it before it starts coming down.

I head for a bench and pull on my skates, lacing them up before heading to the counter to pay for admission.

The rink is only open for another hour on a weeknight, and the number of people here is starting to dwindle. Only about twenty people are left on the ice, but I'm happy to be in a public place with other people around when I meet Win.

I don't feel unsafe to be meeting him, but it doesn't hurt to be cautious.

The music is playing as I spin around in the middle of the rink.

I'm glad I got out here a little early to calm my nerves, though my eyes dart around every so often when I think I might see someone with flowers in their hands.

Out of nowhere, I feel a few raindrops hit my head, and then other people in the rink start to feel it, too.

It doesn't take long for the rain to pick up and it's raining hard.

Everyone is skating to the exit, but I still have five minutes before Win is supposed to be here.

I pull my hood over my head a little tighter as I watch people flee the rink and head for the parking garage or public transit.

It doesn't take long before I'm the only one left on the ice, and the rain is starting to soak through my jeans. At least my rain jacket and hood are keeping the top half of me dry.

I recheck my phone to make sure I have the time right, and then I see a figure moving from the parking garage to the rink.

He's dressed in jeans and a green down jacket with a hood. From here, he looks tall, and though the down jacket mostly covers him, his legs look muscular, like he works out.

I look for the bouquet, and sure enough, he's holding one, but I can't see what flowers are inside the cellophane wrapping.

His eyes lock onto mine, but I still can't determine if I know him from school or not with his hood over his head.

He doesn't stop to put on the skates he has strung over his shoulder. Instead, he walks up to the rink and carefully takes steps out onto the ice.

Finally, I can make out the flowers in his hands.

Pink peonies.

It's Win.

Each step he takes brings him closer to me and I'm surprised at how well he's doing walking on the ice. Most trained ice skaters can but Win never mentioned what kind of experience he has in a rink. I guess I never asked, and he never offered.

The rain beats down even harder with every minute that passes by.

Win surprises me by pulling back his hood and that's the moment when I realize it's not Win... it's Slade.

"What are you doing here? And why do you have pink peony flowers in your hand?" I ask, my eyebrows furrowed, watching the rain soak Slade's hair, water dripping off his slightly crooked nose.

"Pen..."

There it is again. The nickname that only Win ever uses for me.

"Why do you keep calling me Pen? You've done it twice. And why are you here? Win is going to be here any minute," I say.

What if Win sees Slade and bolts?

"I don't even know how to say this," he says, swallowing hard. "Pen... I am Win, and I should have told you sooner than this.

I'm sorry. I didn't mean to lie to you or lead you on... it just sort of happened and then I didn't know how to stop it."

He's Win?

That's impossible. Why would he say that?

"What are you talking about? You can't be Win. Win is a 2.5 average GPA student who needed my tutoring help. You were a pre-med honor student. It couldn't have been you," I argue.

Why would he come out here and make this up?

Doesn't he know that Win will be here soon? Then I'll know he's lying. But how did he know to bring the same flowers?

Slade takes a step closer, and I take a step back. He recognizes my retreat to his advance.

"I lied to you. I didn't need your help with my classes. I just wanted an excuse to get close to you after that night at the frat house when I found out that you were Sam's daughter. I knew Sam wouldn't allow me to date you so I found out that you were tutoring students in one of my professors' classes and I asked him for your email."

He went to my professor?

"You mean that you knew my father would bench you, so you thought the next best thing to do was to trick me into thinking you were someone else?"

I think about any clues he could have given me. And then I consider the timeline of everything.

Win reached out after the night at the frat house, and his "Dear John" email came the day before Slade left. Win reappeared in my inbox a little while after Slade showed up in Seattle.

I feel stupid for not knowing it was him. And how quickly I fell for Win... but I did.

"Why would you do this to me?" I cry out over the loud rain that beats against the ice and the metal roofs around us.

Yet again, Slade found another way to hurt me.

He fabricated the perfect man, and the moment I fall for him, he rips it out of my grasp.

"Pen, I didn't mean to hurt you. I swear—"

"Don't call me Pen," I bark.

"Ok... I won't. Just please..." he says, taking a small step forward again. "Let me explain what happened."

"I see what happened. You didn't have the balls to challenge my father and ask me out on a date, so you took the coward's way out and pretended to be someone else who I learned to trust. I told you things, Slade. Things that I wouldn't have said if I had known it was you," I say, my arms gripping around each other as the wind blows harder against my wet pants. "I told Win things in confidence about you, and you used that to manipulate my thoughts and feelings to your advantage."

He shakes his head.

"I never used Win to make me look better or to manipulate you into trusting me. Win was there to comfort you when I kept fucking up. And I know I fucked up Pen... Penelope." He corrects himself quickly. "And you're right, I was a coward. I didn't want to risk your father's good opinion of me, but not because he might bench me. He's the closest thing I've ever had to a father who cares about me, and I was afraid to lose it. But I didn't realize that losing you was far worse. And I've lived with that decision for the last four years. And maybe if I had asked you out, you would have never agreed to that date with Sean and none of the next set of mistakes would have happened."

He's blaming not dating him as the reason why I ended up without a skating partner.

Really?

"Right, because if you had been dating me, then you wouldn't have acted like an asshole and threatened to beat Sean to a pulp just for asking me out. You couldn't handle the jealousy? Is that what it was?" I ask, throwing up my hands.

I don't want to listen to any more of his excuses. There are always excuses when it comes to him.

"That's not what happened with Sean. That punk kid had to be dealt with."

Of course, he's not going to take responsibility for his actions.

"Then tell me what happened," I demand.

"I can't tell you, but I promise it was in defense of you. You deserve better than Sean Klein or any of those fucking jocks that thought they were going to come anywhere near you."

So, he didn't cock block me as my father's class pet, he did it because he was mad he couldn't date me. That might almost be worse.

All I know now is that I'm freezing cold, and there's no emoji I could send Tessa to explain how I feel right now.

"You know what, Slade? Don't come near me anymore. Don't call me. Don't text me. Don't make up a fake email and weasel your way in again. I'm done with you... officially. You can't be trusted."

I start to skate around him and he reaches for my wrist to stop me. His fingers slide around my wrist, and I hate how well I know his touch and how, for a moment in time, I felt safe with him.

I whip a glare at him.

"I promise you that Sean's intentions were not what you thought they were, and they weren't meant for your benefit."

"Then tell me what they were," I challenge him because I know he's full of it, and he'll say anything at this point.

"It's better that you don't know."

"Goodbye, Slade... for good this time."

He releases me, and I skate off the rink, slipping on my blade covers. I don't bother to change into my shoes that I left under the bench. They're soaked anyway, and the parking garage is only across the street.

I keep walking until I make it across the crosswalk and head under the cover of the parking garage.

I send off a text to Tessa with the steaming red face emoji and a broken heart emoji. This interaction deserves two.

> Penelope:🤬💔

> Tessa: Sending Autumn up with cookies. Sending Lake and his lucky pregame pillow down to Briggs's. Isla is dropping off Berkeley at Sunny's. We're here for you. See you soon.

I look back to find Slade still watching me from center ice. He hasn't moved an inch since I left him. And that's exactly where I want him to stay.

As far away from me as possible.

Slade

I watch as Penelope makes it safely across the crosswalk.

I wasn't expecting a better outcome than that, but I was hoping for it nonetheless.

She has every right to be pissed off at me.

I consider calling up Seven to grab a beer, but we have to leave in the morning for our away games for the final round. If we win this round, we'll be headed for the Stanley Cup.

As much as I want to figure out how to make this right with Penelope, I have to keep my mind focused on the things I can control. And right now, the only thing I can control is how I play out there and being the teammate that the Hawkeyes deserve.

What does or doesn't happen between Penelope and I will have to wait, even though I'm fucking tired of waiting.

CHAPTER TWENTY-FOUR

Penelope

The next morning, I show up to practice with Toby. The anti-puff under eye cream that Autumn let me use worked like a charm and you can't even tell I spent the night crying in Tessa's penthouse.

I'm a few minutes late when I walk through the player's tunnel. I really would rather curl back up in a ball and lay in bed all day than have practice with Toby, who is going to kick my butt all around this ice rink, but he's only here for a week, and I need to take full advantage.

The second Toby comes into view on the ice, I see a second figure.

Jenny McPherson.

"Jenny!" I yell out and skate quickly over to the pair waiting for me.

"She was feeling left out so I told her she could join us," Toby smirks.

Jenny smiles at me as I get closer.

"I called Toby to see how things were coming along and he said it's like the old days. I had to come by and see for myself," she says, rubbing her black gloves together to warm them.

"You came out to watch us skate?" I ask, my eyes widening.

Jenny is a very busy and highly sought-after figure skating coach in the Northwest. Toby and I were lucky to skate under her guidance for as many years as we did. It means a lot that she carved out time to be here this morning.

"Yes. And if Toby is right about you two being in tip-top shape, I would like to invite you to come back to my rink and practice with me.

I look over at Toby, and Toby grins.

"You want to coach us again?" I ask. I had never even considered getting back into competitive skating, but Jenny is suggesting that, or she wouldn't waste her time asking Toby and me to take up valuable ice real estate on the rink she coaches at.

"I'd like to see you two in action first, but yes, if you two skate together even half as well as you did before Toby's accident, I'd like to discuss coaching you again. With nationals coming up, you two have to show you're worthy to enter."

I flash a look over at Toby and I can see that determined look in his eyes already. He wants to do this.

"You want us to compete and place during nationals so we can get an invitation to the Olympic tryouts?" I ask, almost not believing this.

"Why not? Toby has been a solo skater at the top of his game for the last three years, and from the sounds of it, you haven't lost your step, either. What would it hurt to try?"

I'm almost too giddy to skate at the thought that I might get one more shot. It's still a longshot, as Toby and I haven't been in the pair skating world in forever, but what do I really have to lose?

"So... where do we start?" I ask.

Jenny looks at Toby and then me.

"Let's skate."

Slade

Getting on the jet this morning is the last thing I want to do, but giving Penelope space for the next three days is necessary. She said she never wants to see me again, so space is the one thing she needs the most.

When we get to the hotel, I flop onto the bed with a grunt.

I hear Seven give an annoyed sigh.

I can feel him eying the door and debating a great escape, but then he speaks instead.

"Everything ok over there?" he asks.

I sit up on the bed and face him, knowing full well that I need to tread lightly if I'm going to bring up Penelope's name. Otherwise, the Hawkeyes might be in need of a new center again.

Do I want to discuss this with anyone? No.

But will I take this to the ice if I don't get it out? Maybe.

"I fucked up,"

"Not a shocker there. Can you be more specific?" he says, barely interested in this conversation.

There's a high likelihood that Seven might toss me out of the fifth-story window of this building, but there's no one else I can unload this shit with, so here it goes.

"Four years ago, I lied to Penelope about who I was in a tutoring email to get close to her in college. She asked that guy to meet up with her yesterday, and I came clean. Now she's probably googling how to kill a hockey player and get away with it."

"For fuck sake. Do I have a sign on my back that says, "Please tell me your deepest, darkest secrets? Why in the hell do people tell me all of their shit?" he asks, running his hand over his short dark hair.

"Because we all know you won't tell anyone. Trust me, it's not because of your warm and inviting disposition," I say.

"Fuck off."

"I'd be happy to, but you're the one who asked."

He doesn't like that answer and his frown deepens.

"That's because I want to win tomorrow, and you sulking in the back of the jet the entire flight isn't going to win us the finals. I need you ready to fight."

"Yeah, I know," I say, looking down at my boots on the vibrant swirl hotel carpeting.

"I warned you not to get involved, remember?"

"I've been involved for years. Your warning came a little late, not that it would have stopped me then either."

He sighs with a grumble.

"Sounds to me like she has a valid reason for being pissed."

"Yeah, she does. And I may have inadvertently cost her a chance to compete for a spot in the Olympics."

"Jesus Christ, Matthews. What the fuck did you do? Does Sam know about this?"

"Why do you think I was in Canada for four years?"

His eyebrows lift in surprise.

"It was that bad that Sam kicked you out of the country? That's fucking brutal but not surprising. He'd kill for that girl."

"Yeah, I know."

Seven slumps down on the second queen bed in the room.

"I don't understand how catfishing Penelope over email cost her the Olympics. And give me the PowerPoint presentation version. I don't want to be here all day."

This is the part I don't want to explain but at least I know that Seven won't tell anyone.

"I threatened to break the kneecaps of a soccer player who was trying to date her to win a bet. Word got around, and no figure skaters would partner with her. They were afraid of me, I guess."

"And Sam sent you to a farm team to defend Penelope? That doesn't seem right."

"Sam sent me to Canada for a rumor that got spread about Penelope. A rumor that I didn't start," though I had hoped it would get around campus. "What do you think he would have done if he found out some asshole was only trying to date her to win a bet for dating the coach's daughter?"

He doesn't have to answer. We both know that Sam Roberts would probably be in prison for murder by now... assuming they ever found Sean's body.

I made the right call even though it cost me.

"Ok, I get it... but you gave up four years of your career for Penelope. That's insane..." he shakes his head. "You're fucking in love with her, aren't you?"

I just wet my bottom lip and glance back down at my boots.

Seven's smart enough to know the answer. I doubt it was even a question.

"You're going to have to tell her," he says.

"I can't."

"Why not?"

"Because she gave up her skating career when this happened. If I tell her that the truth is worse than the rumor, how do you think she'll take it? I need to find another way to get her to forgive me."

Seven stands back up and then grabs his cell phone from his bedside table. I'm guessing my five-minute therapy session is just about over.

"She's pissed off at you for lying. If you want forgiveness... you'll have to tell her the truth. That's the only way out of this.

And considering all the times she thinks you fucked up, I'd say it's your only shot. There's my advice," he says, slipping his phone into his back pocket. "Now I'm hungry. Want to get some food?"

His resolution doesn't help me. I'm not telling Penelope about the real reason I threatened Sean. But I don't think he's wrong.

I might have no way back to redemption for WinForToday067. And that one is no one's fault but mine.

I stand and grab my wallet and phone off the nightstand by my bed.

"Yeah, let's go."

CHAPTER
TWENTY-FIVE

Penelope

It's been a week since I found out that Slade is Win.

With the craziness of the final round in the playoffs and the team in and out of town, I've been fortunate enough not to see Slade around the stadium.

I've used studying for my college courses as an excuse for not coming to any Oakley's celebrations when anyone outside of the girls asks. Tessa, Autumn, Isla, and Toby already know the details of what happened that rainy night out at the rink with Slade.

Now that Toby and I are skating with Jenny's team again, I don't spend my mornings at the stadium risking a run-in with Slade.

He's honoring my wishes to stay away, and even the morning dirty chai and sticky buns have stopped showing up on my desk.

Toby and I are skating better than ever, and with Toby having been actively competing for all these years and Jenny pulling for us, we secured a spot to skate in our district championship. If we can pull this off and place high during competition, we could be looking at tryouts for the Olympics. It's a long shot... but it's still a shot.

I never thought I'd be back in competitive figure skating again. Least of all, looking at my chance to compete in the Olympics after so many years out of the world of figure skating, but here we are. And though I don't want to admit it, I wouldn't have done it without Slade calling Toby.

Right now, the Hawkeyes game wins against the other team are tied 3-3. Whoever wins tonight takes home the Stanley Cup, and since we rarely lose at home, we have a good chance.

Toby and I get to the stadium a little early so that I can show him the owner's box and a few other places he hasn't seen since we have spent most of our time practicing on the ice for the last couple of weeks.

We pass by the life-size cardboard cutout Juliet and Shawnie had made for today's event.

Toby looks at each one as we pass by the hall until suddenly, I don't hear him next to me.

I look back over my shoulder to find him standing in front of Slade's cut-out.

I wish I could punch the cut-out and knock cardboard Slade on his ass. But a Hawkeyes employee hitting a player, even if it's a cardboard version, would probably look odd to the VIP ticket holders who paid extra to get into the stadium early.

"Is he really this tall?" Toby asks, standing right up to the cutout for reference.

Toby is no slouch either at five foot eleven, but Slade still has a few inches on him.

I walk up, not wanting to lose my friend to the mob of crazed hockey fans who will soon stream through these halls.

"Yep, that's spot on. And trust me when I say that the event planner that puts this on is precise about everything. They came in during practice and measured everyone's height to be sure."

Shawnie didn't mind coming in after practice when all the guys had just showered and were walking around in only towels or boxer briefs. She volunteered her services since Juliet was adamant that the heights were to be exact.

"I guess it's been a while since I saw him in college, and he was gorgeous then... but did he get hotter, or is this photoshopped."

I don't want to stare back at the very real and very accurate life-sized cut-out of the man who is on my lifetime shit list.

"All he's missing in this picture is the knife in his hand that he plans to stab you in the back with. Other than that, yeah, sure, it's accurate."

I turn again and start walking back in the direction we were headed. If Toby wants to go on a self-guided tour, he's welcome to it. I'm certainly not going to stand around staring at the man I despise, especially since I'll have to watch him play for a good part of an hour tonight.

I hear Toby's loud footsteps behind me.

"Hey, hold up, I'm coming."

It doesn't take long for Toby to come up alongside me. His legs are about twice as long as mine, so he can get places faster than I can if he wants to.

"I'm still surprised you two aren't dating. He had it so bad for you back in college and now you two are back in the same city and working for the same team. Not to mention that you live in the same building."

He had it so bad for me back in college?

What is he talking about?

"Do you need a refresher on what happened between us back in college? He ruined my life. Don't you remember that? He definitely didn't have it bad for me," I say.

"I know I was back in North Carolina at my mom's house recovering when all the shit hit the fan with the tryouts, but you know he didn't mean for it to get out to every jock on campus, right? It was only meant for the jocks in on that bet and the rich kids at that frat house that put up the money."

"I have no clue what you're talking about. What bet? What money?"

"You're kidding, right? I heard about this from one of the kids in my biotech class who was sending me his lecture notes. Even he knew about the bet. Are you honestly telling me you didn't know about the fraternity that put up the funds for the bet?"

I stop in the walkway, irritated that he keeps bringing up all this stuff I know nothing about.

"Toby, I have never heard about a bet, or rich kids, or money, or the jocks that were involved. All I know is that Slade threatened Sean Klein not to date me, or he would end his soccer career, and that he would do the same to any jock who tried."

Toby pulls me out of the hallway so that I don't get trampled by the ever-growing number of fans coming in.

"Yeah, that's what was being pushed around school because the fraternity didn't want the Dean to find out about them betting on a faculty member's daughter. They worried the school board would shut down their daddy's fraternity alma mater."

"Wait," I shake my head. "What does that have to do with me?"

"I was told by a reputable source who was really close with Sean at the time and told my friend, that Sean got drunk one night at a party that you attended. A bunch of his friends wagered that he wouldn't be able to get a date with you. He saw an opportunity to make some money, so he went to a couple of rich kids to see if they would sponsor a wager to any jock who could..."

Toby pauses for a second and looks at me.

"Who could what, Toby? Spit it out already?"

"Who could sleep with you on the first date. And since you were the hockey coach's daughter, the stakes were a little more interesting."

Oh my God, I was a rumor even before Slade's threat.

"How much money?" I ask, though I'm not sure if I want to know.

"A grand, paid out by six guys in the fraternity."

I feel bile rise in my throat and I think I'm going to be sick.

I agreed to that date without any idea what Sean had planned. To him, I was just a payday.

To be honest, I wasn't even that interested in the guy. It was obvious he bleached his hair, he was a little rude to people on campus, and he was really cocky with his pickup line. But I was new to school, and I figured one date wouldn't hurt.

How stupid was that?

"How did Slade find out about this bet?" I ask.

"Slade was by far the richest kid in school... by a long stretch, and they knew he played hockey. They thought he might want to bet money on which jock he thought would win."

"Like picking a racehorse? This was all for sport?" I ask.

I cross my arms over one another, gripping around my arms for comfort. This is not what I thought Toby was going to tell me.

"Shit, Penelope, I thought you knew all of this?"

"Did Slade bet?" I ask.

My heart was racing at the thought that he would have put money on someone screwing the coach's daughter. If he did, I'm definitely going to lose my lunch, knowing that I slept with Slade three times without knowing all of this information.

"After he found out, he hunted Sean down and threatened to end his career if he didn't cancel your date. Then he went to the frat house and broke the nose of the guy who was running the betting pool."

My eyes flare as I stare back at Toby.

"He did? I never heard about that."

I can't believe he did that.

"You didn't because the kid wanted to press charges, but the Matthews family is a very powerful family with a lot of money and even more lawyers. The kid's dad pulled him out of school, and then the rumor got spread around that Slade was threatening any jock in school not to touch you to cover up what had happened so that they didn't get expelled."

I stand there, staring back at him, my jaw almost to the floor.

How could I not have known any of this? I went to the same school. Toby was states away and had all the details.

"I can't believe you didn't tell me this!" I say, my stomach starting to cramp with guilt that Slade spent four years paying for this. "Are you absolutely sure?"

"I have it on pretty good authority, yes. I saw the fraternity brother a couple of years ago at a charity event, and his nose looks like it got a lot of work done, but the plastic surgeon didn't do a good enough job. It's still crooked. Slade must have shattered it."

Why didn't Slade tell my dad about this?

If this is true, he couldn't have held that against Slade, and neither could I. But if he had gotten ahead of the rumors, I could have maybe found a skating partner if I had told them the whole story and explained that Slade would not break anyone's leg for skating with me.

What a complete mess this whole thing was.

It doesn't change the fact that he lied to me about Win, but it does change many other things that I thought I knew about him.

"Personally... and I never could confirm this, but I think the fraternity singled you out on purpose because someone knew that Slade had a thing for you."

"Why would you think that?"

"Because Slade and I started school the same year and that fraternity had been trying to get Slade to pledge the entire time. He denied them repeatedly. Slade didn't want people to know he had family money. He had a condo and a nice car but besides that, he didn't flaunt it. The fraternity didn't like that he thought they were just a bunch of spoiled rich kids that paid for their grades, whereas Slade graduated with honors."

"Pre-med, right?"

Toby nods.

"So you think they used me..."

"To get to him... yeah, I think so. But that's just my theory," he says.

I can feel my heart begin to race and my hands sweat. I think back on everything I said to him... the years he put the NHL on hold for me... the tattoo... everything.

Why didn't he tell my father the truth?

Why didn't he come to find me on campus and tell me what was happening?

I don't understand any of it but he's the only one that can answer those questions.

"I have to find him," I say, looking right and then left, trying to think of where in the stadium he is right now.

"Yeah, go," he urges.

"You have your ticket for my dad's season seats?"

"I got it," he says, patting his pocket.

"Ok, I'll meet you there after I find him."

"Good luck."

I turn and race down towards the locker rooms, dodging between people to get there as fast as I can before the game starts.

I reach the lower level and wave my badge at security to let me through.

I see a few players walking back from PT, probably getting taped up before the game that starts in less than an hour.

I see Lake, then Seven, and then right behind him... Slade.

"Slade!" I yell before he makes it to the locker room.

He stops and looks over as I run down the hallway towards him.

There's not a smile on his face as I run up. He almost looks ready to get yelled at again.

Slade

"I need to talk to you," she says.

She looks even more beautiful than ever, which fucking kills me. But I also haven't seen her in days since she's been avoiding me.

"Right now?" I ask.

"Coach wants us back inside," Seven says, looking at her and then me.

"Thirty seconds? I'll be quick, I promise," she pleads with Seven.

The last thing I want to do right now is get my ass handed to me by the little blonde standing in front of me before I go out of the ice. I've put my heartbreak out of my mind to give everything I have to this game, and now Penelope decides to show up right before the puck drops.

It's not the best time.

Seven heads inside without saying another word.

I take a few cautious steps towards her, unsure of what I'm in for.

"I have to get back in there. So, say whatever you need to say that can't wait until after the game," I tell her.

"I want to talk about the bet."

My ears perk up at the word "bet".

How does she know about that and how long has she known?

"What do you know about the bet?" I ask, taking another step closer.

"Toby had a lot of information and I want to know what's true."

I hear clamoring behind Penelope, and when I look up towards security, I see the two people I could have avoided seeing before the game.

I hear my dad's voice echo through the hallway.

"Slade."

Penelope looks over her shoulder to see the two people getting their IDs checked by the guard, and then he lets them through when he sees I know them. So much for high-security measures around here.

This is not how I wanted Penelope to meet my parents. In fact, if she had agreed to be with me, I would have been happy to live our entire lives without her ever meeting them.

"How did you guys get back here?" I ask, as they continue towards us.

Penelope turns to face them, coming back to stand beside me.

"We're your parents. Of course, they're going to let us through."

My mom is dressed in white linen pants and an expensive cashmere shawl with her hair perfectly in place, and my dad is in designer slacks and Hawkeyes limited edition jacket, his hair more peppered than the last time I saw him.

I look over to see Penelope's face plastered with a smile. She knows enough to know that I don't get along with my parents.

"Congratulations, honey," my mom says.

"At least you've accomplished something. I'll be less of a joke at the country club tomorrow morning at tee time with the guys on the golf course if you can pull a Stanley Cup win off tonight," my dad says.

I glance over at Penelope, watching her perfectly placed smile falter a little bit at my dad's words. Embarrassment doesn't express the full extent of how I feel with Penelope witnessing my father's unwavering disappointment in me.

"Chad, you promised you'd be supportive," my mom whispers in my dad's ear, but he waves her off.

"Well, who is this?" my dad asks with the same smile that I inherited and the charm I learned to go with it.

"You are absolutely beautiful, my darling," my mom says, beaming over at Penelope.

"Yes. Finally, someone normal. Please tell me you're done sleeping around and you're getting serious with someone," my dad says.

"Jesus, dad..."

My eyes clamp shut.

The last thing Penelope needs is to be reminded of the reputation I had in college.

"We're not—" I start but Penelope cuts me off.

"Hi, I'm Penelope Roberts. The administrator of the Hawkeyes' GM and Slade's girlfriend."

I whip a look over at her, but she doesn't pay attention as she shakes my mom's and then my dad's hands.

Did she just say girlfriend?

For the first time in over a week, Penelope's introduction gives me the smallest amount of hope. Although it's possible that she's just using the title to help defend me against my father.

"You work for the franchise?" my dad asks.

"She's getting her master's in sports management. She wants to become the GM when Sam retires."

I don't know if that's completely true, but I am making the assumption to brag about Penelope. She's sure as hell smart enough and capable.

"A woman who understands the importance of higher education. I like that. Will you speak some sense into my son and tell him to take his future seriously and go to medical school?" my dad asks.

"Mr. Matthews, your son is one of the best hockey players on our team. He was offered an unprecedented contact amount for a rookie coming into the NHL, not to mention that his contributions to this team have unarguably contributed to why we are playing for the Stanley Cup tonight," my dad lifts a finger to interrupt, but Penelope doesn't stop. "And if you spent any amount of time on any of the sports networks on television right now, you would know that Slade is predicted to possibly become one of the greatest centers ever to play the game." Penelope looks up at me, a glimmer in her eye, and I could fucking kiss her right now. "You should be very proud of your son; I know I am."

My dad doesn't know what to say back.

He stares back at her, then at me, and then back at my mom.

My mom smiles at Penelope and then reaches out her hands. "I'm Lisa Matthews, and this is my husband Chad. It's lovely to meet you. I see that my son has picked well."

"Slade," I hear Seven say, poking his head out of the locker room door. "You're out of time."

I turn my head to give him a nod and then look back to my parents.

"I'll see you later... or I won't. Thanks for coming," I say without any enthusiasm.

And then turn away from them and face Penelope.

They didn't tell me they were coming, and it's just as well because I would have told them not to. But knowing they're here and my dad will be watching me play in person gives me a little more incentive to win this Stanley Cup right in front of him.

They take the hint and turn back for the main part of the stadium, leaving us alone.

"I really have to go," I tell her even though I want to stay and talk about whatever Toby told her but I have an entire team and a championship game to win.

"I know... go," she says.

"Will you be right here when I get out?"

"Yes, I'll be here."

I want to bend down and kiss her but I still don't know what she knows and if she's still pissed at me. And with Seven standing at the door waiting on me, I can't use up any more of his patience.

"I'll see you soon," I tell her.

I turn and run to the locker room door grabbing the door from Seven.

"Good luck," I hear her call out.

I turn back one last time. I want to remember what it looks like to have Penelope waiting outside of the locker room for me.

It's the image I'll have in the back of my mind for the rest of this game and the motivation to make sure that I don't show back up empty handed.

I've dreamed of winning a Stanley Cup since I could walk. And now... I want to win it to prove to her that I'm all the things she told my dad that I am.

Then the door closes finally, cutting my vision of her completely.

It's time to win a championship... and a girl.

CHAPTER
TWENTY-SIX

Penelope

Sitting in the stands gives a whole different feel to the game. It's been a while since I sat this close to the action.

There's not a single open seat in the entire stadium. We're into the second period, and with the scores tied and this being a winner-takes-all game, I'm doing everything I can not to bite my fingernails or cover my eyes when the opposing team tries to make a shot.

It's also been an aggressive game, with more hits and dirty tricks on the ice. Everyone is pulling out anything they can to gain the advantage, and this is far from a clean game.

I can't keep my eye off Slade, and I watch him skate from one end to the other, shifting out with his alternates and playing his ass off every time he's on the ice.

One player on the opposing team seems to be giving him as much trouble as he can. Maybe it's just because I'm sensitive to number 67, Matthews, on the ice, but I swear that the player on the other team is gunning for Slade more than anyone else.

We're at the end of the second period, and Lake gets the puck. He heads down towards the goalie, but he's getting a lot of heat on him as the opposition is closing in.

Lake sends the puck to Briggs, but Briggs can't make the shot.

Slade gets himself mostly clear, lining up to be in perfect position, and Briggs waits for the ideal moment, trying to shake off the players on his ass.

He shoots the puck to Slade, and just as Slade's about to take the shot, the opposing player, who's been out to get him, comes out of nowhere and clotheslines Slade, knocking him flat on his back.

I watch Slade's helmet smack against the ice. My stomach squeezes uncomfortably at the sound of plastic and ice colliding, echoing through the stadium.

A resounding groan from the crowd breaks out around me as everyone witnesses Slade hit the ground.

The referee blows the whistle immediately. He saw it happen.

It's a bad hit, and you know it when everyone in the stadium stands up and boos at the offending player.

It only takes me half a second to realize that Slade isn't moving on the ice.

The moment I see Seven leave his goalpost and sprint for Slade, with Lake doing the same from close by, I know this isn't a normal hit.

"Slade!" I yell out of instinct, but I know he can't hear me.

I immediately start pushing past people on my left, trying to get past the five seats between me and the railing of the player's tunnel.

"Is he going to be ok?" Toby yells after me.

"No," I yell back as I climb over the railing and jump five feet down into the access point for the rink.

I don't look back at security as I race out to the rink's opening and step out on the ice. I know how to walk on ice, and I get out to Slade in record time.

Seven is already down by Slade's head, trying to get Slade to answer, with Lake and Briggs there too. The other Hawkeyes players surround Slade to protect him from spectator view and protect him from the opposition or fans throwing things onto the rink. You never know in a high intensity game what can happen.

I slide down onto my knees, to the right side of Slade's head, with Seven on the left and Lake near his hip.

"Slade, can you hear me?" I ask.

"You shouldn't be out here," the ref warns.

A few seconds later, we hear a moan coming from Slade.

"Then you'll have to physically remove me yourself," I say,

The in-house doctor comes around to Slade's head next to me and leans over, scanning Slade's body quickly for visible injury.

"She's with the team," Seven tells him.

"Slade, you suffered a bad hit. Can you hear me?" the doctor asks.

Slade barely nods his head, but any movement is a promising sign.

I want to lift Slade's head and lay it in my lap, but I can't until we know if he suffered a neck injury.

"Let's get a stretcher out here," the doctor tells the two medics who ran out here with him.

"We're going to move you, Slade. To do that, we're going to take off your helmet to secure your neck for transportation."

Slade barely nods again.

The doctor takes the neck brace he has and nods to Seven to take Slade's helmet off.

I wrap my fingers gently under Slade's neck so that Seven can access the helmet better and then I continue to hold it until the doctor has the neck brace secured.

I lay Slade's head in my lap and gently brush my hands through his long hair as I watch the medics race out with the stretcher.

"You're going to be ok. I've got you," I tell him.

"Pen?" I hear him mutter softly.

He makes another mumbling sound for a second, and then, before I know it, they pull him out of my lap and onto the stretcher. I get up immediately, following the stretcher the entire way with my hand locked between his limp fingers until we get to the ambulance.

"I'm going with him," I tell the paramedic.

The doctor nods at her.

"I'll meet you there. I have to grab his medical file. I'll get a police escort. Just go!" he yells as he, turns and sprints back for the stadium building.

Slade is still a new player, and the doctor probably needs to review his file for possible medications and prior injuries.

I load into the ambulance with the two paramedics, and we take off.

I ride the entire way with my hand in his. His grip has tightened a little, but I know what it feels like to have Slade's hands on me, and I hate how weak he feels now. Can he really feel me? Does he know it's my hand in his?

The ride to the hospital feels like a blur. Before I know it, the doctor shows Slade's detailed medical history, and they all disappear with Slade to run every test known to man.

I hear Slade's groggy voice down the ICU hall as the doctors start asking him yes and no questions. At least I know he's conscious. There's some comfort in that.

One of the nurses shows me to the reception area in the ICU.

A soap opera is playing on a small TV in the corner of the room, and two vending machines—one for snacks and one for hot beverages—sit against the wall.

Twenty minutes later, I still haven't gotten to see a nurse or a doctor, though knowing that our own doctor is with him gives me a small amount of relief. I field dozens of text messages from Hawkeyes staff and friends, all asking how he's doing. Unfortunately, my answer is the same for everything—I haven't heard yet.

I call my father to see if he or Phil have heard from our doctor yet, but they haven't.

"As soon as I hear, I'll let you know, Peanut," my father says. "Keep me up to date if you hear anything on your end."

Next, Tessa calls and puts me on speaker with the rest of the girls, and just like everyone else... I have no news. Only, that's not their only question.

"How are you holding up?" Tessa asks.

At that moment, tears started to stream down my face. I hadn't let my own emotions sink in due to the high adrenaline keeping me laser-focused on him. Now, hearing Tessa's concern for me, I can't stop the tears.

"Is there anyone else there with you? We'll leave the game and come straight there," Isla says over the speaker.

"Yeah, we can be there in thirty minutes with traffic," Autumn assures me.

"No. Stay and be there for the team. Slade would want you there and I'm not much company right now. I'll let you know when I hear from the doctors."

In my peripheral vision, I see a man I already recognize as an older Slade practically running through the hall with his wife's hand in his as he pulls her behind him. She can barely keep up in her heels, but I see the worry immediately on both of their faces.

"Penelope!" I hear Lisa, Slade's mother call out my name.

"I have to go," I tell the girls. "His parents just showed up."

"Let us know if you change your mind. We'll be ready to leave here the second we get your call, ok?" Tessa says.

"And I'm sure we'll be down after the game. The guys will want to see Slade," Autumn adds.

"Thanks, girls. I'll talk to you later."

We all hang up, and I stand as Chad and Lisa approach quickly.

"Where is he? Is he ok?" Lisa asks in a fluster.

"He's still in the back. They haven't told me anything."

"I'm going to see what I can find out. I want only the best surgeons working on my son. I'll pay to fly them in myself if I have to," Chad says, though more to himself than to either his wife or me.

Then, he releases Lisa's hand and makes a beeline for the nursing station.

Hearing him mention surgery has me even more worried than before. Could Slade really need something like that? How bad are Slade's injuries that he would need to be operated on?

Lisa stays with me, and she draws closer.

"Does Chad really think that Slade will need surgery?" I ask.

She rubs my arm quickly and then offers a forced, polite smile. Her son is behind the doors of the ICU, and he hasn't heard anything; of course, her smile is for the show, and I don't blame her.

"We know even less than you do at this point, but my husband is distraught and tends to bark orders to cope when feeling out of control. We left the minute we watched his stretcher get pulled off the rink, but Chad couldn't get through the mob of people to make it to the ambulance before it left, and getting our car out of the parking garage delayed us."

I nod, "Downtown Seattle is tough to get around. Especially on game days."

"He almost left me in traffic to run the rest of the way to the hospital. We're so worried about him."

This is a different sense than what I got from Slade about his parents. The picture he painted is of parents who couldn't be any more unattached to him if they tried. And hearing the way Chad talked to Slade earlier near the locker room... I was beginning to see that. But this version of them seems polar opposite of how Slade described how much his parents care for him.

"Forgive me for asking, but I thought Chad and Slade didn't get along. In fact, the way that Slade describes his father's disdain for his chosen profession, I was surprised to meet you at a game."

She sighs and then shrugs. "Those two are cut from the same cloths, Chad and Slade. Headstrong, hard-working, inability to let go or give up on the things that are important to them. But they are different, too. Slade has a protective spirit and the ability to love in difficult circumstances," she says. "He may have a hard time understanding his father, but make no mistake that Slade still loves him... he's just tired of feeling that his father holds prerequisites for his affection. And that's not fair of Chad to do because Chad's actions come from a place of fear. A fear that Slade will have nothing to fall back on and no true skills if something ever happened to the trust fund."

If something ever happened to the trust fund?

A fear that Slade won't have something to fall back on?

"I don't think I'm following your meaning. What do you mean that Chad comes from a place of fear?" I ask.

"Slade and Chad are both trying to disassociate themself from their upbringings. One from being a rich kid with a privileged life, and the other from growing up poor and moving from foster home to foster home and having to work hard for the scholarships to get into that Ivy League school—the same Ivy League school that his son rejected."

"Slade didn't tell me about Chad's upbringing."

"That's because my husband doesn't talk about it if he can avoid it. He doesn't want to associate himself with his past. He thinks it makes him look weak amongst his peers," she says, giving me a sad smile. "I've loved three men in my life, Penelope. My father, my husband, and my son. And none of them have come complete without flaws, though I will tell you that my husband's imperfections hurt me the most because those are the ones that hurt our son. But they are also the ones that hurt my husband in return and rob him of a relationship with our only child."

Hearing her say this shocks me. She's so much different than how Slade described her.

He made her seem weak and controlled, but really, she's a woman torn between the two loves of her life and she has to wait for them to resolve their issues before there will be peace.

"If you don't mind me asking, what are your husband's flaws that prevent them from developing a relationship?"

"Pride, honey. My husband isn't embarrassed by Slade's success, as he claims. He's just hurt that Slade has rejected the course of life that Chad took to pull himself out of his situation," she says, glancing over at her husband, who's standing by the nurse's desk, pacing while he's on the phone with someone. "If you saw how Chad lights up when someone on the golf course brings up Slade's goal and assist stats, you'd never question how proud he is of Slade. I just wish he could show Slade that too."

She and I sit for a while together while Chad keeps busy, making calls to specialists he knows regarding concussions and head injuries. The Hawkeyes doctor on staff comes out at one point to talk with us and tells us that they are exhausting all tests as a protocol for Slade's sports injury. At least they tell us that he's stable and communicating.

The tests seem to take forever. Players come and go after the game, hoping to see Slade, with a limited amount of people allowed in the ICU, everyone is asked to go home for quiet hours. They allow one of us to stay, and though Chad immediately volunteers, Lisa backs him down.

"I think the first face he'll want to see when he wakes up in his room is Penelope's."

He's reluctant to leave but agrees after finding a hotel suite open in a hotel right next door.

"Call if anything changes... or if he wants to see me," Chad says, his voice almost breaking at the end.

Maybe Lisa is right. Maybe Slade's father is a man of two minds. I hope these two strong-willed men find some common ground.

Chapter Twenty-Seven

Penelope

A small movement catches my eye over in Slade's direction.

His eyes flutter open for the first time since they carted him in, fast asleep. I lock my phone as soon as I send off the last group message, which says that I still haven't received a full report from the doctor yet but that Slade is sleeping soundly and doesn't seem to be in any pain.

I set my phone from vibrating to silent and set it on the hospital tray next to me to eliminate any distractions.

"You're here," he croaks, his voice heavy with sleep and probably whatever they gave him for pain.

"Of course, I'm here. You took a pretty big hit out on the ice. We're all worried about you." I should call the nurses back in now that you're awake. They wanted to know when you woke up," I say, pushing out of the only other chair in his room to head for the door.

"No, wait," he says, reaching out a hand towards me. "Come here first."

He pats a small sliver of bed next to him.

"You want me to lay next to you?"

He nods slowly with the padded neck restraint they have secured around him. Then he reaches for it and yanks it off.

I don't take any steps closer to him. A part of me feels guilty for all the awful things I said to him before I knew about the bet. I feel bad that I've harbored this hate for him for so long when, in truth, he did everything he did to protect me... and my father.

I want to use the fact that he lied to me about being Win to counteract my guilt, but that's hard to do when I'm relieved that they are the same person. I don't have to choose between the two men I'm falling in love with because they are one and the same.

"You should probably keep that on until they clear you," I say.

"I'm fine. They ran all of the tests before I fell asleep. It's a concussion and minor whiplash, that's all. No real damage to my neck," he says, rubbing the back of his neck with his right hand.

I'm sure it's sore, though. And I'm confident that whiplash is considered damage, but I'm not going to argue; he's a grown man.

"You said everyone's worried about me?" he asks.

"Yes, the entire team has been calling and texting me nonstop, wanting an update on how you're doing. The team came by to check on you, but it was past visiting hours, and you weren't out yet, so she sent everyone home."

"But you didn't leave?"

Does he want me to admit that I fought my way into that ambulance with him when the EMTs told me I would have to drive my own car? Or does he want me to admit that the nurse would have had to call security on me to kick me out before I would have taken a single step out of this hospital?

"No, I wasn't going to leave. You took a hard hit during the game. Do you remember that?"

"Oh fuck," he says, running his hands through his hair that's even more wildly messier than usual but just as sexy. "What happened? Did we win?"

God, I wish I could tell him yes so that this wasn't all for nothing, but Slade getting pulled off the ice on a stretcher left our team distracted with concern for his well-being. At least that's what Tessa told me when she broke the news of the loss.

I shake my head. "No, we lost in overtime."

His eyes clamp shut at the news.

It's so hard to be so close and lose at the final buzzer but our team fought hard.

"There will be next year. Everyone just wants you to be ok."

He opens his eyes finally and nods in understanding.

Nothing can be done now—it's over for this season.

"Come here," he says again, leaning his head back against the bed and then opens up the grey-weighted wool blanket outstretched over him.

I do what he asks this time because, truthfully, I've been dying to touch him.

Seeing him go down like that and get knocked unconscious scared me more than I ever have been in my life.

I thought I might have missed my chance to tell him how I feel.

I walk up to the bed and crawl in next to him, laying sideways along the edge of him, trying to ensure I don't disrupt any attached monitors.

He raises his left arm to tuck behind my neck, and I lean forward to let him. I want to be in his arms more than anything, and I'm glad to see he wants that, too.

He gives me a small smile, looking over at me.

It feels good to see him smiling after witnessing that hit.

"I'm not sure if it was a dream or not, but did you ride in the ambulance with me?"

"Yes," I say. "And your parents were here."

"Are they still?" he asks, glancing over at the door.

"No. It's past visiting hours. I pulled the short straw, so I had to stay with you," I tease.

He smirks over at me. "Thanks for staying."

"I wouldn't want to be anywhere else. But I'm not kidding, I almost had to fight your dad for the spot."

He grunts in annoyance when I mention his father.

"Your dad got a suite in the hotel next door instead of leaving tonight. They'll be back in the morning to check on you."

"Call them back and tell them to leave," he says, staring up at the blank screen of the TV.

"They're worried about you. I know that your dad can be a jerk, but he spent two straight hours calling up every specialist he could track down for sports head injuries and sent copies of all of your scans to every single one of them to get a second, third, fourth, and fifth opinion. He would have chartered an aircraft to fly each one of them out here, but they all assured him that you would be ok after a night in the hospital for observation."

"Still, he can head home now. I'm fine and he can go back to whatever charity function he has this week where he'll pretend we're not related."

The doctor recommended keeping things mellow for a few days while he recovers. The last thing I want to do is stir up issues with his dad, especially when we have so much to discuss about us, but I can't let this issue go without telling him one more thing.

"He secretly watches every televised game in his study; did you know that? Your mom told me tonight. And though he says you're an embarrassment to him at the country club, she says he always mentions you in conversation, even though he doesn't know he's doing it. She said his eyes light up when people ask if his son is Slade Matthews, the Hawkeyes's new starting center and the kid with the wicked slap shot."

He keeps his eyes on the TV, his jaw clenching for a second.

"What does that have to do with anything?"

"I think he's just a proud man who can't admit that he's been wrong all these years and that you were destined to find your own path and be successful."

"Can we talk about something else?" he asks.

Not a problem. I did my best, but at the end of the day, this feud is between them.

Besides, I have a specific question I would love answered.

"Sure. Why didn't you tell me about the bet?"

He finally turns to look at me, his eyebrows drawn together. The same look he gave me when I stopped him by the locker rooms before the game... but then we got interrupted.

"How do you know about that?"

"Toby told me. But why didn't I hear it from you?" I ask.

His lips purse for a second.

He doesn't want to tell me about the bet and I don't know why.

"With the way you reacted to the rumors by dropping out of college and figure skating, I'm glad I didn't."

"Did you tell my dad about the bet when he confronted you about everything?"

"No," he says, shaking his head.

"Why not?"

"Because I didn't want him to think that he's the reason you had a target on your back. He wouldn't have taken it well."

I let his explanation sink in for a second.

"So you let me hate you for all these years, thinking it was your fault?" I ask.

"Yes."

There's a look of vulnerability in his eyes that I've seen so rarely. I've never seen him show it to anyone else.

No one else but me.

"And you moved to Canada, putting off your career to protect my father and I from knowing what was really going on. Why?"

"Because sometimes you take the arrows to the back to protect the one you love."

My heart thumps against my chest and my belly flips at his words. He's said them before, but I doubt that I'll ever get tired of hearing him say it.

"You love me?"

"A little more every day since the first time I saw you in the kitchen of that frat house."

It's crazy to think of how our lives would have turned out if we had met under different circumstances.

"I wish you hadn't known I was Sam's daughter that night."

He reaches his hand over and cradles my jaw.

"Walking away that night was the wrong decision, Penelope. I regret it every day. I should have taken the risk to get to know you, even if it meant spending the season on the bench. I can't take that back now, but I've been waiting four years to get a second chance with you. And if Sam wants to trade me for that, I'll take the consequences like I did before."

The consequences—like the farm team.

"He won't trade you. Not after he knows what you did for me—what you did for me and him."

"Don't tell him... please?" he begs.

"He should know."

"It's in the past. He'll only feel like shit that he brought you to that school and caused you pain."

Slade's right.

My father's guilt for the bet placed on me and for sending Slade to Canada isn't worth it.

"Alright, I won't say anything to him about it."

"Thank you," he says, releasing his hand against my jaw. "Are you disappointed that Win doesn't exist? Would you still have picked him over me?"

"Win does exist. That's just not his real name. And in the end, I don't know if I would have gone through with dating him. He was the safe bet," I admit.

"And I'm not safe?" he asks, his eyes locking on mine.

"I was worried I might not make the starting lineup and live my mother's life. A daughter set to repeat her mother's mistakes," I say.

"Pen, you're number one. You always have been. Hockey is just the damn bench warmer. How can I prove that so you believe it?"

He's offering to prove it to me.

How could I have almost passed on this man?

"You already did prove it the day you threatened Sean and the entire athletic department not to come near me and then ended up putting your career on hold for me. I'm sorry I didn't see it before."

"Don't apologize. I would do it again if given the chance. But now there's only one last thing I need to know."

"What's that?"

"If Sam does trade me or sends me back to the farm team when he finds out that you and I are together... will you go with me this time?"

I know he's kidding about my father sending him back to the farm team, but there's no guarantee that my father won't trade him. As the GM, it's part of his job to make trades for the team's betterment. Any player could be traded at a moment's notice.

There's hope in Slade's eyes as they search mine, and I know my answer immediately.

"Yes. I'll follow you wherever you go."

He grins down at me.

"Can I kiss you now?"

"Yes, and hurry. I've been waiting all night."

He twists his body to press his lips to mine, and before I know it, Slade makes a swift move, and I'm lying under him in the hospital bed as he adds pressure to our kiss, one of his hands slipping under my shirt.

I don't want him to stop but our history suggests that Tessa should be barging in at any moment.

"Someone might walk in," I mumble against our kiss.

"I'm sure they've seen worse," he grins.

"I love you," I tell him.

I knew it before this but it's time he knows.

He pulls back for a second and stares down at me.

"Will you be my blind goby fish?"

I laugh.

"Does that make you the ghost shrimp? Are you going to dig me a hole next?"

He nods. "You'll always have a home with me, Pen. I'll always keep you safe."

"I believe you."

A few seconds later, two nurses come barging through his door in a panic and catch Slade on top of me.

"Hi," I say.

One of them grabs at their chest with relief.

"Your heart monitor jumped dramatically. We thought you were in distress."

He looks down at me and laughs.

I just shake my head. "I told you someone would catch us."

EPILOGUE

Six Months Later

Slade

Standing next to Jenny McPhearson behind the sideboards of one of the Olympic rinks here in Paris for the Winter Olympics, I almost can't believe what I just witnessed. I watch as Toby and Penelope end their performance without a single misstep.

Jenny and I immediately start applauding and cheering before they even take their first bow.

"They nailed it!" Jenny yells over to me.

The bleachers go wild as Toby swings Penelope around to all four sides of the rink and waves to the crowd. I can barely hear my own applause over the fans' roaring.

Their unheard-of comeback to pair skating and whirl-wind winning streak that earned them an invitation to the Olympic tryouts garnered mass media attention leading up to the Olympics. The underdogs fighting for their shot at Olympic glory after Toby's tragic skiing accident, were the headlines and fans ate it up.

It's been a wild ride for Penelope and Toby as they've fought through to get to this point. But if anyone can do it, Penelope can.

They nailed their routine today but that doesn't mean anything. They're playing at the height of their sport, and the competition here is tough.

My eyes shift to Sam in the stands with his phone out. He gives me the thumbs-up that he's recording. I don't want to steal Penelope's thunder tonight, but after clearing it with Toby, and Jenny making sure that the Olympic committee approved it, I reach into my coat pocket and pull out the small velvet box.

I wanted to ask sooner but I didn't want our engagement to be a distraction for her. She needed to stay focused on skating. But now that she's finished her lifelong goal, I can't wait another second.

I don't take my eyes off Penelope as she grips Toby's hand and they skate back towards us.

The glitter in her eyes and her smile as she finds me in the crowd of people has my heart racing.

She just made her dreams come true tonight, and I can only hope that she says yes to my question and makes my dream come true too.

I didn't wait more than a couple of days after I got out of the hospital to tell Sam that I planned on marrying his daughter and that I wanted his blessing but that I could live without it. He took it better than I expected he would, though it took him off guard at first. He gave me what I asked for.

Just before they reach the opening of the rink exit, Toby stops and keeps Penelope out on the ice.

"What are you—" she says, looking to Toby for an answer.

Then, her attention flashes to me when she sees me step out onto the ice.

"You shouldn't be out here," she argues.

She glances around quickly with concern that security is going to come after me, but they already know.

The committee didn't give me long to do this but with all the media attention that Toby and Penelope have brought to the viewership, they liked the idea of the happy ending to add to the P.R.

Toby releases her hand and skates past me.

I take a few more steps towards her onto the ice and drop to one knee.

The fans go wild again when they realize that I'm not a crazed fan but a boyfriend proposing.

"Oh my God," she says, covering her mouth with both of her hands.

Immediately, tears start to stream down her face. Although the emotions of today are running high, I'd like to think all those happy tears are for me.

It took us a long time to get here, but I did what I set out to do.

I made it to the NHL, earned back Sam's respect, and made it up to Penelope.

She pulls her hands from her mouth but keeps them clasped together in front of her.

"Are you serious?" she asks with a huge smile.

I hold up the velvet box and then open it. Her eyes connect with the ring, solidifying how serious I am.

She turns her crystal blue eyes back on me and now it's time to convince her.

"I don't deserve you, Penelope. I fight too much on the ice, I've been called a puck hog a time or two, and in every way I could have, I screwed up with you. But I swear that if you give me a chance, there is no one on this planet who will fight for you harder or love you more than me. Will you marry me?"

She beams back at me and nods yes. The crowd erupts with applause, people standing to their feet as she bends down and kisses me, sliding her hands around to cradle my jaw and pulling me tight to her lips.

I take the diamond ring from the box and slide it onto her finger.

I stand and she wraps her arms around my neck.

I yell next to her ear so she can hear me over the continued applause.

"Congratulations, Pen."

"I couldn't have done this without you. Thank you for never giving up," she says back.

"I never gave up on us."

"I know," she says, pulling me in for another kiss.

"Come on, our time is probably up and you have a gold medal to win. Plus, I wouldn't let the girls see the ring until you saw it first. They've been hassling me about it for weeks."

I wrap my hand in hers and pull her with me off the ice.

"The girls?" she asks.

I point to the bleachers where Sam, her mom, both of my parents and half of the Hawkeyes team are all sitting together in a section.

She looks over to find Tessa, Autumn and a very pregnant Isla, jumping up and down in the bleachers.

"You did all of this for me?" she asks as soon as we step off the ice.

"Baby... I'm just getting warmed up."

The End

Want to keep reading? Continue the series with Book 6 LUCKY SCORE!

To be in the KNOW about all the NEWS, subscribe to Kenna King's newsletter so you don't miss a thing click HEREwww. kennaking.com

Thank you for reading and supporting my writing habit ;). If you missed any of the other books in the series, you can find the series in Author Central. or on my website!

Feel free to reach out via email (kenna@kennaking.com) or Instagram (@kennakingbooks)! I love hearing from you.

Thank you for reading Dirty Score!

To read the next book, Lucky Score, you can find it on Amazon or on my website.

Keep up with Kenna by following here:

Made in the USA
Monee, IL
28 October 2024